For Debby,

who made it all happen.

Legacy: A Novel
by Kerrigan Valentine

Edited by Kassandra Sojourner. Certain book design by Eva Bee
Cover illustration and design by Anne Marie Forrester
Author photo by Lynn Grace

ISBN–10: 0–9760604–6–9
ISBN–13: 978–0–9760604–6–8

Published by *Creatrix Vision Spun Fiction LLC*,
A *Creatrix Books LLC* company

Creatrix

P.O. Box 366
Cottage Grove, WI 53527

Printed in the USA

LEGACY

by KERRIGAN VALENTINE

LEGACY

Prologue

My mother died before I was born. It sounds odd, saying that, but I can't find any other way of explaining.

She was fifteen when I was born, the first in a long line of unwelcome daughters. A year later, my mother had Beth. The following autumn brought the twins, and then with each year came all the rest. The one boy that Mother bore brightened our father's life for only a few days. We buried him in the men's graveyard, my father grieving more for this untouched soul than he ever did for his other living, suffering daughters.

Women lived hard in the Valley. Married at twelve, first childbed by thirteen, they were bent-backed grandmothers by the time they were twenty-six. My mother must have been despaired of when no baby appeared those first years of marriage. Father could have divorced her, on grounds of barrenness. He was nearly thirty then, home from warring, and ready to start a family. But in the Valley, a family meant sons. Daughters were of no importance, except to grow up to breed and rear sons. Those like my mother, who failed to do even that, were truly worthless. As I grew, she turned from dead to a ghost.

I played in the grass one morning, after the twins were born, while my mother drew a stained shirt up and down the washboard. A butterfly lifted from a flower and I laughed, clapping my hands, turning to see if she had noticed. Her dead eyes were still as stone, frightening me. I knew one day those would be my eyes. Their emptiness would be just the same.

By the time I was eight, her hair was white and broken, with spots of scalp shining through like scattered coins. Her head withered into the stalk of her neck, her bloodless arms sunk to bony hands. The pale blue of her eyes had leached away, until they looked as white as her hair. She was an apparition that wisped and disappeared when I turned to see. Rarely speaking, never smiling, never scolding. In our tiny living room full of noisy little girls, she simply vanished.

I looked at my father, tanned from the sun, robust at his work, and yet he was so much older than my mother. One day, I stood up from my child's game and began helping. Not as much as I could have or should have, but some. If I had expected her to express thanks, I would have been disappointed. It was Father who approved.

"Maybe you'll be a proper woman yet," he said once, watching me sweep the floor as he downed ale.

Something dark and evil within me rankled at his praise. For I had made a promise, that day in the grass with my mother washing. I did not know how, but my life would be different. Her eyes would never be mine.

Chapter One

Going Home

I'm twelve years plus a season and already an old maid. The thought made me giggle, though at this vast age, I knew I should be beyond childish laughter. San and Teff looked shocked, their insult falling flat beneath my snickering. Beth elbowed my side.

"It's not funny!" she said prissily, fussing over the pleats in her skirt. "Look at you, Shannon! A few more months and you really will be an old maid."

I mussed her thin hair with my free hand. "Better that than a wife, eh, boys?"

Teff's mouth fell open as San stiffened and moved back from the fence they were leaning on. I hefted the market basket up to my shoulder.

"Well, we're off!" I said too loudly, pulling Beth along the road. "Why should I bring a husband's children into the world to starve, when there's not enough food to keep my father's from hunger?" I smiled in satisfaction at the sound of three throats choking.

"I can't believe you said that!" Beth hissed while San and Teff muttered behind us.

"You're not natural, Shannon Wrightsdaughter!" one shouted. The wet sound of spitting followed.

"What if someone heard you?" Beth flinched away from me and tried to fix her hair.

"Spinsters' cursed empty womb, brings lonely life from home to tomb!" the boys called as we neared the end of the Trel farm fence.

I rustled around in the basket. "Think I could peg Teff with an apple from here?"

"No!" Beth said, slapping my hand away.

"It'd be a waste of an apple," I said sagely. "Pity their wives one day. But then who'd marry those cracked brains? I wouldn't."

"Well, you have to marry someone," Beth said.

I started to retort, but she had already begun to wheeze. Children born in the Dark Winter never fared well. Beth and then the boy, both Dark Winter children. And irony of ironies, Beth, the too-early hard birthed baby, translucent-skinned and kitten-weak, had lived. The full-born, rose-colored boy born eight years later had not. Father, the odd time he looked at any of us, made sure to let his eyes skip over Beth. Had she been healthier, more of his rage would have poured down upon her. As it was, his anger was thoughtfully doled out in equal parcels to me, our mother, Beth, the twins, and the others.

Beth tried to even her breathing. I slowed and pretended not to notice her rasp. The sun was setting over the Valley, turning the crop fields a fiery gold against the flame red of the sky. Threads of darkness spread like talons behind us. The road was pale yellow beneath our feet, and the colors of land and sky together were as lovely as Jadan Trelson's paintings before he had gone to war.

"Marriage," I grumbled, hoping to draw Beth into conversation. It wasn't thoughtful, with her trying to breathe and all, but I couldn't bear the silence.

"What else are you going to do?" Beth said with a shrug, sounding exactly like Old Mother Nhilde in the market. "Cut off your braid and take up a plow?"

"Oh, don't be tiresome," I said. "I just don't want to marry, that's all. I mean, honestly, do you want to?"

Her voice was tired. "Of course I do. It's not a question of wanting to, anyway. It's a matter of doing what we should."

"Goat drops to that! I'll do what I please!"

"And that's why your life will be so much harder than mine," she said. I made a horrible face at her and shifted the basket to my other shoulder. We'd gone to market that afternoon and were late returning.

"We're really late," Beth said. I nodded, judging a mile or so left. I loved going to market, the bustle in the square and commotion from the stores, haggling down prices as Beth tugged on my sleeve in embarrassment. Her face would get redder still when some charitable man with many sons gave us a coin for our poor, unlucky father. Poor Father, naught but daughters. Poor Father, unable to plant all his fields with no sons to help. If Father ever found out we had accepted the money, would his fists fly! I always smiled my gratitude to the giver and pocketed the coin. I had one hidden in my dress right now. Taking it out, I watched the deep blue coin flash and sparkle in the last of the afternoon sun. I went to flash the light in Beth's eyes, but thought better of it. I stroked its smooth surface instead and slipped it back into my pocket. A full twenty-pence piece, compliments of San and Teff's father himself.

The road wound south. Suddenly, a rabbit skittered over the yellow gravel and vanished into a patch of thick grass. Beth grabbed my arm before I could give it chase.

"You're no fun," I scolded. "I wouldn't have done it, really."

"Yes, you would have," Beth said. The catch in her voice made me look back. Her face was deathly pale, and beads of sweat trickled down her cheeks to drop onto her dampened collar. Her brown eyes slid around sickly, going in and out of focus when they tried to steady on me. She clutched at me to keep herself from falling. Ignoring her protests, I made her sit down along the side of the road.

The Dark Winter came with a vengeance every eight years, with icy winds scrabbling at the cabin walls and the Valley in near blackness for months at a time. Candles and fires gave the only light while thin blankets gave too little warmth. The oldest and youngest quickly died of lung illness and, by the time spring

rolled in, the hale and healthy were near death themselves. I
had been too young to remember the winter Beth was born,
but I could remember the next one with crystal clarity. Father's
mother, Old Luol, sat in the rocker, going back and forth, back
and forth through the days and nights. I could not tell one from
the other. Firelight flickered on her lumped fingers twisted over
the armrests. The only sound but for the shrieking wind was
her voice, mumbling stories to us about the beasts in the Beyond. I had been nine, Beth eight, and the boy child lived to see
his third day before dying. Had there been some light, Father
no doubt would have gone to the tavern. But he had to remain
in our cramped, tiny cabin until travel was possible. Beth and I
huddled with the twins in a cold corner to avoid his rampaging
about, while the rest of our sisters shivered along the other wall.
Mother was still bed-ridden in our parents' room.

"Dead! Dead! Dead!" he screamed. "Look at my son! What
have you done to my son?" He held the bundled body to his
chest, poking at it now and then, as if to make sure. I had only
caught a glimpse and gotten slapped for my trouble, the boy's
whitish face eerily still in its swathe of wool blanket.

Dark Winters were long and hard. Had they come about
more than once every eight years, I would probably go mad.
That first spring day, when the sun gave the earth no more than
a late evening's dimness, we all spilled outside and would not
go back in until nightfall."Don't worry, Shannon," Beth said. I
jumped at her voice. "I don't think San and Teff will tell anyone
what you said. They know it was just foolishness." I stared at
her in confusion.

"I wasn't thinking ..." I began to protest, but realized she
didn't need to know what I was really thinking. I helped her to
her feet.

"I'm better now. Do you want me to carry the basket?" she
asked.

"No, I'm all right," I said as her chin got a stubborn set to
it. "Maybe you could carry one or two of the loaves; that would
lighten it some."

She took three and started off. We went the rest of the way

in silence. She shouldn't have come with me to market, as fast as she tired, but it was better than being home.

We turned off the road and walked down the dirt path to the cabin. No cook fire came from the chimney.

"What do you ...?" Beth stopped as two of the Nameless ran for us. After Roaninblue were born, Father had forbidden us to waste even names on other useless baggage. I had names for them, but only when Father wasn't around.

I looked over their heads at the cabin. The door was ajar. Father started shouting.

"Come on," I said. "We'll go into the barn and play games." I gestured to the other Nameless, huddled on the porch. They clambered to their feet. All of them ducked when a particularly loud shout cut the air around us.

"Hurry, hurry," I said as I ushered them into the barn, glancing at the cabin. It wasn't much—uneven boards and cracked glass windows that never seemed to get clean. Old Luol's rocker lay in a heap in the front yard. I pulled the barn door shut and counted ... seven, eight, nine. Everyone was here. Roaninblue each took a hand of another sister and tried to pull them into a half-hearted ring game. Roan or Blue gave up, and then the other twin followed suit. Father never called either one by the same name, so they became Roaninblue, like a single identity.

"Come on, let's play hide-and-seek!" I said loudly to cover the sounds from the cabin. "I'm it!"

Beth took the basket from my shoulder. I had forgotten it was there. I ran to the barn door and pressed my face against it, counting noisily. The three youngest shrieked and footsteps pounded away. Beth chuckled. I heard her sit down with an exhausted sigh.

"Twelve!" I called out. Two giggles came from the horse's stall. Greda and Keluu, probably. They always hid together. The twins' voices whispered behind me.

I opened my eyes and looked out a crack between the boards. For a moment, Mother's face was barely visible through the gray glass of the cabin window.

"*Why doesn't she just hit him back?*" I had demanded of her, when I was Greda's age.

My mother looked out over the market. One of the Trelson boys had slapped his mother and ripped a coin from her palm.

"Thirteen!" I shouted, looking at my mother's eyes.

Her face disappeared. I turned back to the musty barn.

"Ready, steady, on I come!" I ran blindly into the dust motes.

The Trelson mother had pressed her hand to her stained cheek. She looked down at the ground. Mother didn't do anything for a moment. Everyone had paused at the ring of that slap, and then they were in motion again around us, slightly faster than before, to make up for the time they had lost.

I ran, not caring if I tripped, keeping my hands in front of me to push off posts and sagging doors and bales of hay. Why had the other girls been so pleased when it was time to put our hair in braids? Who wanted to be a Valley's woman?

I stumbled over a loose board and fell, skinning my knees and tearing my dress. I scrambled to my feet. This time when I ran, like a foolish little child, my eyes were closed.

Chapter Two

The Valley

The northern Valley was a storybook place, each season a gilded glory in its own way. The lacey frost of a first winter's day had no equal, each particle of ice catching the delicate sunlight to make the world sparkle like it had been sprinkled with jewels. I loved the way my feet crunched in the snow, the way an icicle felt cold and smooth under my fingers, how the white winterlarks called sharply in the chilled blue sky. Every year I forgot the hunger and sickness of the winter past.

Beth, who believed I liked the winter only to be contrary, preferred the spring. She cheered it like a friend who visited too little, trying to cajole it to stay just a bit longer. Summer was too close to autumn, which dipped quickly to winter, and with winter came the illness, the cold, and the starving. Better that spring last forever, the farthest point from the year's end. And spring was a beauty, I admitted, though not to her, perhaps my second favorite.

Once spring's sun crept into the Valley, yellow star-flowers burst into life closest to the forests of the Beyond, reaching down the slope into the Valley to mix with redflags and tiny orange clovers. At the Valley's bottom, the clovers gave way to a sea of purple and blue bangle flowers, their colors deep and brooding as they spilled across the earth, stopping in a blunt line at the farmers' fields.

The little ones liked the summer best, of course, since it

meant festival and no school. We had two festivals a year, one at summer's start, the other at autumn's finish. The Summer Festival was my favorite. For an entire day, everyone went to the town square to eat and dance and eat some more. The square was filled with tables of food, a banquet for our winter-starved eyes as well as for our famished stomachs. The old men were enticed (usually by means of ale) to pull out fiddles and play by the square's fountain until the sun was deep in the western sky. The next morning, the men went to the fields, the women to the kitchen, and the children to their morning chores before escaping to play. We stole apples from the orchards and chased each other over the boggy ground to climb the wrinkled trees in the Mooring. The older boys did errands in town for a penny or two, only to spend it on candy at Old Durk's store to share with the rest of us. Heaven, we knew, was to sit against a tree resting our tired legs and licking our fingers clean of sugar. It always took several blasts of the dinner horn to call us back home. Leaving each day was like walking away from paradise. Especially for the girls.

For us, the yearly returns to summer play were more limited. Once a girl put her hair in a braid, she no longer climbed trees or shouted, but stayed home all day long to prepare for the Autumn Night festival. The eleven-year-olds spent their last summer playing longest, fighting hardest, and shouting with every ounce of strength they could muster. They lingered under the trees long after the dinner horn had sounded. Laughing nervously, they spoke of marriage and children while touching their loose hair as if it might suddenly pull itself into a braid of its own accord. Touching, touching, like they weren't aware of it, the short hems of their little girl dresses, the baby fat still on their cheeks, the tops of their kneesocks that would soon be traded for women's fullclothes. Touching and laughing, for they were nearly women and knew by how much they were still children.

The summer ended with a drying of the land. The crops turned golden and the trees turned scarlet, leaves falling to the ground until we kicked through red piles of them. The younger ones returned to school with lagging steps. The older boys helped with the harvest. The older girls remained at home out of sight, not even permitted to market. Everyone was hurrying to finish the fields, store away the food, get ready for Autumn Night. This festival was a far more lavish affair than the summer's, as it coincided with the warriors' return from the Beyond.

The cry of the curlew announced them, a cry echoing from the eastern part of the Valley and continuing on from countless throats until it reached the western end. And then everyone, except the marriage-bound girls, ran to see the northern Valley warriors marching home in long, shining lines. We cheered until our cries were ragged. The last-year warriors came first, features hardened by too much time warring. They were cheered the most, for now they would settle down and start a family after choosing a wife at Autumn Night. The swords at their waists would be passed on to their firstborn son. On the parade went as we shouted and pointed, mothers and fathers searching for their sons, children for brothers. Warriors who had fallen had their swords held aloft by the other warriors of their year. Women screamed when a family sword went by in an unfamiliar hand, but choked back their cries if the family sword was angrily flung at their feet. Those warriors had not died. They had deserted. The family of a deserter rarely had the courage to show their faces at the festival.

Autumn Night was soon after. The women who lived in town decorated the square with every bit of finery they could get their hands on. A rainbow of ribbons, interspersed with lanterns, extended from the fountain to the tops of the buildings. Tables were brought out and placed in a wide circle around the fountain. Each was covered with a white silk tablecloth, polished silver utensils, and a cream-colored napkin folded into the shape of a crown. Two red candles glowed from every table, and a stiff menu leaned against the centerpiece, a gourd filled with fresh green cuttings and the scarce golden autumn flowers. Only two or three of the flowers were genuine, deep in the middle of the piece, since they were so poisonous one touch could kill. All the rest were made of gold-dyed cloth.

Through the morning and afternoon of Autumn Night were games and contests for the young children. We played fox-and-geese in two huge teams and tried to outdo everyone else in running races, relay events, and shouting loudest. I won that three years strong until Hild Gunthersdaughter projected a voice even more shrill than mine. But it was all in fun, and I made a great show of bowing in deference to her after her glass-shattering screams had at last receded.

The young warriors drank ale all day long, re-enacting favorite battles while they downed jug after jug until they passed out all around the town. The matrons competed for best cook, the older ones with grown children fighting tooth-and-nail and the younger ones just looking tired, sick, or disgusted. Many of them were last year's marriage-bound girls, their bloom fast faded. Some were carrying, their bellies low and distended, looking rather like overripe fruit. Sometimes their husbands wandered over, speaking sharply, and from then on they tried to sit up straight and smile. They received little sympathy from the older women, who wondered about the fragility of women nowadays, and whether or not they were capable of bearing healthy children, much less feeding them. The younger the wife was, the more her fruitcake for the contest looked like a cow patty. I said as much to a wife I had played with in the Mooring not five years before.

"Why do you think?" Gella almost shouted. "I work all day with two crying children and now I've got a third coming. This morning I had to wake up before sunrise to bake a cake for this stupid contest and ... "

She had plenty more to say but never had the chance. I stood with my mouth open at her tirade as her husband appeared and slapped her across the face. The older women looked on with approval. The younger ones glanced at each other furtively. I ran back to the children's games as fast as I could. Gella died birthing her third child the next spring. Everyone talked about how sad it was, such a young, happy woman dying in her prime. I thought Gella was probably relieved, wherever she was.

By mid-afternoon, the older women vanished into the town kitchens to prepare dinner for those in the square. The rest of us spread our blankets in the field outside town and picnicked. As usual, the parents wondered if it would be too cold for us children to stay outside in the evening and through the night, but we always stayed until the next morning, shivering in our blankets under thick canvas tents. We weren't supposed to watch those dancing and eating in the square, but we peeked between buildings anyway until a matron noticed and shooed us away.

For the marriage-bound girls, the Autumn Night evening was a magic time. They had been sequestered all day long in one of the shop buildings, preparing for the dance and dinner with prospective husbands. Once the sun began to set, the girls appeared in the town square. The last-year warriors watched as the girls were introduced one by one by Hugh Donaldson, the town Crier, a kindly-faced old man. The girls then circled the fountain to begin their dance. A ribbon was snipped from the decorations for each of them, and as they wove about, the ribbons wound about the fountain in a braid.

I saw the Autumn Night dresses the girls had been making all summer long under the soft lantern glow, rich velvets, satins, and silks. The girls' fathers chose the colors. Many wore purple for luck or white for modesty, several had blues for staidness or green for promised fertility. Yellow was for a particularly happy disposition. Occasionally, a girl was in red for high-spirits that needed taming, but had a good dowry as a lure. I wondered what color I would wear, should my father ever decide to marry me off. Probably purple. It was a matter of honor among men to be honest about the virtues and failings of their daughters, I had heard. The lack of dowry, it seemed, was the daughter's fault.

A lone flute guided their steps. No matter where Beth and I huddled year after year to spy, we never saw the musician. I grew bored with the dance soon after it had begun, but Beth never stopped sighing over the gowns fluttering in the autumn breezes. The dance was finished once each girl had performed her own little routine and let go of her ribbon. Then the dinner began. The girls hurried to the kitchen for an apron while their parents came forward to sit at a table. After the parents sat, a warrior approached the table and asked permission to join them for dinner if their daughter had caught his fancy. Some good-natured bickering occurred when more than one suitor came to the same table, but these conflicts were usually solved by the Crier.

The girls came to the table, waited patiently as the three perused the menu, then took the selections from the warrior first, her father, and then her mother. She served the meals in that order before finally serving herself. During dinner the father and warrior spoke while the mother and daughter ate silently, smiling at jokes, looking thoughtful at politics, blushing at more ribald remarks. When the food had been eaten, the girls cleared the plates and returned to the table to serve after-dinner drinks to their parents. Then the warriors asked the girls to dance.

This dance was wilder than the one before, with fiddlers and drummers playing around the fountain as the couples danced. Had the warrior been disappointed in his dinner choice, he was free to ask an unaccompanied girl. Hours passed. Then warriors and fathers argued about dowries, and if found suitable, shook hands to seal the marriage bargain. After that, the fathers danced with their daughters. The last dance was for the newly married couples.

The next morning, everyone went home, except for the few girls who had not been chosen. They would be escorted by their fathers to another festival the next night. The Dance of the Dregs, we called it, and those unwanted girls often married the widowers in the Valley, men with motherless children besides. Gella's husband had been there three times choosing a new wife. No girl wanted to marry him, as if they would have had any choice in the matter.

Then the winter was upon us again and the next group

of marriage-bound girls began braiding their hair. Last year, I had been one of them, grateful to have my waist-length tresses finally out of my way. But neither my father nor my mother said anything about next Autumn Night, so I continued to play with my sisters and attended school the next spring. The students looked at me in surprise when I entered the schoolhouse, but I stared them down and took a seat. People were talking, but I ignored them and went to school and market as usual.

Our family was the poorest of the poor, living like mice on the throwaway scraps of others. There was no money for my Autumn Night dress. I had no dowry. And I was relieved. That summer I dragged my sisters to the Mooring and kept on returning even when the boys ran me off and shouted at me to go home and learn to be a woman. I let my hair down and came back every day until they grew bored of chasing me and forgot I was there. Beth was mortified. The other eleven-year-olds pointed at me and giggled, so I contented myself with the little ones who were too young to care whether I was marriage-age or not.

"You should be with your mother," the Trelson boys never failed to say whenever they saw me. I was glad when they went to the fields to harvest from morning to night. Women and girls were forbidden to work in the fields, no matter how impoverished the family became for lack of help. Our small crop was planted, tended, and gathered by Father alone, as was all the wild hay he cut in the Mooring for horse feed, and for cheap sale to traders headed to the cities in the Southern Valley. The only outside work we girls did was take care of the garden. I thought it a ridiculous rule.

"It's low class to have women in the fields! What would everyone think?" Father roared when I offered to help that spring since I wasn't in the kitchen learning how to be a good wife.

"It's low class to let your family starve for lack of crops!" I roared back, dodging his fist. The long winter was still fresh in my mind, the sharp pains of hunger a clear memory. But of course, I wasn't allowed to help. Mother made no effort to make me stay inside, so intent was she on her cycle of cooking and cleaning, mending and washing. I tended the garden with my sisters and did nothing else, knowing the next winter would be as hard going as the last. Father sulked wearily at the table after a long day in the fields. I refused to feel sorry for him.

The Valley was like one of the golden flowers in the Autumn Night centerpieces, beautiful but deadly. The men raged and warred in the Beyond for our safety, giving lives and limbs so that we might live without fear. But the real battle was taking place in the Valley itself, I thought at Gella's wake. Her throat was distended, as if she had died screaming. The doctor had told her husband it was the mother or child to be saved, but not both. The husband had picked the child, hoping for a son. Gella had died. Her daughter had lived. This was the war. And the women were always the losers.

Chapter Three

Through the Schoolyard

I woke to the hiss of water hitting fire. The night's dreams balanced for a moment on the borders of my mind before plunging into oblivion. Rubbing my eyes, I sat up and kicked the blanket away.

Our cabin wasn't much. We slept crowded together for warmth in the center of one big room. Greda and Keluu were the littlest, so they slept in the middle and the rest of us formed a circle around them. Our worn pallets sagged between the uneven floorboards. The nine of us shared three blankets, the third only a clumsy stitching of rags and animal skins I had made in desperation one winter. We once had a fourth blanket given as a gift, but that soft, thick fleece had been buried with the boy baby at our father's insistence.

That one room was our bedroom at night, living room and kitchen in the day. Our parents shared a tiny bedroom near the fireplace, separated from us by a flimsy door. Father had woken, and started swearing in protest at the morning. The little girls jerked out of sleep.

"Where's breakfast?" Father shouted. I grimaced, looking around for Mother, but she had already gone out to collect eggs. There were biscuits on the counter. By the time I had pulled my dress over my smock, Beth had already put the biggest biscuit on another plate with a dab of butter and taken it in to placate Father. I rolled up her pallet after mine and shoved it in a corner with the others. Beth shot out the door like a warrior's arrow and threw a warning look at me.

"He's in a mood, isn't he," I remarked. She took the biscuits away from Balasar, who would take two if no one stopped her, then handed one to each of us before putting the plate in the washtub. I shoved mine in my mouth and ran outside to help Mother. She wasn't in the chicken coop and the hens gave me an absolutely black look. Mother must have already stolen their eggs.

She wasn't in the big room either, when I ran back. Beth put her finger to her lips and pointed at the door to the bedroom. She had set a grumbling Balasar to sweeping while the twins whined over washing the breakfast dishes.

"Just shut up and finish it!" I snapped at them. "The longer you take, the later we'll get to school."

Beth's mouth dropped. "You're not going with us!"

All the girls my age had stopped attending school after last year's Autumn Night. This fall would be Beth's final term, and mine should have been one year in the past. Now that I was twelve, it was time to be a woman and fulfill the destinies carefully laid out for us in the Valley's Codes. School learning was finished. Wife training took its place at home. It had been odd for me to be in school last spring, but not half as odd as it would be when I showed up today. Deep in my stomach, fear and excitement blossomed.

I mimicked her voice and reached down to pull Keluu's dress over her arms. She was four now, finally old enough to go to school. I tweaked her pug nose and slapped her backside in the direction of the water bucket to wash the biscuit crumbs off her chin.

"What's everyone going to say?" Beth exclaimed. "You're supposed to be here preparing for Autumn Night!"

"I went to school in the spring," I protested. "And no one said anything."

"They did so," piped Dir and Synde together. Roaninblue snickered.

"In the spring it was odd," Beth said. "In the autumn, it's indecent."

"Learning is indecent?" I said stupidly.

"You know what I mean."

I knew what she meant.

"Come on, school time. Get your writing slates and let's go," I called. Mother still hadn't appeared from the bedroom, and I wanted to make my escape before either she or Father made a half-hearted attempt at making me stay home. It was unlikely they would anyway but best to be gone.

Beth glared at me as we spilled outside. The twins ran on ahead with Greda on their heels. I took Keluu's hand as we started down the path to the main road. Dir and Synde hung behind, squabbling in loud voices. Balasar, lost in her solitary world, vanished into the fields. Sometimes she made it to school, more often not.

"'A marriage-age girl ought never to be seen outside her goodfather's home, lest her impressionable mind be swayed by corruption,'" Beth recited at my back. "The Codes of Life, On Women, the twenty-third verse."

"Tiresome." I waved her off. "And that's the twenty-second verse. The twenty-third is the one about ..." I faltered, "... something else."

Beth continued undaunted. "'She ought to remain indoors and eat sparingly, so that her complexion grows not too lusty of life, and her appetite adjusts to the pain and righteousness of sacrifice.' The Codes of Life, On Women, the twenty-third verse then."

"The righteousness of sacrifice!" I hooted. Our shoes crunched on gravel as we turned onto the main road. "What's so righteous about starving?"

"We starve so that our men may have more to eat," Beth answered. "After all, they fight for our lives in the Beyond."

"What proof of that? I think they sit around and drink ale, belching out songs from dawn to dusk."

A slate thumped against my shoulder. "Don't listen to her, Keluu. Come walk with me and we'll sing together." Keluu trotted to Beth, who walked as fast as her weak lungs and Keluu's short legs would allow. I hung back, yawned loudly and watched the lemon-yellow sun slide higher in the pale sky. Maybe I should have stayed home. Old Mother Ica taught the girls' side of the school each spring and autumn, an unpleasant affair indeed. She kept the fire roaring so we boiled like eggs in a pot. Often enough her voice would trail away during lecture, her chin would droop to her chest, and out of her mouth would wheeze a snore. We learned little but reading (and that none too well), usually just enough to make out the rules for women in The Codes of Life. She taught the town girls the basics of ciphering, so they might benefit their husbands in whatever trade they worked. Town girls married town husbands more often than not, and farm girls more often than not, had farmer husbands. What need had farm girls for ciphering, Old Mother Ica mused every term. Did we need to count the chickens in the coop? But since she taught both town girls and farm girls in the same room, the rest of us could pick up a bit of ciphering just from listening during their lessons. I did listen. Most didn't. And my eavesdropping paid off. When I went to market, I knew how much change I should be receiving if I gave a ten-cent piece for a two-cent order of bread. The Old Mothers in town "accidentally" shortchanged far too often for their goods. The looks they gave me were scalding when I innocently inquired if they hadn't shorted me a penny or two. All of them liked Beth better. Well, everyone liked Beth better.

I raised my head and looked down the main road. Keluu and Beth had become two pinpoints in the distance, and the rest of my sisters were nowhere in sight. I was going to be late if I didn't hurry. I broke into a run, letting the slate tied around my neck bounce over my chest and shoulders until I pushed it behind me so I could run faster. I crossed my fingers for luck as the Trel farm appeared so no one would see me passing. Then the Emons' at my left, and the Shingolds', until the path finally twisted northward away from the farms. It changed then, too, the yellow gravel turning to dark pink clay. I shouted for Beth and Keluu, but my voice came out more a strangled squawk than a cry. They didn't turn around. I gasped for breath and slowed to a quick walk. Old Mother Ica rarely punished for being late, but when she did, she sent us skipping around the room with her leather switch stinging against our legs.

'The schoolhouse, a squat building with two porches and a heavy-glassed window at each side, had two rooms, one for boys and the other for the girls. The front yard was our playground; the boys stayed on the right side by their classroom, the girls to the left by theirs. The field to the east of the schoolhouse was for the boys' throwing games. Girls who wandered over there were chased away.

Beth and Keluu paused at the trail to the schoolhouse. I caught up with them just as Beth nudged Keluu, who ran down to the yard where the little girls were playing touch tag. Old Mother Ica wasn't in sight yet, nor the boys' teacher, and all the children played around the school.

"Please don't go in," Beth said before I'd opened my mouth. "You're a woman now, don't you understand?"

I shook my head. It was she who didn't understand. I pushed past her and walked down into the schoolyard. Slowly, the voices receded. Play stopped. A gaggle of girls sitting on the porch steps began to stare and giggle. Everyone looked at my hair in a braid.

My cheeks flushed even as I tried to stop them. Several older boys ran around the side of the house, stopping when they saw me. There were only a few, the rest having stayed home to help finish the harvest.

"Go home!" someone demanded. The suddenness of the voice made us jump.

"I said, *go home!*" Obal shouted. I raised my chin defiantly and started for the schoolhouse steps just as Old Mother Ica opened the door and rang the bell in her hand. The girls on the steps cringed against the railings as if I were diseased.

"Come in, come in!" the teacher called with a frown. I swept past her into the classroom and sat at the desk farthest in the back. If only she wouldn't say anything ...

The girls came in one by one, each gazing at me and then

at my braid with long, significant looks. I busied myself with straightening my dress and placing my slate at the exact middle of the desk. The desks were built for two students to share, but no one sat by me. I should have expected as much.

Old Mother Ica came in, her girth forcing her to walk sideways between the rows of desks. The little girls giggled. Keluu and several other new students shifted awkwardly in the hard seats. I felt each second go by as if it were a year.

"Slates to the side," Old Mother Ica wheezed once she had planted herself on her cushioned chair. "We will begin with a story."

Nothing would be said. I relaxed and pushed my slate to the edge of the desk. She pulled The Codes of Life from her teacher's desk and opened it to the very first page. Every family had one, it was the only book most owned. The town families had ornate copies, the heavy covers trimmed with gold leaf and set jewels, each word inside written on thick, creamy paper. The farm families had the cast-offs, scruffy and dog-eared, with stains on the cloth covers. Our family didn't have one at all. In the fury of the last Dark Winter, after Father had buried our warmest blanket with a cold son, I had tossed it on the fire for heat. The beating I had received marked the skin on my back for life.

"Does anyone know what the first chapter is called?" Old Mother Ica asked with a pointed glance at the younger girls.

"Advent," several chorused.

"And what does that mean?" she asked, looking meaningfully at the older girls.

"The beginning," Dir said.

"Genesis." "Origin." Old Mother Ica nodded to our calls.

"Very good. The Codes of Life begins with Advent, a story of how our people began. Would you like me to read it to you?"

The little ones nodded. Someone in the middle rows said impudently, "I've already heard it." But the old woman pushed her glasses up her nose and squinted at the small print as if she hadn't noticed.

"In the beginning was Chaos," she read. I fidgeted. She read the story every term, sometimes more than once. I knew it by heart.

In the beginning was Chaos. The people were lost to wickedness. Where once there were just laws and strict order, there was now only wild feasting and fighting. Men dallied with impious knowledge while women danced with satyrs in the forests. Every sort of indecency was committed and celebrated. The Great Father grew angry.

Yet there were still a handful of righteous men in that land, and the Great Father came to them, saying, "Leave this place of transgression, for I will destroy it. Take with you your women and children, for though they may resist, I will grant to you such power as to teach them the ways of virtue."

And their women did resist. Like harlots, they wailed and lusted for their iniquities. The Great Father prevailed through the hands of his loyal men, and at last the women were convinced to leave the realm of the damned.

On that very day, the Great Father rained down his wrath with fire and plague. The wicked people did not blame their own evilness for the Great Father's punishment; instead, they pursued the righteous. Through the Beyond the Chosen ran with the bays of hellhounds ringing in their ears, their pursuers intent on destroying them. Finally the righteous, exhausted and despairing, staggered down a slope into a beautiful Valley and sank to the ground. They trembled to kneeling prayer as the cries of their pursuers sounded behind them. Even as their enemies made to rush through the trees and down upon them, those in the Valley prayed for salvation.

And lo! A grand light burst from the sky, and the triumphant whoops of the enemy ended as the Great Father's sword cut them low. The wicked perished as the Chosen watched, and then the women of the righteous jumped to their feet, ululating, and began to dance wildly, but the Great Father's voice rang down on them.

"Why should I not do the same to you, wicked women?" The men pulled the women down to the ground and chastised them

most grievously; the Great Father was appeased. He gave all Holy Authority to men over the women, admonishing the men to teach the women His ways in all matters.

The Great Father was pleased with His men. He granted them the Valley for all of their days and those of their children and their children's children so long as the men tended the land with love and enforced the Great Father's Holy Will. The men did so and their descendents spread across the blessed Valley.

Old Mother Ica closed the book with a snap.

"The end," a little girl added.

"Not the end, but the beginning," Old Mother Ica corrected. "Now take out your slates and let's begin."

I stayed inside at recess, aware of the boys peeking in through the window to stare at me. Old Mother Ica stayed in as well, sleeping at her desk. I had joined Beth's age group for lessons, and Old Mother Ica had not said one word to me other than to correct my spelling. The eyes on me were daunting. I drew on my slate. Should I have stayed home? Tried to teach myself to sew a dress, bake, and mend, to ready myself for a marriage to someone like Father? No, no, it was better to endure the boys' eyes and remain a girl for as long as I could.

When my sisters and I left the schoolhouse, the boys were waiting for me.

"Go home!" Obal shouted predictably.

"Where else would I be going?" I shouted back. "School's out, half-wit!"

His face reddened, but he turned east and walked toward his farm. Where he left off, the Trelsons were more than happy to take over.

"What are you, a man-hater?" San sneered.

"She's not a man-hater! She thinks she is a man!" little Com Trelson chortled. "Will your father give you his sword?"

I stalked down the path, raging inside. My sisters walked in front of me, listening to every word. We passed the Shingolds' farm, and their two boys left the group of hagglers. Both made horrific faces at me before tromping away. Now it was just the five Trelsons, for none of the Emonsons had made it to school.

"I bet she'll be taking a wife, too, along with Jadan when he comes home!"

"Perhaps our father will give you a job in the fields!"

"Man-girl, man-girl!" Com always had been a little on the dim side. But his brothers laughed and chanted it with him.

"Do you think she'll grow a beard and wear pants?" one asked when they tired.

"Yes, she's just like Annen, the warrior woman!" Teff screamed with laughter.

They all screamed with him. "Take that, you naughty man! And that! And that!" Their voices rose into girlish cries. "I can't fight, my hair's not yet dry!" "But it's dark in the Beyond!" "Do you have a good cold cream? This battle is giving me terrible blisters!"

I gnashed my teeth together and kept on walking.

Finally, finally, I passed the Trel farm and the boys went away. Their shouts of "man-girl, man-girl" did not fade for several minutes. I rubbed tears out of my eyes and hurried to catch my sisters.

"You see?" Beth said softly, fresh tear tracks down her cheeks. "I knew they'd be awful."

I pulled several twigs out of Balasar's hair. She never had made it to school. Her lips and chin were stained with berry juice.

"Were you in the Mooring?" I chided.

"Last of the berries," she shrugged.

All summer long, we picked wild berries in the Mooring before play. She reached into the front pocket of her dress and pulled out an over-ripened strawberry to eat.

"Ask Synde what the homework was for your class, then," I said. Synde learned slowly and was always a few grades behind her age for lessons.

We started down the path to the cabin. "Let's do our homework outside," I suggested, not ready to go in. Keluu and Greda settled under the tree next to the barn, the others grumbling as they followed.

Beth stayed back. "You don't mean you're returning tomorrow, do you?"

I didn't answer.

The boys seemed disappointed when I returned the next morning, striding up the stairs and into the classroom. Again, Old Mother Ica took no notice of me, even when one of the eleven-year-olds said, "But she has a *braid!*" when I stood up with them for a reading lesson.

The boys were just as awful as the day before, maybe worse because they had been so convinced I had been shamed off. They threatened to follow us home and tell our father, for surely he had been duped by feminine wiles to think I stayed in the cabin while he worked in the fields. Their boasts outstretched their courage, and I was glad to see them vanish down their own paths after following me all the way to the end of their father's fence.

And so it went on, day after day, while their frustration grew and mine sank to acceptance. What could their words do to me anyway? Beth and even Roaninblue begged me to stay home, but the younger girls began to walk around me for protection and occasionally shouted something rude back at the boys.

Then it was the last day of the week, and the school children had had enough of me. Several of the girls spat at my feet when I passed, while the boys openly threatened. Obal, both Shingoldsons, and the Trelsons followed the nine of us down the main road, discussing loudly how severely I should be thrashed. I forced my feet not to walk too fast, for I'd let the Great Father damn me himself before I showed them any fear.

Thump. A rock slammed into my slate, which I had pushed around to my back. I whirled and saw another rock rush past my face. Several boys reached down to scoop up more.

"*Go home, woman!*" Obal's wide-open mouth seemed to swallow his face whole. His wildly thrown rock missed me and hit the back of Dir's head. She shouted in pain and covered the place with her hand.

"Leave us alone!" I shrieked and scooped up a rock myself. I threw it as hard as I could at Obal. It struck him dead center in the chest and he doubled over, howling.

A pelting of rocks showered down on me. One raked my forehead, another slashed my arm. I grabbed rocks and flung them back, but I was sorely outnumbered. One of my rocks struck Teff's cheek, and a wide streak of blood coursed down his face. I cheered viciously.

Then Dir snatched a rock from the ground and threw it. Synde took one from my own hand. I looked for Beth.

"Stop it, stop it!" she cried. A rock hit her shoulder and she screamed. Dir, Synde, Balasar, and I all threw our rocks at Obal, who had hit Beth. He fell down in a fury of curses and stone. The twins were running down the main road, Beth staggering after them.

Greda and Keluu cried from their own wounds and threw rocks at Com. He cried as well, blood seeping from a cut on his knee. Ged and Landar, the Shingold boys, advanced on us, brushing away our rocks like pestering flies. I gulped and almost stepped back.

"What's going on?" a loud voice demanded. I threw my last rock, which glanced off Landar's chest. He grunted in pain and threw the object in his hand. It was a book. I grabbed it in the air before it could strike me, but my fingers fumbled and it dropped to the ground and opened. Dust sprinkled the pages.

The warrior Annen took up her spear, I read, before snatching it up so I might throw it back.

Trel himself, his flame red hair standing up like demons' horns, bellowed and cuffed Com for crying. I saw our chance.

"Run!" I hissed at my sisters. We turned and ran for home, Trel's shouts sounding behind us. We caught up with Beth quickly. She wheezed and motioned for us to keep on running. The others sped on. The twins were out of sight. Beth wouldn't speak to me or even walk by my side. I thought miserably that this had, without a doubt, been my last day in school. I couldn't let all my sisters be hurt just because I wanted to attend lessons I had mastered the year before. School had ended.

In surprise, I looked down at the book in my hand. I had forgotten I was holding it. A trash book from the look of it, with a stained cloth cover and the word *Rebellion* printed in an unsteady hand. Boys kept such things, stories of pirates on seas, virtuous maidens in distress, glorious battles on foreign lands. Their teacher always took them away when he found them, I heard, and threw them in the waste bin. The boys rummaged around the waste bin during recess to retrieve their books. This one had obviously passed through many hands and waste bins.

I looked up at Beth. She hadn't noticed. Girls never read anything but carefully marked sections in The Codes of Life. I slipped the book into the front pocket of my dress and pressed my hands over it like the delicious secret it was.

The warrior Annen took up her spear.

Chapter Four

A Gentleman's Offer

School was indeed over. Trel himself marched over to our cabin with a sniffling, scraped Com in tow to show Father what "his pack of hooligans" had done. By a rare bit of luck, Father was near passed out from ale at the table, so Trel had to satisfy himself with a mumbled, "yah, yah, I'll see to it, Trellie" and left to the accompaniment of a belch and snore. On the off-chance Father remembered when he woke, I set my sisters and myself to hard work in the garden. He rarely bothered us when we were preparing food for his belly.

Women did not work in the fields, but all kept a vegetable garden to supplement the harvest. The women in town took great pride in their gardens, growing nothing but flowers and spice beans, and some spent all day working in them so that they might rival the neighbors' in beauty, arrangement, and form. Farmwomen planted a few token flowers on the borders but used the rest of the soil for food. I told my sisters years ago to let the flowers rot. We needed all the soil our father gave us for food, not finery.

Keluu and Greda weeded around the tubers while Balasar plucked out any that seemed ripe. Dir and Synde tended the bean vines. Not spice beans, though, since they were fickle and hard to grow, better left to town women with time for wasting. But wax beans, red beans, and two-bean snaps, which had to be picked before they were fully ripe. Those grew in lengthy vines and had to be supported with poles. Dir took care of them, while Synde knelt in the dirt for the wax bean bushes. Beth checked the carrots. We grew lots of carrots, for they seemed to grow best in our cramped garden. The twins moistened the cabbage line's dirt and then picked bugs off the heads. I went to the radishes and tomatoes before stepping outside the garden to look at the squash. Father hadn't noticed them yet. They grew where the flowers should have been.

Perhaps an hour passed. I sent Balasar inside to get the big vegetable basket and, as we filled it with food, some for dinner and the rest for winter storage, she whispered that Father was still snoring at the table while Mother was just starting dinner.

"Be brave," I said to the little girls. "He may be in a temper when he wakes." They protested only a little when I sent them to the water jug we kept outside for washing. I hefted the heavy basket up and walked in the cabin.

Father jerked where he lay slumped on the table when the door closed behind me. I took the basket to Mother at the stove. She pointed wordlessly at the carrots and beans. I nodded and took them to the washtub for a rinsing. Beth soon joined in, carrying the vegetables I washed to Mother to be sliced and added to the cook pot. The rest of the girls trailed in, one by one, and sat down along the walls, as far away from Father as they could manage.

A long time later, Father woke. He rubbed his bleary eyes and clutched his head. The cup of ale sat overturned beside him on the table, the liquid long since run out between the table's cracked boards to form a puddle on the floor.

"Wha ... where's dinner?" he moaned. No one answered. Eventually he managed to turn his head toward the stove, where the cook pot was simmering. Did he remember? I hoped not.

He wobbled out of the cabin, probably to the outhouse. All of us except Mother let out a sigh of relief. Beth had set the table by the time he returned.

"What was Trel here about?" I stiffened at his words and tried not to look at him. But Father was a big man, a giant in the tiny room. His arms were thick and muscular with war scars webbing them from wrists to shoulders. Huge knuckles dwarfed his large fingers, and the flat of his hand was near twice the size of my face. I shivered.

"Something about . . . about Com, wasn't it?" he muttered. I hurriedly ladled stew from the cook pot into a bowl and brought it to him. The vegetables were still a little crisp, but I thought he was probably feeling too much of an ale-ache to notice.

Luck stayed with me. He ate the meal alone as he liked it, then retired to his bedroom. Slowly, the rest of us let out a long breath and sat at the table while Mother served. We ate silently. Even the youngest had been scared from speaking. Once finished, they unwrapped their pallets and blankets to sleep, though it was too early for bed. Everyone wanted to leave this day behind.

Mother went to the bedroom after tending to the chores. I lit a candle in the evening dimness, even though it was a waste, and sat at the table beside it.

"What are you doing?" Beth asked.

"Just drawing on my slate," I answered. She shook her head and turned away. I remembered the book and pulled it from my pocket.

Rebellion. I caressed the worn cover for a moment, tracing the letters of the title, before I opened it and began to read.

The warrior Annen took up her spear. It was the first battle-day of the war.

I looked at my sisters, rustling for comfort on the thin pallets. None of them paid any attention. Roaninblue were whispering to each other, but quieted at a sound from the other room. I almost shoved the book into hiding, but the sound stopped.

She had pulled her long locks into a tight band, and admired the golden sheen in the mirror for what she knew could be the last time. Today she might die. Many of them would.

She strode from her tent and joined her regiment, all nervously gripping weapons in their hands. General Huss stood atop a fallen tree and looked down at them.

"My warriors!" she called, "Be steadfast today, for the

enemy is ruthless. Never doubt that what we fight today is evil in its darkest form!"

Not their sons or their fathers or their brothers, the warriors told themselves. The enemy.

Then, too soon, the battle was upon them. An endless wave of the enemy covered the plain. The women shook with fear and their spears rattled against their side armor, and then one broke ranks and fled.

I read slowly for hours, sounding out word after word to understand them. The candle burned low as the battle scene raged through the chapters, warriors dying horribly with every moment recorded. It was boring and painstaking to read, but for some reason I didn't put it away. At last one of the women warriors set fire to the brush on the plain, and in the confusion, Annen and one of the men warriors were separated from the battle. The fire drove them deep into the forest.

Annen rubbed her eyes, but the ash still felt like hard bumps under her eyelids. Than washed in the stream, modestly shielding his body with his fire-blackened shirt. She remained sitting on the log when he decided to go hunting for dinner, and she relived the day's battle. When he brought back a rabbit, he cooked it alone on the small fire he built. Even when he gave her a large portion of meat so that she would not go hungry, she did not thank him.

The candle burned out with a gasp and crackle. I tucked the book back into my dress pocket and went to undo my pallet.

In my dreams, I stood reciting at my desk in the schoolhouse. Old Mother Ica's back was to me as she wrote on the blackboard, the students watching her moving hand with great intensity. I fumbled my way through the verses On Women, the six relating to marriage-bound girls. When I finished, the girls stood up from their seats and turned around. They were wearing men's battle garb, and all of them were holding spears.

I woke, that morning when everything changed, to a silver piece slapping into my forehead as Father grunted at me and stalked out the door. Probably he was headed to the trade road connecting the northern and southern Valley, where Old Durk paid him to load heavy barrels onto wagons. Both of Old Durk's sons had died long ago battling in the Beyond.

It was a market day. Though the town shops were open during the week, it was only on market days that all the farm families went shopping. The square was alive and bustling, and the good smell of bread was everywhere. On market days, counters were set up outside the shop to sell specialty items. Old Mother Nhilde made booties for newborn boy babies; they dangled from the counter's bar. Farm husbands often gave expecting wives money to buy them, happy with Old Mother Nhilde's guarantee that the booties could be returned if the baby was a girl. Father had visited Old Mother Nhilde's home in the dead of a Dark Winter to buy three pairs when Mother had had his long-awaited boy. After the baby died, Father tried to return them. She wouldn't refund more than one since the baby had been a boy, after all. So Father reclaimed only a single piece of his silver and came back home with two pairs of unneeded booties. The baby was buried wearing one pair, and the last pair of booties Father kept in his pocket.

One silver wouldn't feed us well for the next week, but then I remembered the blue twenty-pence Trel had given me and brightened. I checked my hiding place and there it was, tucked into a hole I had dug in my pallet straws.

Beth groaned when her eyes opened. "I don't feel so well." Her face was whiter than chalk.

"I'll do the marketing then. Lay back down!" I exclaimed, but she forced herself upright.

"I'm well enough for that, I suppose," she said. "How much did Father give you?"

I flashed the silver piece at her, leaving the blue coin in its hiding place. Best to keep it hidden until we left for market. Beth nodded, her jaw clenched. We put on our dresses and I started winding my hair in a braid. Several of the old mothers in the market had refused to sell to me, now that I was marriage-age and should be home. I took my business elsewhere, knowing there would be at least one old woman poor enough or greedy enough to take my coin.

"Do you hear someone outside?" Beth asked.

I shook my head. "It's just Fath ..." And then the door slammed open, and Father walked in with the town Crier behind him. He looked small and delicate next to Father's bulk, his black suit fresh and crisp. The few hairs left on his head had been carefully combed over his scalp.

"Get up!" Father barked. Beth and I yanked our dresses down right in time, but the rest of the girls were still in their smocks. Father gave me a meaningful look, then the Crier. I smoothed down my dress.

The Crier glanced about our pathetic cabin. He brushed his pants, as if invisible dirt was clinging to them.

"So, what brings you all the way out here, sir?" I ventured boldly, since no one was saying anything.

"Just a small matter." He looked at Father.

Father cleared his throat noisily. The little girls jumped. "Yes, yes. I had to come speak with you, Wright, about your oldest daughter. Will she be joining us then, for the Autumn Night festival?"

Someone had told. The Trelsons must have told their father about me going to school with a braid. Actually, anyone at the schoolhouse could have told. Even an old mother in the marketplace could have complained about me.

While I wondered, Father was stammering an answer. "Well, Crier, it's been so busy lately with the harvest ... ah ..."

"Say no more." The Crier held up his hand. "I understand perfectly, Wright. You're working in the fields all day, little time left over to deal with women's affairs. But Autumn Night grows near, I'm afraid, and this girl will need to get married! I know you're trying to raise your daughters properly, eh?"

"Of course, of course," Father said.

"Of course," echoed the Crier, "so I have a proposal for you. Does she, by chance, have a dowry?"

Father's face hardened. "Well, now, Crier, I'm doing the

best I can but there's little help I have with no sons!" He threw an accusing look at the Nameless.

"No need for anger! She doesn't then, no shame in it! I'm here to offer a solution to your problem. My daughter, Damess, has offered to foster ... Shannon, is it? ... in exchange for a percentage of your wheat crop next year. Not a large amount, just enough to afford Shannon's Autumn Night dress material and lessons in the wifely arts. Perhaps a small dowry as well."

I stared at the Crier, aghast. To be fostered meant that I'd have to leave!

"Damess is Lake's wife. He owns one of the bread shops in town, you know. Their daughter Ekklia's marriage-bound as well. Taking Shannon in would present no problem."

"Thank you, Crier, but ... " I began, but both men ignored me.

"Does she know how to bake?" the Crier continued. "She can work off her keep by helping in the shop. Not selling, of course, that would be indecent at her age. But she can help Ekklia in the back kitchen."

I couldn't bake worth a cent.

"She can bake," Father said with a thoughtful look. "But let's talk crop percentage."

Did they even realize I was still in the room? I tried to intervene.

"I don't really know how ... "

"To sew," Father broke in, giving me a glare. "She would need help learning. My wife is too busy at times to remember to teach these things."

The Crier laughed. "She could keep Ekklia company, learning how to sew! My daughter Damess told me Ekklia's all thumbs."

There was a reason for that. Ekklia had only eight fingers, after all. She wore gloves, and stuffed the missing fingers with cotton. They stuck out stiffly and never moved.

"Does she know her Codes then? The verses On Women?"

"Answer him, girl!" Father ordered, though the questions had been asked of him.

"I know them," I said.

"Good, good. A fine girl. She'll make one returning warrior a very lucky man!" He clapped Father on the shoulder and stood. "Is it a deal?"

Father nodded and shook the proffered hand. "I'll see Lake in town this evening. We can work out the crop details then."

"Wonderful. Come on, Shannon, let's be going." The Crier gestured impatiently at me.

"You heard him, pack your things," Father said. "Don't keep him waiting."

I needed to catch my breath. I was leaving? To live in town, work in a kitchen, and learn how to sew with an eight-fingered girl? I looked over to Beth. She glanced at me strickenly from where she stood among the others.

"Can't I have a minute to decide?" I begged. Their faces froze.

The Crier said gently, "You have no decision to make, child. Now come, pack your clothes, and let's be off."

Chapter Five

Living in Town

Father and the Crier stood outside while I packed my few things and said my goodbyes. My ears burned at the conversation going on outside as I kissed all the little girls.

"She's a good-looking thing, that's certain," the Crier was saying. "She'll do well on Autumn Night."

"Yes, that," Father said. "And she'll breed well, too, if her husband can convince her to drop boys."

I gritted my teeth. I hoped I would prove to be barren, then, and to Chaos with the consequences!

"If I know those boys finishing their last year in the Beyond, then I know she'll drop plenty of sons. They'll give her all the persuasion she needs!" The Crier guffawed. And I had once thought his face kindly.

"Mine's carrying low right now. I know I've convinced her this time." Father's laugh sounded more like a bark. Surely he didn't mean ... I looked around frantically for Mother. She wasn't in the room.

I knocked on the door to the tiny bedroom. No one answered. I opened the door and went in. Mother lay still on the bed, staring at the ceiling. I looked for a long moment at her belly. Again, I realized how little I looked at her. She was carrying, but not as low as Father boasted. Perhaps seven months along. I couldn't leave her now!

"Mother?" I went to her side. Her eyes stayed on the ceiling. "Mother, the Crier wants to take me away to be fostered for Autumn Night. But I'm going to tell him I can't go. I'll stay and help."

She didn't answer. I hadn't expected her to.

"I'm sorry," I said in a rush. "I'm sorry I didn't know you were carrying again. I would have helped more. I will now, don't worry."

I closed the door and absently took the bundle of clothes Beth handed me.

"Get out here, now!" Father roared.

I tried to hand the bundle back to Beth. "I'm going to tell him I can't go. Mother's with child again."

She wouldn't take it. "He won't let you stay, Shannon."

I walked to the door. "I have to stay. She needs me."

"Get out here!" Father screamed. I bounded out the door in pure reflex.

I approached the Crier. He smiled down at me.

"Sir, I appreciate your offer of fostering," I said, measuring my words. "But I can't leave. My mother needs me to help here."

"You'll do as you're told!" Father snapped, raising a hand to slap me. I flinched, but the Crier stopped his hand.

"No need, Wright. She's a fine, caring girl, to be so concerned for her mother." He turned to me. "Aren't you thoughtful? You'll be an excellent mother yourself one day, Shannon. But don't worry about your mother. She's birthed many babies and she'll birth more, no doubt. She knows what to do. Your mother will be fine, and she has many more daughters to care for her and help with the chores."

He couldn't understand. Beth was too weak to be much help, and the rest barely listened to her. I tried to explain, but neither would listen.

"Come now, Shannon," the Crier finally said in a firm voice. "There's no need for you to sacrifice your future by staying here. Don't you want a husband and a family of your own?"

My answer reached the tip of my tongue and died there. Father burst in.

"Of course she does. Every girl wants that."

"Then let's be going." The Crier turned and began walking away. Father looked at me forbiddingly. Slowly, I followed the Crier.

"Perhaps the next time you'll see your family, you'll have a grandson to present them," the Crier said, once we were seated in his wagon and his glossy black horse trotted along the road.

"Won't I see my parents at Autumn Night?"

"No, you'll be sitting with Damess and Lake. There will be six chairs at your Autumn Night table, what with you and Ekklia both, and two suitors!" He chuckled. I blinked away tears and looked down at my hands.

"Ah, yes, it's always sad when childhood ends. I remember how I felt when I first marched away to war in the Beyond."

It wasn't the same. Boys didn't leave their families to war until they were fifteen years old. I was twelve.

"But then, after my first week, I realized the next passage of life, though difficult, is better than the one before. You'll enjoy being an adult, Shannon, and you'll wonder one day why you ever wanted to stay a child."

I couldn't answer. Did Mother enjoy her adult life? She never laughed, never cried, seemed dead but for her shuffling body. I looked back as the last of Father's land passed by. A rabbit ran into the road, jumped over the shallow wheel ruts the wagon had left behind, and vanished into the underbrush.

The Crier's mood was jovial. "Now turn around and face your future!"

I turned around. In every direction, the land seemed desolate.

I fell asleep at some point, waking as the Crier slowed his horse in front of a lovely, white-brick house. A picket fence surrounded the house and front garden. I could not help but gape at the flowers as I climbed down from the wagon.

"Beautiful, aren't they?" asked the Crier, noticing my stare. "Damess tends them every day. She has the loveliest garden in town."

"But what are they?" I asked, unable to stop myself.

"Ice flowers. They're expensive enough, but Lake indulges her. Women do so love their pretty things." He tied up the reins and led me down a short path made of broken pottery pieces. I reached out to touch one of the tall flowers. They were shaped like a spilled cup, with a half-circle piece missing from the top-side. The petals were misted white with a faint blue glow. I tilted the flower up and saw a broad streak of blue on the flower's underside. The rest of the flower reflected the color in its cloudy white. I had never seen anything so lovely.

The Crier knocked on the blond-wood door. It had ice flower shapes carved into it. I tried to look in the two windows framing the entrance, but the glass was frosted and impossible to see anything through save shadows. The knock went unanswered for a long moment, and then a young girl's voice shouted, "Just a minute!" The Crier stepped back. I gripped my bundle tighter.

The door opened with a snap. "Come in, come in," chided a woman in an irritable voice. "Honestly, Father, we're to the shop today for baking, couldn't you have gotten her sooner?"

"Now, Damess," the Crier said firmly, as if chastising a very young child. He pushed me through the doorway and into the living room of the house.

That people could live in such finery! Each wall had been draped in tapestries, ceiling to floor, with only the fireplace, door, and windows for interruption. The smaller tapestries were solid blues, the larger ones had fancy pictures of forests and plains full of animals both real and imagined. Unicorns bent their slender necks down to sparkling white rivers, birds soared high above the trees. Each feather had been stitched ruby red and emerald green. Their wild eyes were sapphire blue.

My shoes sunk into thick carpet. I barely afforded it a glance before turning back to the magnificent room. Two stuffed sitting chairs framed the fireplace, and the mantle above it was lined with porcelain figurines. Light streamed in from a window in the next room, a kitchen with oak cupboards, visible through an arched doorway. I closed my mouth, realizing I must look like a poor relation.

But the damage was done. The Crier looked down at me with an expression that could be nothing but pity, and the woman, Damess, was giving the floor a careful sweep with her eyes as if I had tracked in mud. I put my shoulders back proudly and held out my hand.

"Thank you for ..." I fought for words, "... for offering to take me in. I'm Shannon Wrightsdaughter."

"Yes, how do you do," the woman said, avoiding my hand. "I am sure you will work very hard so we shan't think our concern misplaced."

What to say to that? I didn't know whether to nod or shake my head.

"We are going to the shop today to prepare for market. You will be helping in the kitchen. I shall have Ekklia fetch you an apron." She gave my clothes a disgusted look. "I think you should change first."

Into what? I owned only one dress and that I had on. It was clean, if not stylish. Well, almost clean. A long smear of something had stained a black line down my side. I looked back at her defiantly. I may have been a poor relation, but she didn't have to treat me like one.

The Crier rescued me. "Perhaps she could borrow from Ekklia?"

Damess blinked. Understanding slowly dawned. "Ahh. Ekklia? Come in here, please!"

I hadn't seen Ekklia for almost a year, since last Autumn Night. The girl who rushed into the room was not the one I had played with in the Mooring, nor shared a seat with at school. Her thick brown hair was drawn into a tight, glossy braid around her head and her face had been powdered to a pale white. She was dressed well but she always had been: her everyday outfits were as nice as some girls' Autumn Night dresses. The full skirt was deep green, the perfect shade to show off her hazel eyes. Her face was round as a wagon wheel, but the narrow blouse helped disguise a bit of the plumpness on her cheeks. I felt awkward in the room with her, and more than a little dirty.

"Shannon. It's a pleasure to see you again," she said, a child playing grownup. The powder on her nose was a bit caked. I grinned and felt better.

Her mother turned to her in approval. "Show Shannon your room. She will need to borrow a dress and apron for market."

Even at home Ekklia wore gloves to hide her hands. "I would be happy to. Come, Shannon!"

I followed her through a side door as the Crier and Damess continued talking. As if my hearing only stretched a span or two away.

"I think Ekklia will be a wonderful influence on her," the Crier said heartily.

"I don't know," replied Damess. "Really, Father, I would not want Ekklia picking up any of her ... coarseness."

" ... now, Damess ... "

" ... a lot of work to finish her up, if you will, and not a lot to work with ... "

I hated her. The door swung shut, and their voices muted to sound without words. The hallway was rather dark, but I could see the walls lined with portraits of their family.

"Jadan Trelson did them, before he went warring," Ekklia said, noticing my admiration. They were finely done pieces, but Jadan had always been skilled. "Does your family have one?"

I shook my head. Of course we didn't. "They're lovely."

"Well worth the price, Father said. And they were costly! We got four of them, see? Here's Mother and Father together, don't they look sweet? And the boys, all of them, when Trip, Cessor, and Del were back in autumn. Jame and Reese weren't of age yet. That one is of Father and all the boys, and the last is all of us together. Look, there's me!" She pointed to herself at about seven years old, standing across from her mother with her father and brothers in a tight group between them. The boys had all inherited their father's jutting chin and bumpy nose as well as his nasty expression. I remembered them from the schoolyard and shivered. They pulled hair and killed field mice in front of the little girls to make them cry. I wondered at Ekklia's fond expression. Maybe they were nice to her. Not likely.

"Trip finishes this year. He'll be at Autumn Night for a wife. It'll be nice to have him back."

"You're the youngest?"

"Yes, and was Father mad I wasn't a boy!" She lowered her voice and spoke in a conspiratorial, excited tone. "Mother said he threatened to have me exposed when I was born."

I reeled back in shock. Exposing unwanted girls was not something people talked about. Ekklia continued, unaware of my discomfort.

"But Mother cried and begged, and finally Father laughed and relented. He always gives her whatever she wants."

Bothered, I waved her away. "Oh, stop, no one really does those things."

She drew back and arched an eyebrow. "Don't be a fool, Shannon."

She turned her back and headed down the hallway. But not before I heard her mutter, "Why do you think there are no Trelsdaughters?"

I just thought Trel had been extremely lucky. I bit my tongue as Ekklia sifted through the mass of fabric in her closet, pulling out possible dresses and discarding them just as quickly.

"You could wear this one." She eyed a heavy blue dress doubtfully. "You don't have much of a figure yet, but we could stuff the front so no one knows the difference."

"No one will notice anyway. I'll be under an apron," I protested for the hundredth time. "Just pick one and let's be on our way." Her mother's calls for us had grown markedly angrier.

"Try it on then." She threw it at me. Her play at adult behavior had vanished once I was the only one in sight. I wrestled with the tight buttons while she fluttered around the room, pulling hats and bonnets off pegs on the wall. "Oh, you'll need an apron, too. I'll go and grab one from the kitchen."

She scurried to the door and flung it open. Then, as if a magic curtain separated her bedroom from the rest of the house, her features settled into a matronly smile as she walked sedately down the hallway. I sighed and closed the door. The dress fit quite well, but the added frills, lace, and tiny buttonholes made it quite difficult to put on. No doubt, this was the fanciest dress I had ever worn. My own shapeless gray covering lay in a sorry little heap on the floor. Ekklia's room was not carpeted, but the planks were thin, closely spaced, and polished. Not at all like the uneven, splintery boards at home. She had a canopy bed, a vanity table covered in creams and powders, a small sofa with a pink throw blanket draped over the back, and an enormous clothes closet. I thought of my mother, staring at the ceiling. She should have married a town husband, if they all lived like this.

Ekklia opened the door, an apron in her hands. "Mother's furious. You'd better hurry up."

I strained my fingers pushing the last button through the hole. "I'm ready."

She looked me over, and reached for her vanity table. "You aren't very filled out. Tuck these in the bust." She handed me two little cushions shaped like hearts.

"*Ekklia! I want you out here by the count of three!*"

"Forget them, let's go!"

"Shannon," Ekklia ordered, "you can*not* go outside like that!"

"*One!*"

It was not the time to argue. I stuffed them into the dress.

"*Two!*"

Ekklia grabbed my hand and dragged me to the doorway.

"Coming, Mother!" she called. "Quick, Shannon, don't forget the apron!"

I turned and snatched it up from the sofa where she had left it. We nearly ran down the hall, slowing only when we reached the door to the living room. Ekklia opened it and gracefully swept out, her hands holding the sides of her dress so they would not brush or catch on anything. I followed, but not before noticing the cushion hearts were uneven. I poked the right one down further.

"About time!" Damess said crossly. Her eyes raked over me.

The Crier stretched in a chair and stood. "Very nice, Shannon. Come, girls, get in the wagon." He extended an arm to Damess.

Once outside, Ekklia pointed to the back of the wagon. "Pull up that dust cover. There's a seat under it for us."

I lifted the cover away. Damess climbed into the front seat with the Crier. Ekklia and I folded the cover, put it under the seat, and sat down. The whip cracked and we jolted into motion.

"I'm so glad you'll be in the kitchen. Mother works the front counter and I'm in back all by myself." Ekklia motioned for me to put my head down as we passed a group of boys on the side of the road while she shielded her face modestly with a handkerchief. One of the boys whistled anyway. She was blushing when she looked at me a moment later.

"Rude!" She gasped, fluffing her skirt. "Great Father, a woman's not safe 'til she's married!"

Ekklia fluttered the handkerchief over her stained cheeks to cool them. "It will be great to have someone to talk to. I haven't spoken to another girl since last Autumn Night. Just my mother, that's all, but I listen when her friends come over to keep myself up on the news." Isolation must have made Ekklia a talker; she hadn't spoken this much even at play in the Mooring.

"Last night I heard Father telling Mother that the warriors would be back soon from the Beyond." She sighed. "And Autumn Night is only a month away then! My dress is nearly finished. I can't wait to see it!"

I blinked at her in confusion. "I thought you were making it yourself."

"Goodness, no! Father wouldn't hear of it! He sent away for a seamstress to do it, lots of families are doing that nowadays. It's more fashionable. Anyway, the dress will be arriving any week now, Father says. I wonder what color he chose for me. I'm hoping for yellow. Mother's always called me her sunshine after all, it's a perfect color for me. What color do you want?"

Already tired of the chatter, I blurted, "I don't know, at the rate I'm going, I'll probably attend Autumn Night in my smock."

Her mouth dropped. "Oh ... that must have been a joke! Really, you do have a frightful sense of humor! My dress will be lovely, I know it. I'll have suitors fighting for my hand."

I rolled my eyes but she didn't notice.

"It'll be so romantic! Remember when those two warriors held an honorable duel over Priss Dawidsdaughter? I heard all about it from my brothers. Rown and Kin clashing their swords in front of the setting sun, the last glare of light shining off their hair and weapons. They say when Kin died, his last words were to congratulate Rown on such a fine prize. So romantic!" she repeated. I looked out at the town as Ekklia continued on, undaunted by my obvious lack of interest.

The wagon wheels rattled on the cobblestones as the road we traveled gave way to the town's main street. Small shops lined each side. The fancier ones were still a block away, in the square. Matronly women swept front stoops, hung goods in windows, carried heavy baskets. We passed Old Durk's candy shop. His wife washed the front window as Old Durk stood behind the counter, filling tiny bags with colored sugar.

" ... I asked Trip to tell me just everything about the warriors returning this year. He made me beg something terrible." I realized Ekklia was still talking and reluctantly turned to face her again.

"Trip doesn't sound very nice," I said.

She waved me away. "Oh, you know how boys are. Really, though, I should stop calling him that! Trip will be taking a wife this Autumn Night. He's a man now. I'll tell you all about them, the last year warriors. I remember everything Trip said."

I had no reason to doubt her. The wagon stopped in front of Lake's Bread Shop. It was nearly the largest in town, with a glossy window displaying racks filled to the brim with rolls, breads, muffins, and odds-and-ends, pieces of broken-off bread tossed in a barrel for cheap sale. The shop was expensive. Even the odds-and-ends, which I purchased elsewhere when Father threw only a few quarter-pence at me, were far too costly at Lake's Bread Shop.

I jumped out of the wagon. Ekklia climbed down demurely with her grandfather's assistance. Damess gave me a look of extreme displeasure and opened the door to the shop.

"Ekklia, take Shannon to the back and get started," she ordered. The Crier waved goodbye at us and got back into the wagon. Ekklia nodded her head to me.

"Come on. We need to hurry. Put your apron on." I yanked it over my head as we went inside and walked around the counter to the back of the shop. Enormous ovens stood at my left and right. A long counter ran along the wall and a narrow table stretched across the center of the room. Labeled jars covered the counter between two large washbasins. The kitchen was as big as our one room back home. Ekklia swiftly pulled lids off jars as she motioned me toward the barrels alongside the door.

"Here, take this bowl and start filling it with flour from the barrel." I took a large bowl from her and pried the top of the barrel off with my fingernails. A scoop was half-buried in the flour.

"How much should I get?" I asked.

"Enough for six loaves."

I looked blankly at her back. "How much is that?"

She laughed. "You're great fun, Shannon. I never noticed before."

"I'm serious. I've never ... I don't know how to make bread," I said, determined I would not feel intimidated. She turned.

"Oh, dear. Let me tell Mother."

"No, you don't need to do that!" I did not want Damess' eyes on me again. "Just show me how, I learn quickly enough."

She hesitated. "I really should ... "

"Please, Ekklia!" I picked up the scoop. "How many scoops should I put in the bowl?"

My industriousness won her over. She nodded briskly. "All right. Let me show you."

An hour later, my head swam. "Enough, enough. I'll never be able to remember all this. Just let me beat the dough."

She flipped a mound of dough to me. I pounded it with my fists to relieve my frustration.

"Good, good," Ekklia said, watching me. "I guess it's a bit much the first time around."

A neat row of greased pans lined the counter. She dumped more dough on the table next to me.

"You beat this one. I'll divide the other into the pans." Ekklia had kept her gloves on while mixing the dough, her false fingers jutting out at odd angles. But, as I watched in fascination, she stripped the gloves from her hands. The ring and small finger on her left hand were gone at the base. Eight-fingered Ekklia she was indeed. The skin was smooth over the mounds where the fingers should have been. Her right hand was normal. She worked both into the dough. I tried to look away but kept flicking glances at her left hand.

"Can I ask what happened?" I said softly. She knew what I meant without more explanation.

Her face flushed.

"I don't mean to embarrass you. I'm sorry, it was terribly nosy of me." I tripped over my words apologizing.

"No, it's all right," Ekklia said. "It was frostbite the last Dark Winter."

"I'm sorry," I said again as I finished kneading and divided the dough into the pans. "How terrible."

How could she have gotten frostbite in that cozy house of hers? They had money for firewood all winter long, Dark Winter or not.

"It was my own fault really," Ekklia said. "Trip was mad at me for teasing over something, and so he locked me out of the house. He just meant it as a joke. Del let me back in eventually but it was too late. I had been outside too long. I'm missing a toe, too."

"Your brother Trip is a beast," I said, outraged for her.

"He felt bad about it. I heard him apologizing to Father and Mother afterwards. It was a joke, really."

I stayed silent.

"He was just being foolish, that's all. He didn't mean anything. Trip's not a bad person; I won't have you thinking that. I'm happy he'll be home soon. It'll be good to see him again, the rest of the boys too. Not to mention the rest of the last year warriors!" she giggled suddenly. "I promised I'd tell you all about them."

"Fiery hell," I swore under my breath. She took my mutter as encouragement and tossed another dough mound to me. "Now just wait a second while I get the cornbread you made in the oven and I'll start mixing another batch of bread." Heat belched out into the room as she opened the door to the cavernous oven.

"There are eighteen men in his regiment, all in all. Twenty-five when he started, but they lost six in battle and one was a swish."

"What's a swish?"

"You know, a deserter. That's what the men call them. Anyway, there's eighteen left. Trip told me about each one. The best is Tarien. It'll be a lucky girl that gets him! He led all the regiments this year. I watched for him last year when they returned. I had a description from Trip, but words can only say so much. Tarien's got a hard face on him, but he has eyes as blue as a robin's egg. His hair is thick and brown, with honey streaks from the sun ..."

"I hope there is as much work here as chatter." I jumped at Damess' voice.

"Don't worry, Mother. The corn bread's already in."

"We shall have plenty of customers, Ekklia," Damess said. "That little will hardly please them."

"Shall I make any of the fruit bread?"

"Just a few cranberry and raisin. They haven't sold much lately." Without a word to me, Damess strode from the room.

Ekklia sighed. "We'd better go faster."

"What should I do now?" I asked. Ekklia started reciting a recipe so quickly I near fell over myself hurrying for the ingredients.

"This is for crossbread sticks." I cracked eggs into a bowl as directed while Ekklia covered the pans of sweet bread with damp rags. "These need to rise. Where did I leave off? Tarien, that's right. His second-command is Erlin. Not much to look at, but he's got such muscles in his shoulders ... "

And on she went through the eighteen warriors. Finally, we pulled the cornbread from the oven and sliced it once it cooled. Ekklia threw the pieces that broke away into a basket, which would be taken out to the odds-and-ends rack later. After the bread rose for the second time, she put them in the ovens.

"Now we start on the muffins. They don't take as long." She greased a multitude of muffin tins. I rubbed my shoulders. My stomach rumbled.

Ekklia stopped her Autumn Night fantasies and looked at me. "Are you hungry?"

"I haven't eaten all day."

"Mother will go out and get us lunch. Let me tell her." Ekklia left, calling for her mother. I treasured the few moments of silence. Looking furtively at the door, I sneaked over to the basket of odds-and-ends and grabbed a bit of cornbread. It just made me hungrier.

"It's an hour past mid-day," Ekklia announced when she returned. I swallowed guiltily and turned to her. "You've got a crumb on your chin."

I wiped it away. My cheeks turned red.

She grinned. "Don't worry, I eat some now and then too. Just don't let my mother catch you."

The day dragged on. Damess returned with a lunch for each of us, a wrapped ham sandwich with thick bread slices, a hardboiled egg with a tiny bag of salt for flavor, and one big sugar cookie. It was a feast. Afterwards, Ekklia and I pulled the bread from the oven and replaced them with the muffins. Damess returned to the kitchen more and more frequently to put the bread in racks.

"The crossbread sticks look wonderful, Ekklia," she said.

"Shannon made them," Ekklia corrected. Damess turned to me.

"Very good," she said, as if the words had to be pried from her tongue.

We heard voices from the shop and Damess returned to the front to help the customers. I strained to hear Beth or one of my other sisters. They would not be able to buy any of the breads, but I hoped they would come just to check on me. The afternoon wore on. Damess whirled in with a large, unexpected order of cornbread and Ekklia and I scurried to make it. When we were done, we began cleaning. Flour had gotten everywhere.

I was thankful when I heard the shop door close.

"What will you do with the leftover bread?" I asked, hungry again. "Can we have it?"

"We'll have dinner at home. Grandfather always comes over with cooked meat from the butcher's. Mother will bring some of the leftover loaves for dinner, and the odds-and-ends get thrown out."

The evening moon had risen over the horizon by the time the wagon pulled up in front of the house. Every muscle in my body felt beaten. I accepted the Crier's hand getting down after he had helped Ekklia.

The ice flowers had begun closing in the night air. Damess stroked the deep blue underbelly of one flower.

"They're beautiful," I offered.

"Yes. What flowers do you like, Shannon?"

I jumped at her flicker of interest. "I like these. I've never grown flowers, we always needed the space for food ..." Too late, I realized my error.

"Really, Shannon, the flowers are not just for show. Many kinds of flowers keep insects and other pests from attacking the vegetables. Did not your mother ever tell you that?" She swept away from me and into the house.

The Crier patted my back. "Don't worry, my girl. You can't expect to learn all the wifely arts in one day, now can you?" He chuckled and followed Ekklia inside.

I stood alone in the growing darkness, nearly too tired to think. Even with a full meal waiting for me, I wanted to go home.

"Are you coming, Shannon?" Ekklia stood in the doorway with the Crier behind her.

"Yes, I shall be right there," I answered, my words as formal as any town woman. The Crier looked down at me. His eyes approved.

Chapter Six

The Curlew's Cry

Annen looked up. Than's honest eyes shined down at her, promising protection and security. She looked at him, then at her spear for the briefest moment before deciding.

"Yes, Than, marry me!" she cried, a girlish blush rising to her cheeks. He smiled and took her hand. He would forgive her warrior past, knowing how a woman could be so easily misled. In that instant, she knew happiness. She could see the years stretching before them, full of light and laughter, children and a warm home. She knew she was lucky to have him, and she promised herself to bring him nothing but joy for the rest of his life.

"You'll give me strong sons and beautiful daughters," Than said. And Annen knew that it would be so.

I closed the book in disgust, pushed it deep under the sofa, and blew out the candle. Ekklia snored from across the room. I lay back stiffly and stared into the darkness.

That was it. Annen fell in love and it was over. She traded her weapon for a frying pan and had his babies once a year. Was that all there was to life, then, an endless circuit from oven to washboard to cradle to stove again?

I needed to talk to someone, but the only person I believed could understand was Gella and she was long dead. Ekklia *wanted* this life. Anyone else would beat me for even thinking such thoughts. My shoulders flexed involuntarily and a dull pain burned in them. Damess had beaten me only hours ago.

"You cannot sew?" she had exclaimed the day after my arrival in town. I guessed the Crier had failed to warn her of that. She flung two patches of material at me and told me to stitch them together. I could not thread the needle with her looking over my shoulder and, once I finally did, my clumsy stitches soon had her in a rage. Ekklia watched sympathetically from across the room, her hands still gloved and busily darning socks.

"I never learned how," I muttered.

"Then you will spend the rest of the day learning!" Damess snapped. "I shall not let you shame this family when your husband gives you mending and you are unable to do so."

I pricked my fingers so many times with the needle that I bled onto the material Damess gave me. After the first lesson, she would only give me the most worn rags to practice on so I would not waste her good cloth. I gritted my teeth, temper rising, and took her abuse. If not for Ekklia nodding encouragement, I would have left for home. "You cannot cook either?" Damess' words exploded the next day after I burned the breakfast meat beyond recognition. Her husband Lake barely touched the scrambled eggs I had overdone.

"I never learned how," I repeated.

"Great Father!" she nearly shouted. I flinched. "Am I to waste all my time teaching you what you should have learned years ago? What is wrong with you?"

Ekklia, ever the peacemaker, pushed herself between us. "Don't fret, Mother. I taught her to make bread her first marketday. She learns quickly."

"She had better," Damess said. From then on, she assumed I knew nothing about housework and showed me how to do whatever task presented itself. When I forgot her myriad instructions, Ekklia showed me again. I was indebted to Ekklia's kindness. When Autumn Night came, I planned to cross my fingers for luck. Not for me, but for her. She deserved the best of husbands.

Two weeks passed in a flurry of work. I never left the house but for the shop. There was so much to learn! Cooking and sewing dominated my days. Once I could stitch properly, I learned the rudimentaries of clothes-making, the bore of embroidery, and the knitting of socks and small fancies. Buttonholes were a horror. Though town wives did not need to know of such things, Damess made me memorize detailed instructions on how to make cheese, butter, and cream that she had gotten from a farm wife. Should my husband kill a pig or chicken, or return home from hunting with a dead deer, rabbit, or boar, I learned how to skin, cut, and prepare the meat or salt and store it for winter. Lake brought home fish so I could scale them.

The worst part of the day became late afternoon when Damess taught me how to speak, stand, serve, and sit. How to dance for the routine on Autumn Night. How to behave with company, with men, with in-laws. Every girl needed to know a little music, she announced, so I spent two frustrating hours a day learning to read music, play a lap harp, and sing. No farmwomen I knew possessed such skills, but Damess seemed determined to make both a farm and a town wife of me. She constantly reminded me how grateful I should be for all I was learning. I smiled politely. There was no better response.

During the second week, Damess sat me down at her vanity table. It was covered with even more powders and creams than Ekklia's. In a quiet voice she instructed me how to cover bruises, take care of welts, hide blemishes.

"How to care for myself when I get beaten," I said, just to clarify. Damess blinked.

"It is a husband's rightful duty to correct his wife," she answered. "Now pay attention."

So I learned even that. It made me ashamed, though I could not explain why. And, as a result of my comment, she made sure I had actually learned my verses On Women. She read along in The Codes of Life while I recited them. I had to explain what each one meant after I finished with all of them. It was humiliating.

"The first Code: a woman is to remember she is inferior to

a man, and that he is to rule her on the path to godliness. She must accept his correction without complaint, for thus is the lot of women." I shifted from one tired foot to another.

"The second Code?" Damess prompted.

"A woman is to serve her husband first and then his children . . ." I continued, until my voice was hoarse. After I finished, Damess nodded and closed the book.

I yawned and turned over on the trundle bed. Today Damess had set me to dusting her dozens of porcelain figurines on the fireplace mantle. Twirling dancers, birds with gold-tipped wings, fish riding the crest of a wave, all with tiny crevices to dust. It was boring, painstaking work, but it had to be done since Damess was having company after dinner. As I dusted the heaviest one, the fish on the wave, a sudden knock on the door surprised me and I dropped it. Damess took after me with a switch in her fury. The skin on my back was not broken, but it stung like fire despite the salve and made it impossible to lie in any position for very long.

Ekklia mumbled in her sleep. She was a loud sleeper, snoring and talking and thrashing about. She kept her hands gloved even in her sleep. But it was worth the noise to sleep on her bed instead of a hard pallet on the ground. The blanket was thick and warm. I pulled it over my shoulder in the cold. Autumn Night would not be far away now. The warriors would come marching back any time and my life would change again.

I lay awake for hours, wondering when I had lost control of my life, wondering if I had ever had any to start with.

The next morning I woke to Damess' brisk knock on the door.

"Market!" she called. Ekklia jumped out of bed. I sat up groggily. It was going to be a long day in a hot kitchen. I sank back into my soft pillow.

"Come on, Shannon!" Ekklia shook my shoulder. I winced and sat back up.

"I'm tired," I complained.

"Get used to it," Damess said sharply, nudging the door

open with one foot, a breakfast tray in her hands. "Women's work is never done."

She handed the tray to Ekklia and turned to leave. "Hurry up and get out of bed. I shan't have you be the reason we are short bread at the shop."

I stood up and pushed the trundle under Ekklia's bed. We ate our breakfasts quickly, a bowl of hot oatmeal and sliced apples each. "Did you hear something?" Ekklia said suddenly. I had been too intent on my food to hear anything. Shaking my head, I dipped an apple slice into the oatmeal and took a large bite.

Six whistles broke the silence. Ekklia and I looked at each other with wide eyes.

"The warriors!" She leapt from the sofa and ran down the hallway to her parents' room. "Father! Mother! The warriors are marching back!"

A commotion erupted. I struggled into the blue dress before remembering marriage-age girls were forbidden to watch. But I had to go! My family would be there and it had been so long since I had seen them. I made up my mind at that moment.

Ekklia came back into the room, eyes downcast. "I forgot we aren't allowed to go. Father says we'll go to the shop later. They're going to go cheer the warriors."

"Can you keep a secret?" I whispered, closing the door. Her eyes brightened.

"Of course I can," she said, her eyes lit up.

I held a finger to my lips as footsteps approached the room. Damess and Lake stood in the doorway.

"We are leaving now. Both you girls stay in the house and behave yourselves," Lake ordered. His voice was stern but his eyes were not. Damess looked more pleased than I had ever seen her. It must have been because their sons were returning — if they had survived another year battling in the Beyond.

The same thought must have occurred to Damess. Her lips turned down.

"Yes, well, let's be off," she said to Lake. They smiled to Ekklia and left.

"What's the secret?" Ekklia asked.

"Promise you won't tell your parents?"

"I promise, I promise!"

"I'm going to watch the warriors return. I need to see my family and make sure they're doing well."

Ekklia was horrified. "You can't go to the march! You're marriage-age."

"I know that! But my mother's with child and not well, and I need to tell my sisters to take care of her."

"It's not your concern! Your father will care for her."

"I need to go, Ekklia," I wheedled. "You promised you wouldn't tell."

"You'll be in so much trouble. It won't matter if I tell. Someone will see you and tell Mother or Father."

"I'll risk it." I slid the ribbon from my braid and loosened my hair. "No one will pay attention to me with my hair down."

"It's indecent," she protested.

"Please try to understand, Ekklia. Imagine you haven't been able to see your family for weeks. You know your mother is ill and your sisters are too young to properly care for her. Your father is too fond of his ale to be as attentive as he should. What if your mother needs the doctor? Who's going to help her?"

I knew I was using Ekklia's kind heart against her and felt guilty for it. But nothing else could be done.

"Then go," she urged, "but be careful. And wear my hat with the low brim. That will shield your face some."

"You're a good friend," I said gratefully. She took her hat from the closet and tied the ribbons under my chin. I tipped the brim down over my forehead.

I cracked the front door open and peeked out at the road. The townspeople, in the sharp creases of their best clothing, talked and laughed as they walked east. The farmers' wagons from farther west had not yet appeared. The curlew's cry had yet to reach them, and for the outermost farms like my father's, a message boy would be sent.

"I'll wait 'til the town families are gone. Then I'm going."

Ekklia nodded conspiratorially. Once the shock had worn off, excitement overcame her.

We waited until there was a break in the clusters of families. Then Ekklia pushed me out the door. "Remember to come back early, Shannon. As soon as my parents return, Mother will take us to market."

"All right," I said. I hurried down the path of broken pottery pieces and onto the main road. No one was behind me yet and the people in front were too far away to see me very well.

It would be several miles to walk at the very least. I enjoyed it as I never had before, glad to be outside for more than a trip to the shop. Scarlet leaves covered the ground. I kicked at piles of them with pleasure. It felt so good to have the air skip on my skin again, not like the oppressive stuffiness of the house. Fresh air gave Damess headaches; the windows were always closed.

A long twig had been blown from a tree. I picked it up and swung it over my head, just as Annen had brandished a spear during a battle. Laughing at my foolishness, I dropped the twig and continued along the road. Faint cheers echoed ahead. A nervous lump settled in my stomach. Trumpets blared far away and I could see a crowd of people ahead.

Pulling the hat's brim down farther, I skirted off the road to walk among the trees. It provided enough cover to hide me from the people whose attention was on nothing but the northern Valley warriors.

"Conquering heroes return!" I heard the Crier announce. The warriors were still a way down the road. I edged behind the screaming people and waited. The farm families began arriving minutes later, dividing on each side to leave the road clear, shouting hello to town folk and grabbing excited children who were running about.

A boy was staring at me fixedly. Great Father, it was Obal. I sank back into the crowd and looked down. I noticed thankfully that Damess and Lake had appeared on the other side of the road. The trumpet blare came again as the last year warriors became clearly visible. Ekklia's first choice for a husband, Tarien, led the regiments. He did have a hard face on him. I shivered. Mothers began counting their sons. Where was my family?

"Shannon?" I nearly leapt out of my skin. Hild Gunthersdaughter, the girl who had beaten me at yelling in the festival contest, tugged at my sleeve.

"Hild, don't say anything," I begged before she could speak another word.

"You shouldn't be here," she answered, her lip curling with distaste.

"I know, I know. I'm trying to find my family, have you seen them?"

"You're marriage-age. It's indecent for you to be seen in public!"

"Please, Hild. Just tell me if you've seen them. I need to know if my mother's all right!" She hesitated. "Please, Hild, please. I'll go right back inside as soon as I know."

Hild turned away and looked at the crowd. The noise was unbearable. I moved away from Hild, thinking she was not going to answer.

"Wait," she said, turning back. "You'll go right back into seclusion, promise me?" I nodded. "I haven't seen them today. None of your sisters has been in school for weeks. I haven't seen them at market either."

"Not once?" I asked in confusion. A roar exploded from the crowd. The last year warriors were here. Everyone began pushing forward to see who had returned from the Beyond. Hild and I were separated. Mothers screamed names of sons. Fathers looked solemn, eyes searching. Children yelled even as they jumped up and down trying to see their brothers.

Tarien walked past and, marching in rows of three, the last year warriors went by. I recognized most of the men from Ekklia's detailed descriptions. I saw Ekklia's brother Trip, his face settled into an arrogant sneer, as Damess pointed at him, her face relieved. There was a gap in the last year ranks. One must have fallen. Murr Keliason held a sword aloft. The Cyle family moaned, recognizing the weapon.

The last year regiment continued down the road. The next was upon us. I pushed back through the crowd and looked for my mother, my father, any of my sisters. Why had they not been in school?

The cheers and shouts died down. I turned to watch. A man broke rank with the third year regiment and approached the Trel family. Jadan should have been in that regiment. Everyone watched in shock as the man threw the family sword at the feet of Jadan's mother.

"Deserter!" he shouted in her face. She moaned and sank back. The warrior spat on the ground and rejoined his rank. The people stared at the Trel family. The mother covered her face with her hands. San and Teff reddened at taunts from other boys. Com tugged at his mother's skirt.

"Where's Jadan?" he asked. "Mother, where's Jadan? What's a deserter?"

I did not hear her answer. The youngest regiment appeared. Another man, cheeks still chubby as a child's, broke rank and approached the Sterd family. The youngest regiment ... I shook myself. I had to leave, now, and get back to Lake's house before I was noticed. As every eye turned to watch the Sterds' shame, I bolted for the trees and ran deep under their shelter, hoping none of the marching warriors would look.

One mile, another half. I slowed down, gasping for breath. The road was empty behind me but I made myself maintain a brisk walk all the way back to the house.

Ekklia pounced on me the second I opened the door. "What happened? Were you seen? Did you see any of the boys?"

I waved her off and collapsed on the sofa, fanning my face with one hand and untying the hat strings with the other. "My family wasn't there, I don't understand. Hild said my sisters haven't even gone to school."

"That's odd." Ekklia offered me water. I drank deeply.

"I saw your brother Trip. He's all right. I didn't have a chance to look for any of the others. Jadan Trelson deserted."

Her jaw dropped. *"Jadan?"*

"And I think one of the Sterd boys did as well."

She sat down heavily next to me. "Their poor families. They won't be at Autumn Night this year then. Oh, the shame."

I let my head fall back as the sweat dried on my body and my mind whirled through the information. Jadan had been the only one of the Trelsons worth a cent. His father's mirror image, he could not have been farther apart in temperament. I remembered him in the Mooring, drawing silly things on his slate for the smaller children. I couldn't believe he had deserted. I felt distaste for him as I never had for anyone but Father. He would leave us to be slaughtered by the enemy.

"One more bit of news," I added. "Is it Nandel? The Cyle man in the last year regiment was killed in battle."

Ekklia gasped. She started to speak, but voices rang outside.

"Quick! Let's get to my room so no one suspects." We darted into her room and slammed the door shut. I patted down my hair and hoped my flushed cheeks would be taken as excitement instead of exhaustion.

The door to the living room opened. Loud voices filled the silence.

"Ekklia! Come greet your brothers!" Ekklia opened her door and headed out. I followed to watch, staying at a respectful distance from the happy family.

"All safe and sound," Damess said. She ruffled Reese's hair and smoothed Jame's cheek. They pulled away gruffly from her touch. Trip, Cessor, and Del stood large next to Lake, their size dwarfing the room. Trip noticed me.

"Well, well, who's this?" he asked Damess. His lip curled into a smile, but it looked more unpleasant than a frown.

Damess noticed me. "That's Shannon Wrightsdaughter. She'll be staying with us until Autumn Night. Get back to Ekklia's room, Shannon. It is not decent for the boys to see you."

I left. Trip's laughter followed me.

An hour passed. I fiddled with Ekklia's creams, powders,

and jars of sweet-smelling ointment. I could hear muted voices talking in the living room.

Ekklia finally returned. "It's time for market."

I straightened my dress. "We won't have enough time to bake everything."

"Oh, Mother will help out today. Everyone will understand. It's not every day the warriors return!" She smiled widely. "Father put the boys in the kitchen so they won't see you when we leave."

"Let's go, girls!" Damess called. Her voice was merrier than ever. "The wagon is ready."

"Nearly Autumn Night," Ekklia sighed as Damess whipped the horse to a trot. "Will my dress be here soon?"

"Of course it will," Damess soothed.

"I heard Mother tell Father to order yours too," Ekklia said.

I tried to feign enthusiasm. Ekklia was not fooled.

"Don't worry, Shannon. I'm nervous about Autumn Night myself." She chattered about her fear of missing dance steps the rest of the way to the shop.

"Everyone out!" Damess stopped the wagon and handed Ekklia the key. "You two get started. I shall tend to the horse."

The last of the morning rushed by. I had no time to think of my family or Jadan. Damess' hands flew in the kitchen. So excited was she about her sons' safe return, she was very nearly nice to me. I wished her sons returned more often if it had this effect on her. Ekklia was laughing loudly when I heard the screaming. I dismissed it as children playing, but it came again and again.

"What's that noise?" I wondered.

"Finish wrapping the dough," Damess ordered.

Ekklia listened as well. "Mother, I think someone's hurt."

Something shattered in the next room. I ran out of the kitchen to see glass shards chittering across the floor of the shop, a cracked brick laid near the counter. Damess and Ekklia stopped behind me.

"Someone will pay for ... " Damess' voice broke off as she

looked outside. I followed her gaze to the street beyond and froze, unable to believe my eyes.

Chapter Seven

An Attack in the Market

Seconds, minutes, hours passed as we stood staring through the shattered window. Women, children, old men pushed and shoved, fighting to run faster, looking over their shoulders in fear. An ululating cry pierced through screams wild with terror and pain; a cry taken up by more voices to echo over and over.

A flash of fire scorched past me. The running people shrieked and threw themselves to the ground as a hail of fiery arrows rained down onto the roofs of shops. Ekklia choked on the smoke as the roofs began to burn. The people got up, screaming, and pushed on. I jerked into motion as Damess found her voice.

"Back in here!" she yelled, grasping our forearms. "Both of you, in the kitchen and under the counter!" Ekklia obeyed. But as I turned, I saw a small boy stumble and vanish wailing beneath dozens of legs. Without thinking, I wrenched away from Damess and ran out of the shop.

The ululating cries came again from the square. I heard the child's panicked voice and pushed my way into the crowd. It swept me along, but not before I managed to wrap my fingers around the collar of the boy's shirt and jerk him to his feet. Pushing as much as anyone else, I forced my way out of the crowd and back up onto the sidewalk. We were only a few feet away from Lake's shop. I dragged the child with me and pushed him over the jagged edges of glass in the windowpane and into the shop.

"Go to the kitchen!" I shouted in his face. Blood seeped from a gash on his forehead and several of his fingers looked broken. He turned and ran.

"Shannon! Get down!" Yet another hail of fire streaked overhead. I threw myself down, San Trelson beside me.

"What's going on?" I screamed at him. The fire had caught a woman's hair. Her howl could have shattered the heavens.

"We're under attack! Get as far away from the square as you can. It's the enemy!" He jumped back to his feet and I caught a glimpse of a tall figure, sword aloft in one hand. Its face was completely black with dark feathers protruding from the scalp, a long hooked nose, and a drooping chin that reached its chest. I stared in shock. Whatever, whoever he was, he seemed to be staring back for an instant before turning and running back into the square. Knowing each step was more foolish than the last, I followed him.

An old man lay still on the ground beside the shoemaker's shop. The street turned slightly northward and the square came into view.

First, I saw the fruit spilled across the ground from the overturned counters. Next the clothing and cookware scattered about, some of it on fire, the smoke billowing out of two shops, their windows broken. Then I saw the people among the ruins, some moving, most still. One here, two there, big and small, male and female. A woman clutched her leg and moaned. It took me several moments to recognize Old Mother Ica. A girl lay near her, crumpled on her side. A thin trail of blood stretched from her to form a pool near my feet.

Voices made me look away from the girl. Figures darted along the other side of the square, some smashing windows, others stabbing their swords into the wrecked counters. One last figure stood tall at the fountain in the square's center, surveying what was left of the market.

One of those stabbing through counters let out a sharp laugh. "Found one!" He pulled an old man from under a mass of material and shoved him in the direction of the enemy at the fountain. I recognized the Crier. Blood streaked his arms and face.

The one at the fountain drew his sword. "All of you head back. I'll finish this business." Their voices were odd but I could not tell why.

The enemy strode to the Crier. He shrunk into himself, looking like a frightened child. His knees gave out and he fell.

"No!" I shouted and ran toward them.

"Run away, little girl!" the enemy said. Up close, the face was truly frightening. Dark eyes glittered over ribbed black cheeks. Yellow fangs gleamed dully over the lower lip. Heavy black hair reached the enemy's waist, in tight braids tied with dangling ribbons, a feather dropping from each end.

"Leave him alone! He has done nothing to you!" I shouted, trying to cover my fear. The enemy laughed and slapped me aside with one arm. I staggered and nearly fell.

"Say hello to your Great Father for me," the enemy taunted the Crier.

Men's voices shouted in the streets. The warriors were coming! The Crier moaned. It would be too late by the time the warriors got to us. The enemy raised his sword high and the air hissed as it fell.

I threw my fist at his hooked nose. The sword wavered and went off-course. Something tore across my knuckles and the enemy's face fell away.

The black animal face vanished. A mask. I froze.

A woman stared back at me. A woman.

A long scar ran down her left cheek, a light line in tanned flesh from temple to chin. Her honey-colored hair had been braided and was coiled around her head like my own.

A woman. Had she tried to strike me with her sword, I still would not have been able to move.

"You're a woman?" I asked stupidly.

"Pawn!" She sneered, and then bolted away. The world disappeared around me in a jostle of men's bodies and voices and weapons.

The skin on my back was being seared away. I curled my body and screamed, fighting to get away from the whip. Heat pounded through my head. The whip fell again with a wet slap.

"Recite the third Code, Shannon!" Damess ordered. The Crier stayed the whip.

"A woman ... a woman is never ..." I sobbed in pain. "... a woman is never ..."

The whip lashed down again.

"Recite it!"

I gulped and tried to speak. "A woman is never to...never to raise her hand to ..."

The whip struck my neck, tearing the skin like paper. Blood streamed down my shoulders and over my chest.

"... raise her hand to strike another, for a woman's place ..."

"What, Shannon? *What is a woman's place?*"

But I could go no further. The whip lashed over and over. Finally, finally, I lost consciousness.

Ekklia was ripping one of the kitchen rags into shreds. The shop was silent. I was sprawled on the floor. Someone must have dragged me inside.

"Lay still," Ekklia warned, dipping one of the strips into a bowl of water. "This is going to hurt."

I gasped at the feeling of ice on fire. Willing my body not to thrash, I bit through my lip.

"I'm sorry, I'm sorry," Ekklia wept as she lay the strips down on my back.

"Where is everyone?" I asked, my voice hoarse.

"Father and all my brothers have gone to a meeting in the town hall. Mother went to help dress the dead for burial."

The dead. Still figures on the ground. "Who died?"

"The enemy ... they killed children. Mostly children. Com and Teff Trelson. One of the Emonsons, I didn't hear which one. Rale Guntherson and the baby Swee. There were a few others,

I think. And they killed Old Durk. Old Mother Nhilde's dead, too. She was crushed by the counter."

Ekklia brushed my hair aside to put a rag on my neck. "Oh, Shannon, what did you do out there? Who did you strike?"

I paused. The Crier had grabbed my arm when the warrior woman vanished and beat me about the face with his fists until I crouched into a ball to protect myself. Then he had yanked me up by my hair and propelled me to Lake's shop.

"Damess! Ekklia! Are you all right?" he yelled. They came out of the kitchen, tears streaking their faces. The little boy I had pulled from the stampede peered around Damess' skirt, eyes wide with fright.

"What is going on, Father?" Damess asked, wiping her cheeks.

"The enemy attacked," he said shortly. "Our warriors are in pursuit. Get the whip from the back, Damess."

"Why?"

"This girl," he said, shaking me, "broke the third Code."

Damess went white. Without a word, she turned and left the room.

"I only hit her to save you!" I protested weakly. His eyes bulged.

"If you ever speak of what happened, I shall beat you until you die!"

"Her?" Ekklia asked in confusion.

The Crier dragged me across the room, past Ekklia and the boy, and through the kitchen to the back where the horse and wagon were kept. Damess appeared with the whip in her hand.

It was insane. Dead and dying littered the streets and square, and here I was, about to receive a whipping for breaking a Code. I opened my mouth to protest but got slapped by Damess.

"After all I have done for you." Her body shook with rage. "After all I have done, this is how you repay us? You good-for-nothing farm trash! How many people witnessed our shame, Shannon? How many?"

Anger flared through me. This was not fair. Did it matter if I broke a Code to save someone's life?

It did matter. The Crier pushed me against the wall, hissing in my ear. "One word and I shall kill you." He took the whip from Damess.

He drew his arm back. The whip whistled in the air and struck my stomach. I doubled over and shrieked from the burst of pain. Damess hauled me up and slammed me back against the wall.

"You need to remember what you are, Shannon!" she screamed.

The slightest jolt of the wagon made me want to howl. Everyone sat tense and silent, Lake and Damess in the front, the boys, Ekklia, and I in the back. The boys modestly looked out to the fields and Damess had told me to look at my lap and nowhere else.

"As if you could shame this family any further," she added. Our warrior men were fighting women in the Beyond. All those grand imaginings we had as children, glorious battles and falling heroes against an inhumane, monstrous-like enemy had just been destroyed for me. And all that time, the warriors were just women. Some of them. All of them. I didn't know.

I heard a rustling and assumed Damess was checking on us. Soft tears were rolling down Ekklia's cheeks, splashing on my arm.

"Are you all right, Ekklia?" Damess asked.

Ekklia nodded. "I don't mean to cry, Mother. It's just all those children that were killed ... their poor parents."

Lake's voice rumbled. "Be strong, Ekklia."

I refused to cry, no matter my pain. My eyes were hot and pricking, but I would give no one the satisfaction of tears. I thought of *Rebellion* and found myself wishing I had Annen's discarded spear.

One of the wheels struck a rock and rode over it. I breathed in sharply and glanced up to keep the tears from falling. Trip was watching me. I looked down. I heard him spit over the side of the wagon.

"Why did they do it?" Ekklia asked her father. "I thought there was a truce once the warriors returned."

"The enemy is dishonorable," Lake answered. Ekklia wept again at the thought of the slain children.

Teff and Com Trelson. I could hardly believe they were gone. And Jadan deserted. Once the luckiest of families, today had dealt them a blow I doubted they would ever recover from.

"Home," Lake announced. "Jame and Reese, tend to the wagon and horse. The rest of you go in and stay in the kitchen until the girls are secluded."

The boys went into the house. I crept out of the wagon like an old woman on unsteady legs. Damess' beating had not even healed before this new one was laid upon it. Each step made my back rage like fire. I did not look up as I went through the living room and hallway. Once Ekklia had shut the door behind us, I pleaded with her to help me take off the dress. It was stuck to the bloody rag strips Ekklia had left on my back. We pulled it off and I lay down on my side. She rinsed the rags in her basin and put them back on.

"I'm sure they will cancel Autumn Night," Ekklia said with sudden ferociousness. "No one can celebrate in light of today. It should be put off until spring."

I did not answer her. In humiliation, I heard Damess' loud voice describing how I had broken the third Code. The men made no response, and finally her voice ceased its tirade. Cupboards banged open and shut. Soon I fell into a deep sleep, in which I dreamt that I was being slowly strangled.

Chapter Eight

The Mantle of Womanhood

Ekklia was wrong. Autumn Night would be held as always at the end of the season. The men decided, Lake told us, that there would be no retaliatory attack on the enemy. It was too close to the first snowfall and the enemy's winter camps were not known. The younger men wanted to go to the Beyond anyway and find them, but cooler heads prevailed. The Valley had suffered such a tremendous blow with its loss of so many sons not old enough to battle that there would be no further risking of the ones that were. Not until next spring, at any rate. The names of the fallen boys and elderly men were carved into a block of marble brought from the southern Valley and for one full week everyone wore black in their mourning. No official mention was made of the girls and the women who died. After all, what were women?

What were women? I thought. I watched Jame and Reese pull Ekklia's gloves off her hands and laugh at the missing fingers. They slapped her for crying. The next few market days, I stared at the women setting up their counters. Their backs were bent with work, and yet all the money they earned belonged to their husbands. I thought of my mother. My youngest sisters, not even accorded the dignity of their own names.

Lower than animals, I decided. At least animals, when wounded or incurably ill, were put out of their misery. Old ones were turned out to pasture as a reward for a life of hard work. And women? Old Luol with her wasted hands had still been expected to care for children and do what little work her body could perform. If Father had grown displeased, he could beat her, his own mother. There were Codes protecting animals from undue abuse, but there were none for women. We were no more than what we could give birth to, shuffled from father to husband to son until we died.

We were nothing. I was nothing. The next weeks slipped by like grains of sand through my fingers. Damess' orders sounded hollow to my ears, and I moved through my chores and lessons woodenly, without feeling. Ekklia pestered me to talk and gossip with her, but I needed silence. The only way I could survive was with silence, my body in motion, my mind in hiding, uncaring and still.

I did have to break from my shell at times, mostly to avoid Ekklia's brothers. It became an unpleasant game for me, having to leave a room when they entered, hiding in closets if I could not make it to Ekklia's room in time. Better to hide in the closet with the stench of mothballs than listen to Damess shout at me for my indecency, letting an unmarried man see me before Autumn Night. Autumn Night, marriage, and unmarried men she nattered about frequently, bemoaning my lack of suitability for any. Autumn Night, marriage, and unmarried men Ekklia gossiped about ceaselessly, wondering why I shared not a flicker of her interest. Had I thought any farther than wash, cook, recite, I would have screamed at the words Autumn Night, marriage, and unmarried men.

Late one night, Damess roused Ekklia and me from bed and into clothing. We sat sleepily in the wagon while she drove us towards town, Ekklia's one question rebuffed with a slap. Once Damess pulled the wagon into the square, we noticed other wagons all around us. Mothers stood in a tight circle talking, marriage-age girls remaining apart and curious. I fell asleep with my head in my hands until Damess returned for us. We were led to the fountain, all the girls, and told to wait there. Ekklia whispered excitedly to the girls she had not seen for nearly a year now. I stared at the ground, willing my mind to remain silent.

Two town mothers had coils of ribbons in their arms, which they tied around the fountain. It was shaped like a blossoming flower and they somehow knotted the ribbons about the top of the stem. Working only by moonlight and a few lanterns, the mothers pointed out to us the small hooks protruding from the underside of the flower. The ribbons would be tied to those, and we should be careful not to pull too tightly or the ribbons would lose their hold.

"We're going to practice the dance for Autumn Night!" Ekklia gasped. "Oh, how exciting!" The other girls nodded and talked among themselves. Once the ribbons had been knotted to the hooks, the mothers spread us about the fountain and placed one ribbon at each of our feet, warning us not to pick them up. My ribbon was blue. I stared at it, a wave of depression rolled over me. The girls, about sixteen in all, hushed.

Old Mother Chone, her white hair hanging to her waist, held up her hand. She stood at the north curve of the circle, closest to Ekklia. I slouched at the west curve. Damess hissed at me and I straightened, staring dully at Old Mother Chone. It was unsettling to see a married woman with her hair down. I fought an urge to look back down at my feet.

"A year has passed," Old Mother Choe said, "A full year. You have stayed home to learn all that a woman must know to serve her husband, her children, the Valley, and the Great Father. Childhood ended with last year's Autumn Night, and womanhood is soon to begin. It has been a year in-between, not always a comfortable ground to stand on." She smiled, inviting chuckles of commiseration. "Your childhood toys and fancies have been placed aside, but the mantle of womanhood has yet to grace your shoulders."

She walked to Ekklia and picked up the ribbon on the cobblestones. "Tonight begins your last lesson. Once you take this ribbon, you take upon yourself the burdens and trials of adult life. Are you ready?" The girls stiffened, rather self-importantly. I stifled a yawn and thought of the warm bed I had left.

Ekklia cried when the ribbon was placed in her hand. Old Mother Chone continued eastward around the circle. I would be one of the last to receive the mantle of womanhood. When Old Mother Chone lifted the ribbon to my hands, I kept my face down hoping to convey humility, when what I really wanted to do was take the ribbon and throttle myself with it.

"Turn to the fountain," Old Mother Chone bade us. I looked at the stone flower, my stomach tightening. Ekklia smiled at me through her tears.

"There is a reason you will dance around the fountain for the warriors at Autumn Night. You are like this flower before us. Long ago, each of you was just a seed waiting to break forth into the world. With each passing year of childhood, you grew taller, stronger, and wiser. This Autumn Night, you will burst into a beautiful, womanly blossom. As you dance around the fountain, winding the ribbons over the stem, you are showing the men you are ready to leave your years of childhood behind."

I had thought we danced so that the warriors could determine which girl seemed the most comely. My face flushed. I bit down on my anger with no mercy. Ekklia sobbed.

Old Mother Chone's speech seemed interminable. Perhaps it was practice for marriage, something to be endured. "And after you give your husband his first child, your womanhood will be fully upon you, and never will you want to look back upon your childhood world."

We'll be too busy to look back. Who had time to think about anything when you were tending a baby or chasing a toddler? Ekklia took a long, rattling sniff.

"Do not be afraid. Autumn Night is not an ending. It is, indeed, your beginning."

"Move, Shannon!" a girl hissed. Startled, I looked up from the ribbon in my hands and realized the mothers had begun directing us in our dance steps. I staggered into the beginning sequence, two twirls with my left arm outstretched at eye-level. The mothers walked around our circle, pushing too-low hands up and slapping our backs to improve our posture. Damess struck with a little too much force on the sores from my whipping and I fell over with a groan. Someone snickered.

I clenched the ribbon in my right hand and then transferred it to my left. I turned two and a half times with my right hand tucked behind my back. Damess strode over to my side again.

"Relax your hands, Shannon," she demanded. Both of them were tightened into fists. I loosened them and began the eight prancing steps around the fountain, turn back for four steps, turn back again for another eight until we had circled the fountain completely and were standing again in our original positions. Ekklia was still weeping. The ribbons were shorter now, and we had each drawn closer to the fountain. The stem was partially covered in our multi-colored ribbons.

"Begin the braid!" Old Mother Chone ordered. Total confusion ensued and took minutes to straighten out. Twelve of us were to break into groups of three to form a braid and then unwind it, and none of us could figure out if we were part of that twelve, and if we were, which two near us we were to braid our ribbons with. The remaining four girls were to let go of their ribbons and break away from our circle. While the twelve braided, the four would form a line facing the south side of town, where most of the warriors sat to watch, and begin their individual dance routines. By the time they finished, our braids should have been completed and then taken apart. After they rejoined us, we would begin another loop around the fountain, eight steps forward and four back. Another four would break away during the second braid, which the remaining twelve would have to perform more slowly since the ribbons were much shorter now.

And on it went. Ekklia went with the second group for the individual dance, and I watched during my slow braiding sweep steps with the girls to my left. Her body was sure and her feet confident as she spun and dipped, lifted easily onto her toes, performing without a reprimand from the attentive mothers. Damess glowed with pride.

How would my own mother look at me right now, if she were here? I imagined her flat eyes shining with happiness that

I would soon be a woman like her. A woman like her. I forgot a step and the braid formed a coil without me.

"Shannon!" my group admonished. They tried to right it, but ended up making a knot of the three ribbons.

Colli Axsdaughter griped to the mothers when Ekklia and the others returned to the circle.

"She messed up our braid!" Her voice always sounded whiny. Two of the mothers picked the knot out with hairpins, berating me all the while. Damess' glow faded.

"It's all right, Shannon." Ekklia dared to call. Her eyes were bright and no longer teary. "Just keep working at it. We'll practice all day tomorrow."

The mothers looked at her approvingly. "What a sweet girl," one of them said to another. "She'll make a fine wife, that one."

I thought of Ekklia, married. The thought was unbearable. Her sweetness would fade under her husband's fists and a heap of wailing babies. Maybe Damess had been like her once. Ekklia certainly had not gotten her kindness from her father.

And maybe my mother had been like me once. Our ribbons finally separated, a mother slapped the back of my head and told me to pay more attention. The dance resumed. Maybe my mother had been like me, many years ago, practicing her dance steps with giggling girls and worrying about what would happen after Autumn Night. Maybe she had been as angry and tried to hide the anger with indifference. And that indifference had killed her, turning her into the living dead woman I barely knew.

"Stop it!" I admonished myself. The third group was sent to the line for their routines. I would be next.

Even more slowly now, we braided while the four danced. I shut off my mind and went through the sweep steps without thinking. The mothers corrected the individual dancers and sent them back. Around the fountain like fools again, skirts brushing the stone ledge of the pool, and it was my turn. The last of us left the circle and came forward.

I forgot my routine halfway through. Damess put a hand

to her head as if in pain before demonstrating my next step. Embarrassed that all the eyes were upon me, I did it hurriedly and was sharply scolded to slow down. It seemed an eternity before I had finished and the next girl began.

Then, we picked up our ribbons and wound them the rest of the way around the fountain. The ribbon tails we let slip into the dark water in the fountain's pool. With a curtsey, one at a time around the circle starting with Ekklia, we finished the dance.

"The last time I saw curtsies so badly performed was when my boys were doing them!" a mother shouted at all of us. "Like this! No, don't do it with me, just watch!"

We practiced far into the night. Once the mothers were satisfied, Old Mother Chone raised her hand one last time.

"Welcome to womanhood," she greeted us. Ekklia started crying again and ran for Damess when we were dismissed.

"That was so beautiful!" She threw herself in her mother's arms and sobbed. Damess stroked her hair. All the other girls went to their mothers for embraces and encouragement. I stood alone.

The dresses arrived the next day. Damess told Ekklia and me as we sat wearily in the back of the wagon, our aprons and forearms still spotted with flour. Ekklia threw off her exhaustion.

"They're here?" she squealed. Damess nodded, smiling at Ekklia's enthusiasm. The wagon moved down the road, out of the market and past houses. Ekklia bounced on her seat.

"Oh, Mother, what color did Father choose for it?" she asked.

"Wait until you get home and you will find out," Damess teased. "Besides, I have no idea. He looked very secretive when he pulled up to the shop to tell me it was here."

Ekklia spoke to me. "Oh, *Shannon*. They're here, they're here! What color do you think it is?"

"Why don't we get to pick the color of our own dress, do you think?" I tried not to sound like I was complaining.

"Who knows a daughter better than her own father?" Damess asked stiffly, though I had asked Ekklia.

Ekklia patted my hand. "I'm sure Father went to your home and asked your father what color he wanted for you."

I shuddered. Damess remained silent and I knew without a doubt she or Lake had chosen the color for my Autumn Night dress.

I turned away from Ekklia's incessant chatter and looked out at the town. A vise settled around my chest. Had there been any energy left in my body or mind, I would have leapt from the wagon and run, run for anywhere that was not here.

"This was our last market day." For some reason, Ekklia's voice regained my attention. "Oh, Mother, I'm going to miss the kitchen, silly as it is."

"Perhaps your husband will let you shop in our store," Damess said wistfully.

Ekklia cried. She had done little but cry since the night we had practiced the dance around the fountain. Her tears had steadily increased with every day we came closer to Autumn Night, now only two days away. I rolled my eyes and stared at my lap until we arrived home.

Once inside, Ekklia forgot her usual play at adult behavior and ran from room to room to find Lake. I waited in the living room. The town Crier would be by soon with meat from the butcher's for our dinner. He usually ignored me whenever we were together for market day meals or family visits. Now that the boys were back from warring, I had to take my plate and eat alone in Ekklia's room so they would not see me. See what? What about me was so indecent?

Ekklia returned to the living room. "I can't find him," she said, disappointed. Just then the door opened; Lake and the Crier smiled as they came into the room. They held two large packages in their arms. Thick brown paper and twine covered the contents tightly. Ekklia squealed and clapped her hands.

"My dress!" She fairly jumped across the room. "Can I see it? Can I see it?"

"Now, Ekklia," Lake chastised. "Dinner first. I'll put it on your bed and you can see it after dinner."

"How can I eat dinner?" she pouted prettily. He laughed.

"I'll go out and get the meal." The town Crier placed the package he carried on top of Lake's and went back outside. Lake got by Ekklia and walked down the hallway to the room we shared.

Damess and I sliced the roasted chicken for dinner. It had been spiced and my mouth watered. After filling plates for the men, we carried them out to the table Ekklia had set. Damess pushed a plate into my arms and sent me to my room before calling the boys to dinner.

Footsteps thundered down the hallway. I sat on Ekklia's sofa and ate, looking at the two large packages sitting on her bed. One had been placed on the center of her bed and the other was at the corner. I swallowed my last mouthful and got up to inspect them more closely.

Under the twine of the package in the bed's center was a thick envelope. *Ekklia* had been written on it in beautiful calligraphy. On the other, *Shannon* had been scrawled directly onto the brown paper of the package. Well, what did I expect? I was only a foster daughter after all.

Soon Ekklia bounded into the room. "Dinner's over, finally! Mother and Father told me to go see my dress and try it on, you too. The boys have gone out, all but Trip. He's talking to Father but said he'd go to the kitchen when you come out."

She rummaged through her drawers while speaking and plucked out a pair of scissors. "Do you want to go first?" she offered, her body shaking with excitement.

"No, no, you go first. You'll go to pieces if you don't." She went to the bed and saw the envelope. With another squeal, she snipped the twine and snatched the envelope up to tear it open.

"Oh, Shannon," she said, moments later. "Read my card. It's so lovely. I'm going to keep it the rest of my life."

She thrust the card at me and dove for her package. I set

the card down without looking at it so I could watch her instead.

"*Ohhhh,*" she gasped. The brown paper slid onto the floor as she lifted up her Autumn Night dress.

It was not the yellow I remembered her wishing for. But the look on her face said that hardly mattered. The bodice of the dress was lace over white satin. The lace had been shaped into delicate lilies and somehow edged with gold trim. Ekklia pushed up the neck of the dress. Stiffened material would rise to just under her chin and then spread outward and down like petals with her face as the flower. Unlike the solid one-color of every Autumn Night dress I had seen, Ekklia's had been divided into two colors. The wide skirt flowing over the carpet was a deep blue. Ruffles gathered the bottom, lifting up so her feet would just slightly be visible. Around the waist was a string belt of light blue pearls.

"It's beautiful," I said. Ekklia was speechless. I looked down at the discarded wrapping paper on the ground.

"You missed something." I pulled a small black case from the folds of paper. Ekklia set the dress down carefully and opened the case with a snap. In it was a pair of fancy white gloves, the material so thin it was nearly see-through. The two fingers of the left glove for Ekklia's missing fingers had been stuffed.

Ekklia found her voice. "It's perfect. Completely perfect. It will be the loveliest dress at Autumn Night this year. I bet the warriors will have a duel just to sit next to me in this dress, don't you think?"

"I hope you get the nicest man there," I said sincerely.

Ekklia flushed with pleasure. "I'm going to try it on."

While she fussed with her dress, I tentatively reached out and touched my own package. I knew beyond a doubt it was purple for luck, simply made as well. Father wouldn't give that much of his crop for me to have a dress as fancy as Ekklia's.

"Can you help me?" Ekklia stood in her smock, half out of her dress. I held out the sleeves for her arms once she had torn the gloves from her hands and put the new ones on.

"You can't see my fingers, can you?" she whispered concernedly. "You can't tell two of them are fake?"

I pulled the sleeves up her arms and looked at her hands. Two of the fingers stuck out too rigidly, but I couldn't tell her that.

"Your hands look fine. I can't see anything," I said.

Ekklia looked at her hands. "I'll tell you a secret, Shannon. I've never told anyone this, not even Mother, but you feel like a sister to me. I've always been scared I'd be sent to the Dance of the Dregs because no warrior would want a woman who was... damaged. I thought I'd be one of those poor women at Autumn Night that no man would sit with."

"That's ridiculous," I said, hiding my pity for her. "Every man will want a girl like you."

"You, too," she returned, confidence creeping back. "I had the most wonderful idea last night. What if you married Trip? Then we could really be sisters."

My pity vanished. Marry Trip? The reason she spent years dreading the Dance of the Dregs? She didn't notice my silence as I fastened the back-strings of her dress.

"How do I look?" she faced me after examining herself in the mirror. I smiled weakly. She opened her door and went down the hallway, calling to her parents.

A minute passed before I remembered my own package still waiting. I picked up Ekklia's scissors and cut away the twine. Fingers trembling, I peeled the paper away from my dress.

Red. It was *red.* The color girls wore if they had not been quite modest, maybe kissing boys in the Mooring or eyeing warriors with too much interest. It was the color of a forward girl, a high-spirited girl, one who needed a firm hand like an unbroken horse. It was the color of a girl who had a good dowry, to lure men who might otherwise look to a less challenging girl to be his wife. And I probably had no dowry at all. What would a husband think of that?

I pulled the dress up and held it against me, looking in the mirror. Worse, even worse than the color, the deep cut of the bodice revealed too much of the space between my nonexistent bust. The skirt was not full like Ekklia's, but clingy and barely hung below my knees. Tears came to my eyes. I spied a black case like Ekklia's in my package and dropped the dress to the sofa. Opening the case, I found a large hairpiece inside. Long red feathers had been sewn into red felt and attached to a clip for my hair. Hot tears ran down my cheeks. The point of my Autumn Night would be to humiliate me in front of the warriors and make me grateful to be chosen at all.

I could not wear the dress. But I had no choice. I had to wear it no matter what I thought.

A door closed and Ekklia's happy voice echoed down the hallway. She stopped short when she saw the red dress on the sofa.

"Red? You have to wear *red?*" she said in shock. I nodded and sat on her bed, tears still streaming down my cheeks and dripping onto my lap.

An odd expression settled on Ekklia's face. It took a moment for me to recognize it as anger.

"Why are you wearing that color? Just because of that day in the market? I'm going to go talk to Father!" I grabbed her arm before she could stomp back to her parents.

"Don't, Ekklia. It's too late now."

She considered. "Then you go talk to them. It's not right, Shannon!" Her face brightened. "I know. Maybe one of the girls who married last year can let you borrow hers if it fits. Just go apologize again for the market day. Father's sure to give in once he sees you're truly sorry for breaking the Code."

She lifted the dress from the sofa. "What a horror," she murmured to herself before handing it to me. "Go, talk to them."

I took the dress from her. "I don't know ..."

"If they make you go in that dress, I won't go at all," she said loyally. "There has to be a mistake. Maybe that dress was meant for someone else, like Colli or Latay. You know how awful those girls are. Maybe this is just a mix-up."

As much as I disliked Colli, I wouldn't wish this dress on

her. But maybe it was a mistake like Ekklia thought. She pushed me out her door and down the hallway.

I opened the door to the living room and stepped out. Voices rang from the dining room just past the kitchen. Wiping the last of my tears off my face, I entered the kitchen and stopped short when I heard Trip's voice. I couldn't go in there with him at the table. It was indecent.

"... don't see why I should have to ..." Trip was saying.

"... family duty ... responsibility ..." Damess' voice was hard to make out.

Lake's voice was much easier to hear. "Of course you don't have to, Trip. I've just asked you to consider it. This family has been humiliated enough by her."

They weren't discussing Ekklia then. I listened, completely still, mesmerized by their words.

Trip made a rumbling sound in his throat. "I guess she's a pretty enough thing."

"Yes, yes." Damess' voice sharpened. "She knows all the wifely arts too."

"You're a man now, Trip. A man ready to start a family of his own. I can understand you wanting a calmer, less headstrong girl, one that will be easier to control." Lake's voice soothed.

"Well, now, I think I can handle any girl." Trip became indignant.

"She simply has presented us with too many problems," Lake said. "We took her in at your grandfather's bidding, because she was still attending school earlier this fall. The whole Valley was in an uproar over it. Your mother made an unwise comment to Grandfather about the disgrace it was, and he decided we should foster her until Autumn Night. Since then, we've had nothing but trouble with her."

"This hardly convinces me to consider her as a wife!" Trip exclaimed. "I can hardly expect a dowry either."

"There will be a dowry," Damess said firmly. "Should you marry Shannon, your father will give you half-share in the shop."

"Be quiet," Lake said to Damess. "Trip, you'll have half the shop."

"Half-share," Trip echoed. "I want two-thirds if I take her off your hands."

Silence.

"You have it," Lake offered. "Or it's the Dance of the Dregs with her, and humiliation for the family. And the other reason," he said with great intensity. "You know she will need the firmest of hands on her at all times, something I don't feel too many men in your regiment can provide."

"That's true." Trip liked the flattery.

"What other reason?" Damess asked. She was ignored.

He meant the secret I shared with all the men. That the enemy wasn't monsters, just people, and at least one of them was a woman at that. So intent had I been lately on obeying Damess' instructions, I had not thought of it much.

"I shall consider your offer," Trip said. He reminded me of Ekklia, play-acting at adult fare.

"She'll not be likely to die in childbirth, either," Lake surmised. "Her mother's had near a dozen children, the Crier said, and lost but one of them. She'll bear with ease and not leave you wifeless with a baby waiting for next year's Dance of the Dregs looking for leftovers."

Horrible man.

"Little of girls next year, anyway," Trip said. "Next year's the Dark Winter crop. Dark Winter girls aren't strong, and there'll be only a few of them besides."

I thought of Beth. There were only four or five girls her age in the northern Valley.

"Her mother's had naught but girls," Damess said sulkily.

Trip laughed. "All a woman needs is a little ... encouragement. She'll have boys." He and his father laughed.

I cringed. I knew what kind of encouragement it would be. My mother's face flashed before me. Her baby ... had it been born yet? Maybe she had finally given Father his long-awaited boy.

"So, where is the little harlot?" Trip continued. "Father

told me he'd ordered a special dress for her after that disgusting display at the market."

Lake cleared his throat warningly.

"Now, Trip, you know you cannot see her until the day after tomorrow," Damess chided.

"I want one more look at the goods I'm getting!" Trip protested, only half joking. I stepped away from the dining room entrance.

Out. I had to get out, away from this house and out of the town.

"Ekklia looked lovely, did she not?" Damess said, changing the subject. The men responded, but I could not make out their words. I backed out of the kitchen. Ekklia was singing in her room, her clear voice filling the air like bell chimes. I paused for one moment, torn between returning to her room and running out the door to the street beyond.

But I only paused. Throwing the red dress to the floor, I opened the door and walked out. I closed it gently behind me and turned to face the garden. The ice flowers had closed in the night air. Forcing my body to be calm, I walked on the broken pottery path and looked back at the house. It wasn't too late to go back. Light shone from behind eight-fingered Ekklia's heavy curtains. With her voice ringing in my ears, I ran for home.

Chapter Nine

Autumn Night

Beth's whitish face blanched even further when I opened the door. The twins sat, eerily still, against a wall. Neither Mother nor Father was in sight. The little girls shouted my name and ran for me.

"What are you doing here?" Beth hissed. I pushed the door shut behind me and patted several bobbing heads.

"It's good to see you too, Beth," I said. "Can't a girl come home to see her family?"

Her mouth set in a prissy line. "Why are you here?"

Why was I? What answers had I hoped to find in my father's home anyway? It had just seemed the only place to go as my feet pounded down the road away from Lake and Trip, Damess and man-wild Ekklia. The only place I could sit and think, return to the girl I was before living in town.

A loud cry came from the bedroom.

"Is Father ... " I began angrily.

"No," Beth's voice was short. "He's at the tavern. Mother started having pains this afternoon."

"The baby's coming," Keluu said, tugging at my hand. "Why can't we go see her?"

"She didn't make dinner either," Greda added. "I'm hungry, Shannon."

"You can't go in there because I said so," Beth said to Keluu.

"And I told you Greda, Father will bring home food tomorrow, and then we'll eat at Autumn Night festival the day after."

"Is there really nothing?" I asked her.

"I wasn't given a coin for market today," Beth said.

"So what?" I exploded at her. "There's vegetables in storage, aren't there? Haven't you been gathering the last of the harvest? It's almost winter!" She turned away from me, shoulders trembling. I shooed the Nameless away from me and went to Beth's side.

"It's been awful since you left," she whispered. "Mother's been sick, the twins won't help, and I ... I've just been so tired."

I led her to the pile of pallets and pulled one out. She sat down heavily and crossed her thin arms over her chest. Her skin was cold when I brushed her arm pulling a blanket over her lap. Two more cries came from the other room.

"Get up!" I shouted at Roaninblue. They got to their feet more out of surprise than obedience. I pinched their ears between my fingers and dragged them to the door.

"Get to the barn's winter storage for food. Tomorrow you're going to harvest anything left in the garden."

"But it's dark!" one of them protested. The other squirmed until I let go.

"I don't care. You two are old enough to help. Get out there and don't come back until you've got enough for a stew."

Their protests continued. I shoved them outside.

"But it's dark, Shannon!" one said, wringing her hands. "Spirits of the dead walk the earth at night, we might be taken away." The other one made a sobbing sound.

There was no time for this foolishness. "When I see real tears, girls, I'll care. Go!"

I collared Dir and Synde next. "Get water and boil it."

"Biting spiders are in the woodpile again."

"Good. Then you'll go faster."

"But ..." Synde got out one word before thinking better of it. I told Balasar to mind Greda and Keluu. Then, holding my breath, I dragged my pallet out, slipped my fingers into the straw and pulled out the blue twenty-pence I had hidden there ages ago. I slipped it into Beth's hand. Her eyes widened.

"Has this been here the whole time?" she asked.

"Yes, and it's going to have to buy a lot. Be careful to get the right change for every purchase next market day."

She nodded, head down and fingers tracing the coin. I straightened and headed for the little room.

"We're not supposed to go in there," Beth said weakly. I waved her off with my hand and pulled the door open.

An awful stench filled the dark room. I reached back for one of the candles on the living room table. Mother's sweaty face swam back and forth in the flickering light. She lay on the bed, the blankets pushed to its foot. White hair matted her forehead and cheeks. Her eyes settled on me.

"Beth, have Greda or Keluu dip a rag in water and bring it to me," I called out. I set the candle down on the rickety side table and went to my mother. Her back arched; a low moan rose from her. I pulled the rest of the twisted bedclothes to the floor, but there was little I could do to make her more comfortable. Why couldn't Damess have taught me something useful?

Greda, swollen with importance at her task, handed me a dripping rag. I wrung it out on the floor and touched the cloth to Mother's face, wiping the hair away, cooling her hot skin.

Feverish hours passed in that tiny house. The air closed in around me as I moved between my sisters and my mother. Roaninblue returned with five tubers, a sick-looking cabbage, and several handfuls of runty carrots a rabbit would reject. I set the twins to slicing the vegetables and putting them in the pot of water. The fire roared and pushed more heat and light into the house.

Beth refused to stay seated and insisted on filling a bowl with cool water for the rag I used to wipe Mother's forehead. I felt so helpless at her bedside, hour after hour, with the baby not any further along than when I arrived.

"Maybe we should send for a farm wife or a doctor," I said hesitantly. The twins and the Nameless were long asleep on their pallets.

"'A woman is to attend to her birthing alone, for it is not the business of men, nor will unmarried girls benefit from learning too soon the lot of women. Married women should be kept separate as well, for a gaggle of women produces naught but gossip-mongering and never the child.'" Beth recited.

"To Chaos with stupid rules!" I exclaimed. "When Gella was dying in childbirth, her husband sent for the doctor."

"Only in the most extreme cases does a doctor lower himself to women's problems," Beth responded with similar anger.

"Beth, whose side are you on?" I screamed. *"Mother's unwell and you're quoting Codes!"*

Several of our sisters woke up. "What's going on?"

"Nothing!" Beth and I said together. "Go back to sleep!"

We lowered our voices. "Living in town didn't change you at all, did it, Shannon? You still won't accept how the world works!"

"I never will!" I turned on my heel and went back to Mother. Her breath rasped. Should I send for the doctor? Who could go for him? Beth was too weak, the twins would dawdle, and I didn't want to leave her side. I decided to wait it out. Like the Crier had said the day he took me away, she had given birth to many children and should know what to do. And if she gave birth successfully while I called the doctor for nothing ... The bill for his trouble would be more than enough reason for a beating. Not to mention the one I'd already earned by leaving town without permission.

It was not until the rising sun had stretched weak fingers of light across the Valley that I realized I should have called for the doctor anyway and taken the consequences. Mother's last breath faded as the baby's first was drawn, and I stood numbly next to her wasted body with another daughter in my arms.

"What are you doing here?" Father yelled as I entered the big room. The heavy stench of ale surrounded him. Dazed with exhaustion and shock, I stared at him. The baby squalled in the crook of my arm. Beth and the others watched with wide eyes.

"Mother's dead," I announced. Father's eyes bulged in their sockets.

"Dead? *Dead?* She can't be dead and leave me with all these children!"

I had no response for that.

"And is that the brat that killed her? What is it?"

"A girl."

Father's mouth opened in a wordless howl. The little girls began to cry for our mother.

"I need milk for the baby," I said. "She's hungry."

"Not a drop I'll waste on her!" Father flexed his hands warningly. I nearly stepped back but forced myself to keep my ground.

"Roaninblue," I said, looking past Father, "go to the Trel farm and ask them for some of their morning milk."

"Feed that child and I'll break your neck," Father said. Quickly enough he would take food out of his own mouth if the child had been a son, I thought. "Give her to me and you're returning to Lake right now."

"I will not. Someone needs to care for this child."

"I will give her the care she needs."

I did not like the way he said that. I remembered what Ekklia had said about the reason for no Treldaughters. "No. I'll care for her. I won't be married at Autumn Night anyway."

Father moved closer to me. I held the child to my chest.

"Don't come any nearer," I warned. Out of the corner of my eye, I saw the knife the twins had used last night to chop the vegetables still on the counter. Blessing their laziness, I grabbed the knife.

Father laughed.

"I'm not afraid to use this!" I shouted. The baby cried harder. Behind us, Beth pushed all the girls out the door and into the yard.

Abruptly, Father turned away and went into the little room where Mother lay still. I ran out the door.

"One of the twins went for milk," Beth said when she saw

me. "Come on, Shannon, give me the baby. Father and I will take care of her. You should go back to your foster home now."

"I'm not leaving this child." My knuckles were white on the knife handle. I pushed by Beth and walked to the barn. I would be safe in the hayloft. Father couldn't climb up without me seeing him first.

It was hard climbing the ladder with a wailing baby. I tucked the knife into my bodice, nestled between Ekklia's heart cushions. Slowly, I made my way up to the top and set the baby down in a pile of hay. I had wrapped it in one of Mother's sheets, so it would at least be warm if not fed. It. I couldn't call my sister It. I looked down at the little pink face. Tufts of hair were matted on her head, a darker color than mine, but lighter than Balasar's. Dark blue eyes shifted about, unfocused.

"Shannon? You're being ridiculous, you know," Beth said from below. "It's time for you to put your childhood aside." I peered down at her. Her arms were crossed about her chest like an old mother.

"Don't be bothersome!" I snapped. "What do you think Father's really going to do with the baby once I leave?"

"Raise it, like he has the rest of us. What else would he do?"

"Expose it."

Her mouth fell open. "Shannon Wrightsdaughter, you have a filthy, nasty mind. No one does that to their own child."

"Why do think there are no Trelsdaughters?" I said. Beth stomped from the barn. I shook my head and picked up the crying child. She pushed her face against my dress, looking for milk.

Father came next into the barn. "Bring that baby down here and get in the wagon!"

"No!" I brandished the knife when he neared the ladder. His face reddening with rage, he shook his fist at me and cursed.

"Mother's to have no wake," Beth said later, once Father had left and a twin had brought milk. "He's burying her now in the yard."

I had not expected more. Gathering the baby into my arms, I pushed the bottle back into her mouth and held it there. Trel's wife had sent a bottle of milk and two canteens filled to the brim with more. The child's crying had ceased once milk was in her belly.

"You can't stay up there the rest of your life," Beth said.

"Have the little ones search the garden for food," I said. "Did Father bring anything back like you said he would?"

"No."

"Get to the garden," I bossed.

The day went on. I had feared Damess and Lake would appear at the farm, demanding my return, but they never did. It was the day before Autumn Night, after all, and Damess would be in the square decorating with the other women. Lake, though, …. But the only noise I heard was Father's shovel and the weeping girls. I stopped feeling sorry for Mother by afternoon and pitied more my motherless sisters.

Greda and Keluu ran in by evening to feed and water Father's horse in the stall below and to give me some carrots from storage below. I realized I had not eaten all day. Father was at his ale jug, they told me, and Beth was cooking some vegetables. The rest of the garden had been gathered up. After a few curious looks at their youngest sister, both of them returned to the house. I sipped a bit of the milk and ate the carrots. Exhaustion rolled over me. Once my head touched the pile of hay near the baby, I fell into a deep, dreamless sleep.

I woke alone. The baby was gone. Great Father, she hadn't fallen off the loft, had she? I looked over the edge and yelled in frustration. Father must have sneaked up the ladder while I slept and taken her. Knowing it was already too late, I jumped down the ladder and ran out of the barn.

"Where is she?" I threw myself into the house. Only my sisters were in the big room, sleeping on their pallets. The door to the little room was open, and no one was in there.

"Where's who?" Roaninblue asked.

"The baby, the baby!"

"Come girls, time for festival!" Father shouted outside. His voice was far too cheery.

We spilled outside. Beth's eyes were unbelieving.

"Where is my sister?" I demanded.

"Don't speak to your father that way," he chided. "Your sisters are all there with you."

"Doesn't he remember the baby?" Keluu whispered to Greda.

"I'm going to hitch the horse. All of you get ready to pile into the wagon." Father went into the barn.

The Nameless jumped up and down in excitement. Beth and I stared at each other.

"Don't even think of it, Shannon," she said. "He probably left the baby on someone's doorstep."

"Beth."

"You think the worst of everyone, you always have."

"Beth."

"It's better as it is. There's not enough food for all of us anyway, not including a newborn babe."

The ground felt unsteady under my feet. I noticed a mound of dirt near the house, freshly disturbed. A plank of wood had been plunged into the far end of the grave. Trae had been scratched into it with a knifepoint. Trae. It must have been Mother's name. I had never known.

"Come, girls, into the wagon. Shannon, make sure to cover your head when we near town so no one sees you. It isn't decent." Father tightened the harness on the horse.

Beth and I climbed into the wagon after the Nameless.

"Where's the baby, Shannon?" Keluu persisted. My throat choked when I tried to answer.

"There wasn't a baby, Keluu," Beth said for me.

"But I saw it!"

"Hold your tongue. Do you want to get in trouble and stay home from festival?"

Keluu shook her head.

"We'll be good," Greda offered.

Father pulled himself up to the wagon seat and took the

reins. "Hold tight now!" He lifted an ale jug from his belt loop and took a deep swallow.

Our land passed away to Trel's fields. Their house was silent, as if they had already left for festival. But I knew they had not. With Teff and Com dead and Jadan deserted, their family would not appear at this year's Autumn Night.

"Talked to the Crier, Shannon. Your dress is ready and waiting at the women's quarters in town. You'll go right there when we arrive."

I ignored Father. Mockery was heavy in his words.

"Your dress?" Dir asked. "You didn't tell us you have your Autumn Night dress. What color is it?"

"It's ... lovely," I said haltingly.

"I want blue for mine," Roaninblue said.

"I'd rather have yellow," the other Roaninblue said.

The wagon creaked on. Ahead, voices filled the air. I looked up. Father swung his ale jug wildly. Under his arm, I saw a milling group of people around long tables of food. Beyond them, old mothers were carrying decorations into the square. A canopy of ribbons fell from building tops. Lanterns swung from thick white cords.

"We're going to watch the dance!" Synde said. "The old mothers never check between the woodworker's and butcher's shops, and Dir and I are going to hide there tonight."

How I wished Autumn Night had ended. I did not want to imagine the looks on my sisters' faces when they saw my red dress. Trip wouldn't be the type of husband to let me visit my family either, so I probably would never hear their questions and comments about it.

"Head down, Shannon!" Father crowed. Ale splashed down on us. "Remember, a nice girl doesn't let herself be seen!"

Panic shattered my still body. "Come on, girls, let's play a game the rest of the way to the festival, shall we?" They nodded eagerly.

"Everyone bend their heads and count to thirty. I'm going to hide a button in someone's hand, and then you'll guess who has it, all right?" Eight heads lowered and began counting.

I edged to the back of the wagon. Father's head never turned. The festival was not far away now. I grasped the last board of the wagon floor and swung my body onto the road. Diving under the Emon's farm fence, I looked back only once. Beth watched me.

I held my finger to my lips, pleading with her in my mind. Then her eyes closed, and I heard her voice resume counting with Roaninblue and the Nameless. Staying close to the fence, I ran back down along the road. Through the Emon fields and then the Shingold, wondering all the while if my sisters would tell Father I was gone or if he had noticed anyway. Their count of thirty must be nearly over.

Fire burned in my legs and up to my sides. A cramp formed and I paid it little heed. I could not slow down. Once I reached the end of the Shingold farm, I climbed back through their fence and looked down the road. No one was heading in my direction. Yet.

No time, no time. Past the Trel farm again, onto Father's land. I paused only a moment at Mother's grave to whisper goodbye, then charged into the barn and up the ladder to grab the milk canteens for the baby. Father couldn't have gone far with her.

I stood outside and looked around. Where? Not east toward the town, people would have seen. But that left south, north, and west. South was the Mooring. I crossed that out. It was a flatland that Valley children used for a playground.

North or west. Both led to the Beyond miles away. I compromised and headed northwest, crossing through Father's few harvested crop fields and out into the wild fields beyond. Above the call of morning birds under a chilled sun, I imagined I heard a baby's cry.

Chapter Ten

The Beyond

The Beyond loomed, dark and foreboding, over the Valley. I had never really looked any farther than the waterfall of flowers cascading down the hillside. The trees above were too dense to see through anyway; their branches hung low enough to touch the ground.

When I was very little, town wives traveled to the edge of the Valley every fall to gather the poisonous gold flowers that would grace the Autumn Night festival tables. Then, when I was six or seven, Priss Dawidsdaughter, Ekklia's heroine of exceeding beauty, trailed out of sight in search of flowers and vanished. The women came back to the town in confusion, wondering if she had already returned. But no one had seen her, and the Crier said a bear had likely carried her off. Since then, the men had searched the hillside for the gold flowers. It was a sight: the men wrapping their hands in smock rags so the blooms would not touch their skin. The old mothers shook with laughter when the men returned, baskets of flowers draped over their arms like girls. Old Durk, before he had died in the market, had enjoyed his wife's laughter and worn one of her frilly bonnets every year to make the women laugh even harder. I wished farm men went too so I could see my father in such costume. But decoration of the square was a town job.

I hesitated once I neared my father's outermost fence, the hill to the Beyond just visible. I could still go back to the red dress, Trip, the dance, and my life. My mother's face wavered in front of me, her breath growing lighter and lighter until it simply faded away. I pushed ahead.

I climbed between the fence boards. There was no other place Father could have left her. No one went near the Beyond, much less in it, save the men warring in spring and summer. Warring, indeed. Fighting a woman hardly qualified as warring. But then the woman in the square had worn her weapon as easily as her mask.

Remember why you're here, I told myself, you should be listening for the child. I concentrated but heard nothing. She couldn't have died already. But if a wild beast had carried her off ... I reached the slope and looked up. The flowers had died in the cold air, their brown, withered remains snarling up to the trees above. It would be hard to climb. I tucked the canteens of milk down the front of my dress, next to the knife that was, amazingly, still there. It was a tight squeeze with Ekklia's heart cushions, so I pulled them out and dropped them to the ground.

I dug my fingers through the twisted mat of dead flowers, looking for a hold. The dirt was cool and crumbly and gave way easily. No help there. I looked around and noticed sturdier vines to my left. I gripped some in my left hand but they broke. I fumbled around until I found a handful of vines that held.

"Great Father, help me," I murmured. What help would He provide, though? There should be a Great Mother. The blasphemous thought repeated itself.

I burrowed my left foot into the dirt until the crumbly soil fell away to a stronger hold. Trying to exert as little weight as I could on the vines, I pushed myself up several inches and dug my right foot into the dirt until it also had a steady hold. A vine in each hand snapped and snaked down the steep slope towards me, but I held on. I let go of one handful to grasp another a little higher, but jerked away just in time. A glittering patch of gold flowers sparkled in the sunlight until the vines swung back over them. Heart pounding, I reached again, found a handful that held, lifted my left foot, burrowed again into the dirt and pulled myself up. Slowly, painstakingly, I inched my way up the incline.

Halfway up, I discovered another patch of the gold blooms growing directly above me. I could not safely climb over them, so I edged over to the side, floundering for more vines to hold and cursing the flowers. Once away, I began ascending again. A fair amount of dead leaves and vines showered to the ground below. Should anyone come following, it would be plain as day where I had gone. Maybe being a woman was at last to my advantage. No one would bother going into the Beyond after me. I was just a girl in the end. Not such a loss, even if I was trained in the proper wifely arts.

I reached for the top and grasped a pile of leaves instead of ground. For an instant, panic choked me as my right hand and foot swung free. Leaves rained down on my face, stinging my eyes and filling my mouth. I kicked my foot wildly into the dirt, pushing, pushing until I had a hold. Grabbing an assortment of vines and dry flower stems with a death grip, I caught my breath as tears tickled down my cheeks, cleaning the grit from my eyes. I moved my left foot up a few inches, then moved my right up another few and again with my left until I was high enough to crane my neck and look over the top. Where my hand had been was the only place not covered in leaves. I put my hand back on that spot and dug my fingernails into the dirt. A few more inches, I willed my feet as they wobbled alarmingly in their holds. Just a few more ...

I let go of the vines and threw my other hand over the side. The dirt crumbled under my right foot so I leaned all my weight onto the left and hauled my chest up and into the leaves. I wriggled forward until I was safely over the edge. I stood up and looked boldly down at the Valley. Father's unused land was near wilderness itself. I turned to face the Beyond. My pulse quickened with fear, but there was no time to dally.

Still I could hardly see in between the dark trees. I put my hands forward and pushed into the dense foliage. Twigs snapped loudly against me, their jagged edges pulling at my hair and clothes, scratching along my bare skin as I stumbled over a fallen branch. It would take forever to find the baby in this place. How could anyone fight here?

As I forced my way through, the forest lessened its overgrowth. The trees still huddled together, but the underbrush thinned. A musty smell lay in the air. Weak light filtered between the trunks but the sun was hidden by the tangle of branches above. Only in patches did a thread of light illuminate the ground.

I went east for no other reason than it seemed to have more sunlight. Perhaps Father had done the same. Picking my way over slippery piles of leaves and dead branches, I pulled the knife from my dress and tried to hack at the bushes when they grew too closely together. The knife was too dull to be useful, so I put it back in my dress and broke the twigs and thin branches with my hands. They soon stung from scrapes.

"Cry, baby!" I whispered. The search could take forever, especially if Father had gone the opposite direction, or not come here at all. Perhaps Beth had been right. Maybe he had dumped the child on someone's doorstep. Let her be some other family's problem. But it would be easy enough to figure out whose child it was when my mother was announced as dead. And when the child grew up to look just like my sisters and me. Surely Father could not be that foolish.

"Baby!" I called, hoping the sound of a voice would make her cry. "Come on, baby, cry so I can find you." I felt silly calling for her, but what else could be done? I tried to keep myself from going deeper into the Beyond. He had to have left her right around the edge. Strange birdcalls fluted through the air. Once, I looked up to see a blackbird staring down at me with beady eyes. The only sound but for the birds were my feet crunching through the dry leaves.

What I supposed to be an hour passed and my sister was nowhere in sight. Reluctantly, I turned back the way I had come, but not before pushing through the foliage to see the Valley and estimate how far I had traveled.

Two miles, judging from the part of the Emon's fields I stood over. Far in the distance, I saw smoke from what must be the festival's cook-fires. My mouth watered. Ham and sausage, warm bread, cakes and cookies. Chicken legs. A pain twisted through my belly. I took out one of the milk canteens and took a long swallow, reasoning I wouldn't help my sister any by dying of starvation before I found her. Her. I had to find a name. I shoved back into the Beyond and retraced my steps.

I nearly missed the bit of cloth. A ragged piece hung from a low bush branch, the threads tangled and dirty. But I recognized the light blue of my mother's sheet. Father had been around here! But where had he left the child? I got down on my hands and knees and looked at the bushes nearby. Another bit of material clung to a twig deeper into the forest. Pushing through another line of bushes, I dropped to the ground again once I was clear of them and finally saw her under a bush not ten feet in front of me.

She sobbed weakly, lying on a torn scrap of sheet. She was naked, and her lips and fingernails were blue. I picked her up and pressed her to my body for warmth. Her legs kicked feebly as I crooned. She needed to be covered. The child cried with the cold when I put her down. Taking the knife, I lifted my skirt over my shoulder and cut away at my smock. The knife was not much help, but within minutes I had a large enough piece of material to wrap her in. When the child was covered, I tore a small piece away from the wrapping and dripped milk onto it. Then I pressed the soaked corner of material into her mouth. She sucked it greedily.

"It's all right, it's all right." I cradled her head in the crook of my arm and dripped more milk onto the material.

A twig snapped. My head jerked up in alarm.

"Hello?" I called. "Is someone there?"

Silence. It was too quiet.

"Is someone there?" My voice cracked. "Show yourself!"

No one. I tried to press the material into the child's mouth with the same hand holding her and grip the knife in my other. It required more coordination than I possessed. I put the knife back in my dress and gave the child more milk. She drank a little more and then fell asleep. Her lips and fingernails were still blue.

I started to walk. What was I doing? Wandering in the forest with a newborn, unable to return to the Valley, and too afraid of the enemy to stay in the Beyond. I needed to find people, more milk for my sister and food for me. Shelter as well. It was nearly winter, and the nights would be fearfully cold. Snow would begin falling. It may not have been a Dark Winter, but the cold would kill us anyway. What had I been thinking?

I headed deeper into the forest. Surely it could not go on forever. Something had to be beyond the Beyond. Blast Old Mother Ica for not teaching us girls anything but a little reading. Basic geography would have come in handy right now.

The ground dipped and lifted. I slowly picked my way up and down gullies and once had to balance on a fallen log above a river too fast and wide to try wading through. It rolled once, terrifyingly, but then was still when the far end came up against a boulder. The child screamed when I clutched her too tight. I reached the other bank in record time. I looked back, realizing I was caught. There was no way I would go over that river again.

The world ahead had to be more than just forest. Sooner or later, I would stagger out of the trees into someone's fields if I were lucky, or the winter camp of the enemy if I were not. And here I was, armed with a dull knife, an infant, and a clawing hunger in my belly.

The past few weeks had spoiled me with frequent, filling meals. I drank some of the baby's milk and felt guilty. She and I had consumed nearly one canteen. What had Father done with her bottle? Probably taken it with her to keep her cries from wakening me, then drank the milk himself and tossed the bottle somewhere. Blast him along with Old Mother Ica.

By evening, I stopped walking. Hungry and exhausted, I squinted in the fading light to find some sort of shelter for the night. The noise I had heard earlier had not been repeated. Whatever animal it was apparently decided not to follow me. I did not want to climb a tree with a baby in my arms, but I would have to if a bear or wild boar decided to visit. I hunted for a tree with bushes about it. We could sleep in the bushes and scale the tree if it became necessary.

She wailed when I put her down to clear away some of the underbrush from a half-circle of bushes only a foot from a tree.

"Don't cry, baby," I soothed, tossing dead twigs over my shoulder. I found as many newly fallen leaves as I could to cushion our bedding. Several bugs scurried away, indignant at losing their home.

"What will your name be?" I asked her, needing to hear a voice even if it was only my own. "Ensee is a pretty name, isn't it? A bit overused." The baby cried harder. "All right, not Ensee. How about Pipher? That's a lovely bird with silver and green feathers."

She howled until I picked her up again. "Aren't you disagreeable? Let's see, there's Luvern. I never liked that name, but someone as contrary as you might. Luvern, is it? Maybe not." She quieted when I pushed milk-soaked cloth into her mouth.

"Jetti? Arlice? Penina?" I wearied of my game. My stomach rumbled. Tomorrow I should try to catch some game for a meal. Perhaps a rabbit, but what would I use for a trap? I scratched the side of my right hand, for a fierce burning had started there. My nails sunk deep into the skin. I jerked my hand away and yelled with pain, turning my right hand to see what damage I had caused.

The skin was black. I forgot to breathe. *Great Father ...* It couldn't be! The gold flowers *had* touched my skin on the climb up the hillside. The slow poison had had the whole day to embed itself in my flesh. I moaned. Even as I watched, a bit of charred skin fell away from my hand and onto the ground. I took the baby from my lap and placed her aside so I could stand up and vomit a few feet away.

This was a joke. I should have stayed in the Valley where I had been safe. But it hardly mattered now. I would be dead in a few hours anyway. And then what of the baby? She would have the same fate as before I had found her. All I had done was prolong her death and secure my own as well.

I went back to my sister and held her to my chest.

"I'm sorry, I'm so sorry," I said. She slept against me, content.

"Ekklia Lakesdaughter!" The Town Crier announced. *"I present to you my own lovely granddaughter, Ekklia Lakesdaughter!"* The warriors looked up and down Ekklia as she solemnly walked to take her place at the fountain for the dance. Her dress shimmered in the lantern light. In the darkness, Damess wiped a tear from her eye.

"Colli Axsdaughter!" the Town Crier said, searching for a compliment for someone as distasteful as Colli. *"As skilled with her lessons as she is with her tongue, Colli Axsdaughter!"*

Colli left the line of girls to take her position. I saw Trip point to Ekklia's hand and laugh as he said something to another warrior. Great dislike welled in me.

"Move forward, Shannon, you're next!"

I stepped up to a pool of lantern light. The Crier's eyes glittered when they fell on me. The warriors gasped. I looked down. The red dress clung to my body. I touched my hair in alarm. A feather whispered against my hand.

"Oh, no!" Blood rushed to my face.

"Shannon Wrightsdaughter, foster daughter of Lake," the Crier said. His teeth looked like fangs. *"She'll need the heaviest of hands to tame her, but her rewards will be untold! Shannon Wrightsdaughter, gentlemen!"*

The girls behind me giggled. I slunk to the fountain. Standing above my blue ribbon, I stared hard at the ground and waited for the rest of the girls to be introduced.

Once our circle was complete, a flute pierced us with its crystal pure song. The dance began. I went through the motions, dreading my solo routine. Gentle applause pattered over us each time a girl completed her individual dance. I chewed on my lip when my turn approached.

My dance steps went unnoticed. All the men stared at the dress and the skin it exposed. My cheeks were as bright as the material. Trip's eyes crawled over me as he cracked the knuckles on his big hands, one by one. I knew at least two of my sisters were watching with their mouths dropped in shock. I had never felt such shame.

The flute trailed away when we let the last of our ribbons sink into the dark water of the fountain. The stem was covered in a rainbow of colors. I looked at it for a long moment, hearing the Old Mother's voice saying again my childhood was now put aside.

Goodbye to my sisters, my parents, the two rooms that had made up our home. Summer games in the Mooring, sitting in the schoolroom sweating because of Old Mother Ica's fires. Father slinging his fists, Mother's bent back. I looked up at the other girls, watching their ribbon ends vanish. I knew they were thinking the same thing as me. We turned away and the warriors stood to applaud with our parents.

"*To the tables!*" the Crier said, laughing. We waited for our parents to sit at a table before sitting ourselves. Lake sat at the head of the table, Damess at the foot. Ekklia and I sat next to each other, but Lake made us switch places so Ekklia would be closer to him. The warriors milled around, looking at each girl before sitting.

"*May I join you tonight, sir?*" Trip said formally. Lake smiled at him.

"*Of course, you can, young man. It would be a pleasure to have you at our table!*"

"*I was quite taken with Miss Shannon Wrightsdaughter,*" Trip boomed. Damess failed to suppress an unwifely giggle at her son's antics. The men looked at her in disapproval and she quieted.

Ekklia looked around her nervously. No suitors for her had yet approached. I squeezed her clammy hand under the table.

"*It's time to go to the kitchens!*" she whispered to me when the other girls rose. "*Let's go get our aprons on.*"

We stood. Heat rose to my face again when everyone looked at my dress. All the girls hurried to the kitchens, where old mothers thrust aprons over our heads and put fancy serving placards in our hands.

"Write down their orders carefully, girls!" one said. *"Serving the wrong meal is a ticket to the Dance of the Dregs tomorrow!"*

Ekklia gasped as we returned to the table. Another suitor had joined Lake, Damess, and Trip. Damess' brilliant smile in her daughter's direction meant the suitor was for Ekklia, not a challenger to Trip.

"Thank you, Great Father!" Ekklia said under her breath.

Dinner flew by. The men talked of politics, marketing with the southern Valley, and whether or not girls should be educated to read. Ekklia, Damess, and I sat and smiled.

"May I have the pleasure of this dance?" Trip asked, once dinner had ended. I nodded, too miserable to speak. All I wanted was to cower under the tablecloth until Autumn Night had ended. The older men brought out fiddles and drums. Trip and I danced for what seemed like hours, and then he and Lake formalized their arrangement with a handshake. Lake and Ekklia's suitor began debating. The girls stood awkwardly near the fountain, watching the arguments and then the handshakes that determined their marriages. When it was time for the father and daughter dance, I sat alone and grateful for it at the edge of the fountain, until the Crier forced me to dance with him.

Then Trip shoved past the girls and stood in front of me. The Crier bowed and took his leave.

"It's time for our dance, wife!" he exclaimed, taking me by my forearm.

"My feet are so tired!" I said, trying to make conversation. *"Aren't yours?"*

"Dance!" he snarled. He grabbed me by my waist and forced me to dance in rhythm with him. I stepped on his foot and we staggered.

"Someone needs lessons!" a man chuckled. Trip flared.

"Here's your first one!" he roared. His fists hammered down. I cried out for help. Everyone watched silently, even Ekklia. The drums and fiddles stopped so everyone could watch the first beating of a man and his wife. I shielded myself with my hands the best I could, but his fists snaked around them, striking my chest, my stomach, my face. Finally, he raised his hand high to

slam a blow down on the top of my head. I threw up my hand to block it.

He turned and stalked away. I looked to my hand that had spared me the brunt of the blow. Where his fist had touched it, a pinpoint of black grew and swelled. The skin bubbled around it, and the blackness burned up my hand into my arm, then under the sleeve of the awful red dress. Seconds later, it crept onto my chest and up my neck. When I touched my face, the skin of my cheek began singeing.

Everyone cheered. Their sound grew louder and louder, the resonance carrying to the heavens where the Great Father parted the clouds, looked down at us, and smiled.

I jerked awake. A weak dawn's light filtered through the trees. My sister cried furiously where she lay next to me. I staggered to my feet. Voices were talking, laughing. Just beyond the next trees, just beyond ... The blackness on the side of my hand had spread over my fingers, eating away at the flesh. I fancied I could see the white of bone on my smallest finger. Grabbing up the baby, I followed the voices I kept hearing, their words indistinguishable. The canteens dropped onto the ground. I promptly tripped over a log and fell to my knees, sobbing for help as I stood up. My dress was torn and bloodstained from the cuts on my knees.

The voices, the voices .... I leaned heavily on a tree before continuing. The baby's wailing increased, but I barely heard it. Watch out for that rock, watch out for it ... Though I saw the rock a distance away, when I reached it my foot still caught on it. What was wrong with me? I could hardly lift my feet under the tremendous weights bearing them down.

"Help me!" I shouted. "Please help me!" I wove unsteadily, trying to figure out how to pass between two closely spaced trees. Go around them, I demanded of myself.

"Help!" I shouted again.

Was that a sound behind me? I turned and lost my balance. The baby cried when she fell from my slack arms.

Giggling like an unmarried girl, I sprawled on my side and

rested my head on my shoulder. The baby's mouth was open in a scream, but I could not hear it at all. I closed my eyes. An eternity of time passed. My body was pushed and pulled down a waterfall. I landed with a sickening crash on the rock below. Ekklia waved her eight fingers in front of me. I lay hypnotized by their movement.

A touch on my side. "Go away. I won't marry you!" My words were thick. Had I really spoken?

"I won't marry you either, child," a voice said. No, I was hearing things. I was lost in the Beyond with a baby and no one in sight.

Movement. I opened my eyes to see the trees dancing dizzily over my head. A face with no features appeared and vanished, leaving blurry afterimages. I waited in a red stillness.

"Do you have the baby, Reia?"

"I have it."

It. The baby couldn't be an It. Not another Nameless.

"Is it hungry?"

"She's not an It," I said to the stillness, my loud voice ringing in my ears. "Trae. Her name is *Trae.*"

Chapter Eleven

Ilari

A series of small awakenings ... damp white sheets ... a clay basin with a rag dripping water ... later, a figure in brown bending over the bed with a black object in its hands. My eyes could stay open for only seconds at a time, then sank back down to take me on another journey of glaring lights, pulling sensations, and stretched voices like echoes. My body jerked with the force of the Crier's lashes. A rock struck Beth. Com and Teff's names glowed on the marble block.

I had no idea how much time had passed when someone spoke above me. Claws reached up to pull me back down to oblivion, but I fought for consciousness. A winterlark flew in a cold white sky ...

"She's improved a little," the voice said. The winterlark vanished into the distance. I looked away.

"I hope so. She's loud," a second voice broke in. Younger. Greda and Keluu toddled across the yard after Balasar.

"The cure's as bad as the poison." I tried to open one eye, but couldn't. Father pressed his hand to his heart as we stood over the grave. "Wright Wrightsson" had been elegantly engraved in stone. Mother stood immobile. My sisters sobbed.

Rustling. "Well, I wish she'd shut up!"

"Tell me, Jelsey, why did it take so long for you to get her here? She nearly lost her hand."

Five-fingered Shannon. Ekklia and I had lots in common.

"Narine didn't want to bring her at all; none of us knew she had choga poisoning," spoke the other.

"Ahh. Forget approaching her and offering shelter or food!"

"What does it matter? She's just a Valley pawn. We thought she'd go back."

I tried to open one eye again. One should be easier than two.

"Is the baby well?"

"I checked her last night. She seems none the worse."

"Well, I'm off ..."

The voices were maddening. I tried to lift a hand to force my eye open, but I couldn't feel my fingers and my shoulder seemed locked in place.

"Time for the next dose." A thick, splashing sound filled my ears. I was swallowing something. Then I was flying higher, higher, and the blackness below glittered like crystals under moonlight.

What could have been months or years passed. I traveled on a golden horse, spoke in sharp, clipped tongues unintelligible to my own ears. Rough men in white fell to their knees at the sight of me, their arms upraised in salute as they chanted *Annen* over and over again. Then a sprinkling of sand fell down on us, first a shower, then a wave, blanketing sheets I could no longer see through.

Annen Annen Annen.

Shannon. Annen. I opened my eyes. My mouth was parched, my lips so dry I could not separate them.

"Well, look who decided to join us at last. How do you feel?"

I pulled my lips apart. "Water," I rasped.

A chuckle. Coolness made my tongue prickle. Over the rim of the cup, I saw an old woman's face with her lips quirked in annoyance or amusement. Perhaps both. She took the cup away before I finished the water.

"No point in letting it come up again. You can have more

later." She set the cup down on a small table near me. The muscles in my neck ached when I turned my head to see where I was. I lay on a cot next to several other cots, all empty, in a dim room.

The woman stood on the side of another table, putting a cork in a jar of greenish-brown liquid. She was dressed in men's clothes, her trousers tucked into black boots. She brushed off her hands on the long tails of her white shirt. Around her neck was a necklace from which dangled animal teeth. Her hair was white, but she stood unbent.

"I'm the doctor," she said finally.

Who ever heard of a woman doctor? That was ridiculous. "Where am I?"

"You're in the infirmary. Your hand will be fine in a few weeks. Scarred some, but don't worry about it."

My hand. I looked down at my right hand. It had been wrapped in white bandages, each finger individually with the littlest finger twice the size of the others.

"I touched the gold flowers by accident," I said.

"Choga flowers," this strange woman said.

"But there's no cure for that poison!" I exclaimed. "One touch is certain death."

The doctor smiled. "You Valley women always surprise me. The Great Father you worship gave you the land to tend and respect, and yet you know nothing about it."

"The Great Father gave the land to the men," I snapped. "Where's my sister? And why are you in costume?"

"Costume?" She looked down at her clothes and then back at me. "Your sister is in the Mothers' House. She's fine. And I didn't mean to offend you. Choga poisoning can be cured if you know a little herbal study. Certain mixtures of other plants can break down the poison in your body."

Light flooded into the room. Instead of a proper door, a flap of wall had been yanked aside and a head poked through.

"Is she awake?"

"See for yourself, Jelsey."

The flap fell back as a girl entered the room. I squinted at a

115

riot of curls tumbling over each other in the breeze of the falling wall flap.

"I'm glad you're better," the girl said. "Maybe you'll let us sleep tonight!"

"I don't understand." She was an older girl, but her hair was unbraided and had a blunt cut at the shoulders. Her trousers were black, as was her shirt, and she had three strands of white animal teeth around her neck.

"You've been screaming and shrieking every night. We didn't know how you couldn't wake yourself up yelling that loud. I stuffed wool in my ears at first, but then I got used to it. Some of what you yelled was pretty funny, anyway. Who's Ekklia? And why did you yell out recipes for bread?"

She looked at me expectantly.

"Ekklia's a friend. I don't know why I yelled out recipes."

"I'd try some of them if I baked better. They sounded delicious. I heard you screamed most of the day too, but I was at practice and didn't hear it. Too bad."

My head began to hurt. I closed my eyes briefly.

"Jelsey, it was very nice of you to visit. But she needs her rest." The doctor looked down at me. "What's your name? I forgot to ask."

"I'm Shannon Wrightsdaughter," I said.

Jelsey stiffened and waved her hand. "That's pawn nonsense. What's your mother's name?"

The doctor shook her head at Jelsey, but she continued.

"My mother's name was Trae."

"Oh, did she die? I'm sorry. So did mine. Anyway, you're Shannon Traesdaughter, not Wrightsdaughter. After all, who gives birth to the child? Who raises it? The mother, that's who!"

"Jelsey," the doctor said warningly.

Jelsey grinned. "Don't worry, Doctor, she's well enough. You're too protective."

"*Jelsey!*" the doctor said. "You are going to leave now."

"Good health. I'll visit later, Shannon Traesdaughter. I'm

Jelsey, daughter of Desid, the daughter of Gran, warrior of the Ilari clan."

"Out!" With a sassy grin, the girl turned and opened the flap. The walls must have been made of canvas.

"Rest now, Shannon. I must tell Saasu that you're awake." The doctor followed the girl named Jelsey out the flap, before I had even thought to ask who Saasu was. I shifted on the cot and rested my cheek on the pillow. Commanding myself not to shout out recipes for bread, I fell into a deep, restful sleep.

Sleep, sleep, sleep. That was all the doctor said I was to do. In a fit of boredom some days later, I slipped out of bed and leaned on the table, forcing my weakened legs to hold me up. I had to see outside. Muted voices tantalized me all day long, raised voices sung at night. The doctor had unwrapped my bandages minutes before and inspected my hand, nodding in approval at the fresh pink skin growing in the pits and crevices the choga poisoning had left in my fingers and palm. After picking away the remaining flecks of charred flesh, she wrapped my hand back up in clean bandages and told me she would return to check on me at midday.

It was still early in the morning. Wide awake, my stomach barely filled with the light breakfast she had given me of eggs and cheese, I knew I could not bear to spend one more minute in this infernal tent. Jelsey had laughed the day before when I told her the doctor had said I was in the infirmary.

"She thinks big of it! It's just a tent, Shannon, surrounded by other tents." Jelsey had laughed again. The doctor allowed her to visit each day, for a short while in the evening. Jelsey always left me exhausted, the thousands of words she spoke in a half-hour's time ringing in my ears.

"Are we in a camp?" I had asked her yesterday.

"The Ilari winter camp."

"What's Ilari?" I said, fascinated by this odd, shorthaired girl in men's trousers.

"A clan of women warriors. There are nine clans now, but

we're the only one in the northwest. The Kyata clan is in the northeast, they're the closest ones to us."

Clans of women warriors. I laughed. "Do you fight with men?" I questioned her. "Valley men?"

She looked at me as if I were a simpleton. "Of course we do! Don't you Valley women even know where your men go off to every spring?"

"We know they war with the enemy in the Beyond. But the enemy are monsters ... or are supposed to be, but at least one that I saw once wasn't, it was a mask ... but anyway, they can't be *you*."

"Why not?"

"Because you're just ... you're just *women*. The men should have won by now."

"What in Chaos does that mean, just women? And how can you not know about us? Didn't you ever ask the men in your Valley who they're fighting against?"

I snorted. "Sure, if I wanted a beating."

"If they hit you, hit them back."

"Whips aren't scared of my fists," I snapped.

The doctor had interrupted then, giving Jelsey a dirty look.

"Things aren't as easy in the Valley as Narine tells you, are they?" An undercurrent flowed through all their conversations, one I didn't understand.

"Oh, rot that. If the women had any courage, they'd stand up for themselves and fight." Jelsey crossed her arms over her chest. "Narine is right. The Valley women are pawns, all of them, men's pawns in men's games."

"Shannon's a Valley woman," the doctor said.

Jelsey shook her head. "She's different."

"How?"

"She left." Jelsey looked uncomfortable. "I'm off now. See you tomorrow, Shannon."

"Rest, Shannon," the doctor said predictably.

Carefully, I released the table I clung to. One step. Two. How long had I been in the infirmary? I glanced around the tent, searching for clothes to put on. Under the bed, I found the blue dress Ekklia had given me. I slipped it on, grimacing at the filth staining the material. Nothing could be done about it. I lifted the edge of the tent flap and looked outside.

The smell of a cook-fire swept in. I inhaled it hungrily as I waited for my eyes to adjust to the sudden light.

"What are *you* doing?" I squinted at the dark figure in front of me.

"I need to get out of this tent for a while!" I exclaimed, glad to see it was Jelsey and not the doctor or someone else.

She nodded and looked around. "Come on out, quickly."

Holding onto her outstretched hand, I exited the tent as rapidly as I could and let the flap fall.

"Great Father!" I gasped in amazement. A multitude of light brown tents covered a plain, forest surrounding us on all sides.

"The doctor's in the Mothers' House," Jelsey explained. "She'll be out any minute and we should be away."

"That's where my sister is! I want to see her."

"You can wait until the doctor's gone on her afternoon rounds, or you won't see her at all." I looked at Jelsey for the first time in broad daylight. She was only twelve, but she was much taller and bigger than I was. Suddenly, she shoved me around the tent and down to the ground with one swipe of her hand.

"That was close! The doctor's gone to Saasu. Clear coast, Shannon, let's go!"

"Who's Saasu?" She reached down and put her big hands under my arms. Suddenly I was on my feet again.

"She hasn't been to visit you? Saasu's the Guide of the Ilari."

I looked blank.

Jelsey elaborated as we walked. "She's in charge. The Valley men call them commanders or generals. The women warriors prefer guides to commanders. We're not slaves to be told what to do."

I heard women's voices inside the tents. All those I saw

were dressed like the doctor, men's tan trousers and white shirts. One string of animal teeth dangled around each neck. I wondered why Jelsey had three and wore black. Some of the women looked at me with interest and opened their mouths to speak, but closed them when they saw Jelsey was with me. Was she not liked? I watched Jelsey walk confidently by them, each step taken with utter surety until she tripped over nothing at all and fell over.

"Chaos!" she swore. On her feet in an instant, Jelsey grinned at me sheepishly. Her cheeks were red.

"I do that all the time," I said to reassure her.

She brushed off her clothes. I watched three women walk by, spears in their hands.

"Why are you the only one in black?" I asked Jelsey, after the women looked at us and then looked away without speaking.

"Because I'm not one of the cows," Jelsey said heatedly, loud enough for the three women to hear. They smirked and vanished beyond another curve of tents. Jelsey grabbed my hand and dragged me the other direction.

"I'm hungry. Are you?" she asked shortly, propelling me through rows of tents until we had nearly reached the forest edge.

"Very hungry," I gasped for air. My legs felt watery. Jelsey looked strong enough to sling me over her shoulder and carry me the rest of the way like a sack of tubers until we reached wherever we were going. Just when I had decided it might not be such a bad way to travel, my legs on the verge of buckling, we came to a small circle of black tents separated from the others.

Jelsey led me through a gap between two tents and into an enclosed space. A large cook-fire blazed under a bubbling pot. An older girl yawned and stirred the soup inside it.

"Last night's stew," she said to Jelsey. "Still good if you want some. Bowls are over there." She was dressed like Jelsey. Her eyes flickered when they settled on me.

"Here you go," Jelsey shoved a bowl into my hands. "Maybe you can make us bread sometime."

I grinned in embarrassment. The other girl's expression did not change from its tired, sullen stare at the pot, even when she ladled large portions of the stew into our bowls. Some of it slopped onto my hand and stained the bandages. Jelsey reached into a tent and pulled out two animal hides for us to sit on near the fire.

"Stew!" the girl announced to no one.

"Ness, this is Shannon," Jelsey introduced. Ness grunted and glared at the tents around us.

"Stew!" she repeated.

"She hates cooking," Jelsey whispered. "Come on, eat up. The doctor isn't giving you anything but cheese and eggs, you must be ravenous."

"How did you know what I've been eating?" I asked, watching Jelsey root around in her hot stew with her fingers. She plucked out a piece of meat and dropped it into her mouth.

"I used to be the doctor's apprentice," Jelsey mumbled through her food. Her fingers went back into the bowl, searching. I looked down at my own stew and hesitantly stuck one of my fingers in. Yelping at the burning liquid, I yanked my finger out and stuck it in my mouth to cool it.

Jelsey laughed. "We need to toughen you up, Valley woman. You're too frail. No wonder your men dominate you so easily."

"STEW!"

"Did you run away from the Valley too?" Where had all these women come from?

Jelsey choked. *"Me?* A *Valley* woman?" She coughed a carrot back into her bowl. "Not a chance. I was born an Ilari. We used to have a Valley runaway or two, but they were killed in battle years ago."

"STEW!"

I gritted my teeth and put three fingers into my stew. I snatched a piece of hot meat near the surface and pushed it into my mouth, sucking the searing broth from my fingers. They throbbed.

"A Valley woman," Jelsey repeated with a laugh. "What an idea! I shall have to practice my curtsey." The laugh turned into a growl. "I'll bow my head to no man or Great Father."

The blasphemy was as delicious as the soft meat I chewed on. I looked around to make sure no one was listening. Ness stirred the pot, looking as if she'd rather be anywhere else.

"So," I said, wanting to broach the subject of her clothes again, "Why are you and Ness in black while the rest of the women are in brown and white? Do younger girls wear black?"

Ness snorted over the pot.

"We," Jelsey said, indicating the circle of black tents, "are part of the true Ilari. We don't believe in fighting the Valley men year after year with no end in sight. We fight to win."

"And how do you do that?"

"We'll do what it takes. We won't spend every summer until we're old or killed fighting in the Beyond. We'll march right into the Valley and ... "

I looked at her in horror. "It was you that invaded the market, wasn't it? You killed children!"

"I'm too young still for that kind of expedition," Jelsey said. "And so what if they killed the younger boys? They only grow into the men we have to kill in battle anyway."

"STEW!"

Crumpled figures in the square. Blood pooling inches from my feet. I shook my head.

"I don't think that's right!"

"What do you think would happen if the men marched on our camp? Do you think they'd spare the younger ones?" Jelsey's brow lowered. Her big hand gripped the bowl tightly. "True followers of Ilari know this war has to end. If that is by killing the boys that grow to warrior men and then fathers of more warriors, we will strike there. It's not a pretty truth, Shannon, but neither is this world."

My voice rose. "The Ilari didn't just kill the young boys.

They killed older men as well. I was in the market when it happened."

"So what if they killed the older men? They kept them from having more sons to war against us!" Jelsey's eyes were bright, but as much from wanting me to understand as from her anger.

"They killed women and girls, too!" I nearly shouted. "What did the women ever do to you?"

"STEW!" Ness screamed.

A tent flap ripped open and a head appeared. "Yes, Ness, we know! Stew! Shut up!" The woman turned and saw Jelsey and me. A long scar ran down the left side of her face, partially covered with small, honey-colored braids. Dark eyes widened.

"You!" I dropped the bowl and staggered to my feet. It was the woman in the market who had tried to kill the Crier. The one I had struck to save his life, for all the good it had done me. My back twinged, even though it was mostly healed.

"That's Narine," Jelsey said, still mad. "She's the Guide for the true Ilari. Saasu guides the rest of the cows. Narine, Shannon says you killed women in the market!" I realized Jelsey's anger was no longer for me. "You know we're not supposed to kill women! You could be hanged for that."

The woman called Narine swept out of her tent with the grace of a dancer. Jelsey stood beside me, her eyes glued to Narine's approach.

"What's a Valley woman, Jelsey?" she said. "She's nothing more than a breeder of warriors, an animal with no thought of her own, shuffled and passed around between men for their pleasure and benefit. We didn't kill women, Jelsey, we put them out of their misery."

"We're not to kill women," Jelsey protested. "The only way to win is for all women to unite. We have to stand firm together, Saasu says, and then the men will never break us."

Narine laughed, a nasty sound. "We can't stand firm together in our own camp, Jelsey. You know that, you're a smart girl."

"The doctor says we should be helping the women in

the Valley, not slaughtering them like chickens." Jelsey's voice weakened.

"They are chickens. They aren't really women. They have no thoughts of their own, no will of their own. They exist to do men's bidding. What good is it to kill the men in the Beyond every year when the women are simply raising more of them in the Valley? This war needs to end, Jelsey. You understand that or you would not have joined our group of the true Ilari. The cows in the main camp are little better than Valley women. They march off every spring and march back every fall and how much closer are we to the end?"

Narine's eyes bored into Jelsey's as she put her hands on Jelsey's shoulders. "They are only playing the men's games. The men want to destroy us, force us back to their Valley shackled and shamed, to live as their slaves. Is that what you want? The men want to hold out year after year, weakening us until we can be overrun. You can't let that happen, Jelsey! We can stop this war. We can build a new society ..."

"Narine!" The doctor and a woman I didn't know forced their way between the tents. Narine let go of Jelsey's shoulders and drew back with a smile. It reminded me of Trip. I shivered.

"Stop spouting that radical nonsense to the girl. She's just a child!" The doctor tried to pull Jelsey to her side, but Jelsey jerked away and glared at the doctor.

"Narine, you travel dangerous ground," the other woman said. She was older than the doctor. Her gray hair was drawn into a short tail at the back of her neck, and her skin was wrinkled around the lips and eyes.

"We live in dangerous times," Narine said insolently. "So nice of you to visit, Saasu."

I stared at the woman with more interest. So she was the Guide of the Ilari. Saasu looked over at me.

"It seems you have misappropriated the doctor's patient," Saasu said, turning to Narine.

She spat into the fire and said nothing. Jelsey spoke.

"I brought her here, not Narine. Don't blame her."

"Shannon," Saasu said, ignoring Jelsey's plea. "I apologize. You must be very confused." I nodded. "I am Saasu, Guide of the Ilari clan. Welcome to *my* ..." she glanced at Narine and then around the tents, "... camp."

The doctor looked helplessly at Jelsey. "It's not too late to come back to us."

Jelsey lifted her chin and went to stand at Narine's side. "I'm where all true Ilari should be."

Saasu stared her down. "All of us are true Ilari. Now come with me, Shannon."

I looked at Jelsey. She would not meet my eyes.

"I am more than what Narine tells you," I said to Jelsey, trying to keep the anger out of my voice. Saasu and the doctor turned to leave. I waited a moment for Jelsey to respond, but she seemed fixated on the ground.

As I turned to follow Saasu and the doctor, Narine grabbed my arm and dug her nails into my skin.

"I'd be very careful where I stepped, Valley pawn."

I pulled away. "Don't touch me, child killer."

Her voice was that of a mad person. "You're right. I am a child killer." She stroked back the braids from her face. *"And you have a baby sister in this camp."*

I wobbled on weak legs after the doctor and Saasu. Narine's laughter followed me all the way back to the main camp.

Chapter Twelve

Taking Up the Spear

I hurried to catch Saasu and the doctor. Should I tell them what Narine had just said to me? Could they be trusted? How safe was Trae in the Mothers' House?

"They should be punished," said the doctor. I hung a few steps behind, not wanting to interrupt what seemed to be the beginnings of an argument.

"I don't think we should worry, Ollyn," Saasu answered in a weary voice, as if this were a conversation she had had dozens of times before. "They were severely reprimanded for the attack on the Valley and have done nothing wrong since. You're more worried about Jelsey."

The doctor's voice was clipped. "Her interest in them worries me, Saasu. Many of the younger ones look up to Jelsey. When she considers Narine's ideas, it encourages the others to examine them too."

"There's nothing wrong with Jelsey exploring views we don't have," Saasu said. "She'll come to her senses."

The doctor shook her head. I panted for breath behind them. My legs burned all the way to my toes. Women and girls squatted around cook-fires, yawning and eating. Everyone looked up to greet Saasu and the doctor, and then glanced at me with puzzled smiles. Sometimes one whispered to the others, and the puzzled looks were replaced with pity, pleasure, or interest.

"Recipe for crossbread sticks!" a little girl shouted, and all the women around that cook-fire laughed and waved at me.

"Hungry?" one of them asked, offering a bowl of mash.

"No, thank you, I've already eaten," I said. My stomach felt uncomfortably tight with both breakfasts I had eaten this morning.

Saasu and the doctor stopped arguing and turned when they heard my voice.

"How are you feeling, Shannon?" Saasu asked.

My stomach hurt, my legs burned, and my head pounded with indecision. She didn't seem too concerned about Narine.

"I'm fine," I answered.

"Why don't you come with me? I'm sure you have a lot of questions." Saasu looked at the doctor. "If you think she's ready to be out of bed."

The doctor took my right hand. "What happened to my clean bandages?" I couldn't tell if she was angry or amused.

"Stew," I said.

"Be back in the infirmary by midday. I'll change them then." She let go of my hand and spoke to Saasu. "By midday."

Saasu nodded. "How is her sister?"

I burst in. "Yes, how is she? Can I see her?"

"I'll take you to see her tomorrow, when I do my rounds in the Mothers' House," the doctor said. My spirits flagged.

"But I really do feel fine," I protested.

"Young woman, I did not spend all this time caring for you only to have you fall dead the first day you decide to get up. Tomorrow!" The doctor walked off. I thought Saasu hid a grin, but when she looked at me, her face was completely serious.

"Come, then." She beckoned. I walked at her side back to the center of the main camp. The faint wails of a baby threaded through the air. I wondered if it were Trae. Tomorrow. I sighed in frustration.

"The doctor told me your sister is eating well," Saasu said.

"But who's taking care of her?" I worried.

"We've given her to Jinda."

"What do you mean given? She's *my* sister!" I said indignantly. "*I'll* take care of her!"

"You misunderstand," Saasu said. "We gave her to Jinda to care for while you were ill. She isn't a foster mother. She cares for our women when they are in labor and tends to the foundlings until we find someone to take them in as a daughter. Your sister, once we are certain both you and she are well, will be returned to you."

A little ashamed of my outburst, I stared away to the little tent we approached. It was no more than ten paces across.

"Is this where you live?" I asked. Saasu shook her head.

"No." She opened the flap and motioned me to go in. "I'm taking you to meet Ilari."

I stepped inside. Saasu entered and pinned up the flap behind her. Light illuminated a tall bronze statue. A woman balanced on a stone over a flowing river, actual water running down a slab of black rock to a pool that stretched across the ground. The woman's features had been painstakingly done. Her cheeks were full, almost chubby, and her hair hung over her left shoulder in a loosely made braid. Round eyes stared to the right, wisps of hair fell over her forehead. She wore trousers that had been patched at the knee; threads hung from the hems. Her blouse was open at the top and the sleeves dangled to her elbows. A dagger had been tucked in her belt. Her right hand pointed across the river, and her left held on to the long shaft of a spear.

Water bubbled and frothed on the floor, enclosed in the shallow pit. Tiny tiles shined under the water. Saasu and I stood by the pool and looked at the statue.

"We are presented to Ilari four times in our lives," Saasu said in a quiet, respectful voice. "When we are born, when we hear her story, when we vow our lives as warriors, and when we die."

"Who is she?" I asked.

Saasu smiled. "Tell me the story of Advent."

"Advent?" I said, startled. "You mean from The Codes of Life?"

"Tell me."

Old Mother Ica's voice echoed in my head. "Righteous men took their women and children and escaped from Chaos, chased by hellhounds and the wicked. They stumbled into the Valley and began praying for salvation. The Great Father struck down the wicked and offered the righteous sanctuary if they followed his Codes. Then they had His blessing to stay in the Valley. The Great Father protected the people from evil, provided they obeyed him in all things."

"A nice tale," Saasu said. She drew me away from the pool to a marble bench near the door and beckoned me to sit. My palms tingled with expectation on the cool surface of the bench.

"Now, Shannon," Saasu said with satisfaction, "Let me tell you the real story."

The Chaos had been no more than another land, a month's journey to the north over a great sea. Many millions lived in this land. Long ago, the women of that world rose up and protested their positions as compulsory kitchen help and tenders of children, eventually winning the right to the same advantages in life as the men. Women could become doctors and hunters, writers and council servers. They could choose whom they married, when they married, even if they married. It was truly a golden age for these people, when every role was respected, and valued, because it had been chosen rather than forced.

But a small group fought to return to the past. They claimed a woman's place was in the home and only there was she safe and happy. When the citizenry did not agree, the minority defected. The men built ships and sailed away to find a new world, taking willing and unwilling wives and children with them. The government sent out ships of enforcers to retrieve them. But few had ever traveled the sea's dangerous waters, and not all survived. Waves as tall as mountains slammed ships into splinters, vicious whirlpools sucked ships down to the ocean floor.

Of the four ships full of men, women, and children, three

landed in a new world. Three of the six ships following them made it. The defectors escaped the enforcers into the forests of the Beyond. The men dragged their wives and children with them, but some members of their families pretended to fall and hurt themselves too badly to travel, and others outright ran back to their pursuers. Still, many wives thought what their men wanted was right, and many of the children were too young or too frightened to protest. They reached the Valley. Then word came to the enforcers that one of their own was a traitor, and had burned the ships behind them. They turned back to the beach with the women and children they had recovered. The defectors traveled to the southern Valley and began creating a world to their liking.

The enforcers returned to the beaches to build more ships to return. A few did not want to risk it, and they stayed here. Most risked their lives on the sea again, and no one ever knew if they made it back to their land.

Two generations passed. The women who thought their men were right became disillusioned when they realized just how much of their freedom was going to be restricted in this new world. Some of the young girls who had been too afraid to leave their parents remembered the old way, and were disturbed by the changes. They passed the story of the land they had left on to their daughters. And one Autumn Night, as they were sequestered preparing for the night's festivities, fifteen girls rebelled. Tantalized by the thought of freedom, angry that their mothers and grandmothers had come willingly to this awful new world, they tied up the matrons watching them and escaped into the Beyond on the day of festival.

Enraged, the men pursued them. The girls learned how to hide, to fend for themselves, to kill game and build shelters. And then, when the men nearly caught them, they learned to fight. Many more women and girls joined them in the next few years. Every year, the men who could be spared from the fields returned to the Beyond to bring them back home. Sometimes they succeeded, but those they brought back had to be hobbled to prevent their escape, and they had their tongues cut out, because they spread further dissent among the Valley women. More left. All men of a certain age then were sent to retrieve them. And every year, the women fought them and won their freedom. Some went north and discovered settlements of people, the children and grandchildren of the enforcers, who treated them equally. Most stayed in the Beyond, hoping their mothers, sisters, and friends would join them. And within a generation, the Beyond became their home.

The men in the Valley punished anyone among them who spoke of the old land. The next generation of girls grew up ignorant of anything but the Valley and the truth of whom the men fought with every year in the Beyond. Soon, no more Valley women ran away to join the warriors.

"But who's Ilari?" I asked again. Saasu smiled.

"Each of the women's clans takes the name of one of the fifteen girls who defied tradition and ran away to the Beyond. Ilari was one of those girls. It was she of the fifteen who first made a spear and taught herself to use it. She fought for ten years before falling in battle."

I looked at the statue of Ilari. "Is that what she really looked like?"

Saasu nodded. "The warrior women have always been on good terms with the small settlements in the north. After Ilari died, several of the fifteen who remained went to a settlement and asked one of the artists to draw her picture from the description they gave him." She smiled at the statue. "This statue was made generations later when the Ilari clan broke away from a clan that had grown too large. We have had it ever since we separated."

"Are there still settlements of the people from the other land?"

"They supply us with much of our food while we provide protection from the men in the Valley. They don't war themselves, preferring to farm or work at other professions as their predecessors did. Many of the deserters from the men's army go to live there."

My world had exploded in size in the last hour. Jadan, I thought suddenly. And the thought of him reminded me of something else.

"Have you taken in foundlings from the northern Valley?" I asked.

"Every year." Saasu stood. "Come. I'm returning you to the infirmary. You're tired."

I gave one last glance at the statue. Saasu closed the flap behind us and nudged me to walk. I staggered after her to the infirmary. Falling onto the cot without removing my clothes, I was asleep as soon as my cheek touched the pillow.

I slept through the day and awoke at evening, when the doctor brought a tray of food into the tent and set it down on the table.

"Dinner's on," she said when she saw I was awake. "And Jelsey wants to visit. She said to tell you she's sorry."

"That's all right," I said, reaching for the food. My head heavy with sleep, I hardly remembered why Jelsey could possibly want to apologize. The doctor handed me a plate of meat and bread. She left the tent and I heard her muted voice speaking to someone.

I took a bite of the bread. It was warm and thick.

The tent flap rose moments later.

"... and don't be waving Narine's notions at her right now. She needs rest, not radicalism."

"I won't, I won't." Jelsey peered in at me. "Shannon, is it all right if I visit?"

"Come in." I remembered Narine and lost my appetite.

"Narine's sorry," Jelsey said, once the flap was lowered. She sat on the cot beside me. "She didn't mean what she said."

"Did she tell you that?" I asked.

Jelsey hesitated. "Well, no. But I could see it on her face after you left. She gets carried away sometimes and says things she doesn't mean."

"Threatening a tiny baby is more than getting carried away."

133

"It was the heat of the moment. She wouldn't ever do that to a child."

"She did that to many children in the market."

"But she would never do that to an Ilari child. As long as you and your sister are in the camp, you are Ilari. Ilari's daughters may disagree at times, but they are not supposed to turn on one another. Your sister is safe."

"Narine doesn't seem to be very trustworthy," I said, though I was glad to hear her words. "And why were you surprised to hear that Narine and her followers killed women? Why didn't you know?"

"Nobody knows. And nobody's going to know."

"What are you, her thug?"

Jelsey looked appalled. "No! Look, you two just got off on the wrong foot. She's not a bad person. But please don't tell anyone what happened in the Valley. The warriors in our camp are asking you to keep your silence. Most of them didn't kill women, but Saasu won't care to find out who did what if she finds out. She'll just expel all of us. No other clan will take us, either."

I would not feel sorry for Narine wandering around in the wilderness, but I would feel guilty about Jelsey and the others who had being punished for what they hadn't done.

"Are you sure Saasu would do that? She seems reasonable."

"You're new here." Jelsey got to her feet. "Don't think you know everything about us, because you don't. I'm begging you, Shannon. Please hold your peace while you're with us. Nothing will happen to your sister, I promise."

She looked so earnest I felt bad. "I won't say anything, I promise. But, Jelsey?" I said, when she turned to leave.

"What?"

"Nothing had better happen to Trae. *Nothing*."

"I give you my word as an Ilari," Jelsey said. Then she swept out of the tent and into the growing night.

The next morning, the doctor removed my bandages. The

new skin along my finger and palm was raw to the touch, but the doctor did not want the skin to attach itself to the bandages.

"Fresh air and constant washing," she declared. "If you notice a smell or any change in color, get back here."

"You said you'd take me to see my sister this morning," I reminded. "I need to see her."

"Not until you've eaten," she said implacably. I ate soft cheese and mash with large bites while the doctor rolled my old bandages and put them in a basin for washing.

"All right, I finished it," I said, mouth full of the last bit of mash. "Can we go now?"

"I'm waiting for you," she said. I jumped off the cot. My legs were sore but much stronger than they had been yesterday. I grabbed the table to steady myself only once to smooth down my dress.

"Oh, Chaos. You can't wear that anymore." The doctor leaned out of the tent and called to someone. "Bring me an extra pair of trousers and a shirt." She let the tent flap fall and spoke to me. "I'll tell Quinn you need to be measured properly."

"Thank you," I said to a disembodied hand that thrust a folded shirt and trousers into the tent. I took off the dress and considered the trousers. Men's clothes.

"Come on, one leg and then the other."

I sat on the edge of the cot and put them on. They were too large. I tucked the shirt tightly into the trousers.

"You'll grow into them," the doctor said. "If you decide to stay with us."

I did not know if she expected an answer, so I raked my hands through my filthy hair and tried to pat it into place. It really needed a washing.

"Come then," she said with a wave of her fingers. I followed her out of the infirmary tent and into the camp. She walked quickly and I hurried after, inexplicably pleased that now I looked no different from any other woman in the camp with my tan trousers and white shirt. All I needed was a string of animal teeth around my neck.

"Where am I going to stay now?" I asked the doctor when we reached the tent called the Mothers' House.

"Many of the new mothers and foster mothers stay here while the babies are small. Everyone helps with the children so the mothers don't feel isolated and overwhelmed. Come in, come in!" she said impatiently. I walked into the house.

Four beds, each with a cradle beside it, lined the room. A colorful rug covered the floor. A shelf held many books, and another beneath it had toys and games within reach of a small child.

A noise to my right made me turn. A big woman turned from a long counter, where she was pouring milk from a jug into a row of bottles.

"Jinda," the doctor said, "this is Shannon, Trae's sister."

The woman set down the jug and looked at me. Her eyes were warm and friendly, and I gladdened to see this was the woman caring for Trae.

"It's nice to meet you," she said, capping a bottle as she spoke. She saw the anxiousness on my face. "Your sister's over there, in the last cradle."

I felt Jinda and the doctor watching me as I crossed the room to the cradle. A woman nursed a baby in the bed nearby; she looked at me and smiled.

Trae. I stared down at my tiny sister, who slept on a soft mattress with a little blanket drawn over her back. She had gotten bigger since I had last seen her, and her skin was flushed pink. I touched her hair. It had become a lighter brown, like Beth's. I pushed the thought of Beth from my mind. Right now, she would be practicing her braid for next year's Autumn Night. I didn't want to think about that.

"You'll never have an Autumn Night," I whispered to Trae. She would be so different from my sisters and me. No two-room shack with splintered boards and Father yelling. No memorizing Verses on Women. I smiled.

"You can be an Ilari," I said, before remembering Jelsey's words. "You already are."

She stirred and began crying. I picked her up and held her against me, patting her back to soothe her.

"Here you go," Jinda said, handing me a bottle. I sat on an empty bed to feed her. She cried and moved her head away from the bottle.

"What's wrong with her?" I asked Jinda in frustration. She came to my side. Trae bellowed in my arms.

"She doesn't like mornings, this one," Jinda said, reaching for Trae. I gave her over. Within moments, Jinda had calmed Trae and had her enthusiastically sucking on the bottle. I felt lost.

A woman walked in with a two-year-old. She gave Jinda a tired smile and took one of the bottles from the counter. I stared at the child's livid red hair, just like the Trelsons. Grasping the bottle in one hand, she toddled over to the shelves and began pulling off toys with her other hand. I watched, frozen with wonder, the only sound in the room being the doctor's voice murmuring to the mother with the baby.

Jelsey burst into the mothers' house. After our conversation the night before, I hadn't expected to see her. She came right to me.

"I thought you would be in here!" she said excitedly. The two year old turned at the sound of her voice and crowed with delight.

"Jelly!" the little girl said, holding a hand up to Jelsey.

"Good morning, Enon," Jelsey said, and picked her up. Jinda crooned softly to Trae, rocking back and forth on her big feet.

"Come on, Shannon. I talked to Pasahn, one of our arms-teachers. If you're feeling well enough, you can come with me to our morning practice."

"I don't know ..." the doctor began, from where she stood at the bedside.

"I'm feeling all right," I interrupted, wanting to be away from Jinda and Trae. "I'll just watch this morning."

"Just watch," the doctor echoed me. "You're not strong

enough for anything else. We'll discuss living arrangements at midday, so come back here."

I stood up from the chair. Jelsey looked at my clothes with approval while Enon tugged at her necklaces.

"Come on, we've got to hurry."

Jinda and Trae did not notice me. Jelsey put the girl down with a pat on her head and pulled me toward the door.

"Just watch!" the doctor shouted.

"All right, all right," Jelsey muttered. She and I walked through the camp and into the forest.

If Jelsey was upset over last night, she made no mention of it. She chattered happily about the spear she had carved by herself, how many times out of ten she could hit the middle of a target with her arrows. Narine had made her a scout, a task usually not given to girls until they were thirteen, and Jelsey was still twelve. She had been on her first expedition with Narine and three others of her followers when they saw me wandering about the Beyond. It was a duty that rotated among the members of the camp, to search the Beyond near the Valley for any girl babies that had been left to die.

"We find at least two every year, sometimes three," Jelsey explained. "And we bring them back to Jinda. The doctor treats any wounds or illness the baby has, and once it's stronger, the baby goes to a woman who wants to raise a child."

I took her hand to steady myself over a small stream. Rocks had been placed in the water as stepping-stones. "How many women are in the camp?"

"About a hundred. Some of the women have their own babies as well, instead of fostering. We have a good relationship with the settlement northwest of here. It's a new one called Lorinn, and it's still pretty small. Many of the Ilari have daughters fathered by the Lorinn men."

A dark thought pushed to the front of my mind. "What if an Ilari gives birth to a son? He can't be a warrior then."

She gave me a careful look. "What do you think we do? Expose them? That's a Valley atrocity, not something we do here. The sons stay with their mothers until they are five, then they go to live with their fathers in Lorinn. The mothers of sons often stay in Lorinn during the winter to be with them."

I had more questions, but just then Jelsey pushed between two trees and we walked onto another plain. Twenty girls stood in four groups, each one listening to an older woman. One of the younger groups held wooden swords, carefully watching the movements of their teacher. The other group of younger girls had small bows slung over their shoulders, and their instructor directed them to three trees at the other end of the plain, each with a red and blue target pinned to it.

Four of the older girls cheered, sitting in a circle around their teacher and a tall, stringy girl with blonde hair. As I watched, the teacher's foot lashed out at the girl's knee. She bent her leg so that the teacher struck her shin instead. The teacher nodded and backed away, but their eyes stayed warily on each other. Suddenly the student threw a fist to her opponent's stomach, but before I could blink, the teacher whirled the student around and captured her arms behind her, holding her immobile.

Jelsey tugged on my arm, but I ignored her. The third Code shrieked in my head. The girl stomped on the teacher's foot, and she loosened her grip in pain. Yanking free, the student reached between her legs and grabbed the teacher's ankle, pulling it up swiftly. The teacher fell to the ground. The girls in the group applauded.

"Shannon, you're going to get us in trouble!" Jelsey said, staring down at me.

"Sorry. Where do we go?"

"That group over there. We're first at spears this morning." We joined the last group of girls. Ness looked at me with no recognition in her eyes.

"About time," a woman said in a surly tone.

"This is Pasahn, our arms-woman," Jelsey introduced. "This is Shannon." Pasahn grunted at me.

"Come on, girls, grab your spears, no shields yet, and let's get started." A pile of spears sat on the ground, their metal tips covered in cloth, next to animal hide shields. The others in the class each took one. Jelsey waved me off.

"Why don't you go and watch over ..." she began, but Pasahn overrode her.

"I said, grab a spear!" she yelled.

I stepped back. "I'm just ... just supposed to watch today."

"Oh, that's nice! Jelsey, why don't you just watch today, too? In fact, why don't we all just drop our weapons and watch? Let's listen to the birds! Let's revel in nature!" Her voice got louder and louder. The other groups began to watch. "Let's wait for winter and make snow warriors! Let's just sit around and watch today, because we don't have anything better to do!" She was only inches from my face now. "Nobody watches, young woman! Pick up a spear! *Pick up a spear!* PICK UP A SPEAR!"

I picked up a spear. The girls giggled until Pasahn's icy blue eyes settled on them.

"Is something funny?" she roared. They paled.

"No, Pasahn." "No, Pasahn." Shaking their heads, they backed away and formed a wide circle.

"Mother of Chaos and all that's in it! Watch! WATCH!" Pasahn swore. She snatched up one of the remaining spears on the ground.

"Now, Shannon, fight me!" She shoved me into the circle the girls had made. "Stand there!" I stood across from Jelsey.

"Pasahn, she really is supposed to just watch ..." Jelsey began, seeing the terror in my eyes.

Pasahn barked at her. "When I want your opinion, I'll tell you what it is. Now *be quiet!*"

I gripped the spear in my sweaty hands. It was about five feet long. I shifted it to my left hand and held it in front of me like I had seen men hold their swords.

"Fight, woman!" Pasahn ordered.

"But I don't know how!" I said, hating the whine in my voice. "I've never fought before!"

"Then today you learn!" she thundered. She raised her spear and charged at me. I screamed and dodged her.

"I told you to fight me, coward!" Her chest heaved. "Stand and battle!"

"But ..."

"No! No! NO! This is not a Valley tea party!" She approached me slowly and raised her spear. It slapped against mine, almost teasingly. She did it again, harder this time. I put both hands on my spear to keep my hold on it.

Pasahn smashed her spear into mine. It flew out of my hands. I ran after it. Ness sneered at me.

"Now fight me!" She stalked closer. I swung my spear wildly at her and missed. The cloth point stuck in the ground. I yanked it out and spun around to face her.

"Is that the best you can do?" She spat on the grass. I jabbed it at her. "Come on, try again."

I swung at her upraised spear. She grabbed the shaft of my spear with the tip of her cloth point and wrenched my spear and me with it nearly out of the circle. Dizzy, I steadied myself before turning to face her.

Laughter. She was laughing. I saw red.

"Give up?"

"*I hate you!*" I screamed, and charged for her. I swung the spear to my side, cloth tip pointed right for Pasahn. As I reached her, she lashed out with her spear for my own. Just when her spear neared mine, I dropped it and flung myself bodily at her. I carried her with me to the ground. She had one moment of surprised hesitation when we landed, and I took advantage of it. I sat up on her chest and struck her face with my fists, over and over. The land tilted wildly, my head hit something hard, and suddenly I stared up at the sky. Pasahn stood above me. Her right eye was bloodshot.

"Does this look like the body combat class?" she screeched. "This is spears! Spears! SPEARS!" She grabbed a handful of my shirt and dragged me to my feet. "Get over there and take Jelsey's place! You're going to watch until you learn something!"

Pasahn kicked my spear at me. I plucked it up and staggered over to Jelsey. I sank to my knees beside her.

"Jelsey! GET IN THE CIRCLE!" Pasahn blasted. Jelsey jumped to her feet.

Pasahn attacked her. Jelsey's face remained calm as she

thrust Pasahn's spear away with her own. It was a battle too quick to watch, all over the circle, spears flying so fast it was hard to tell which spear was whose. Finally, Jelsey overreached when she thrust her spear at Pasahn's legs. Pasahn twirled in the air and whipped her spear down onto Jelsey's back. She fell flat on her face. The spear broke into two pieces. Everyone gasped.

"You're going to spend tonight making me a new spear!" Pasahn snarled. She grabbed Jelsey's spear. Jelsey shook her head, her eyes dazed. She got up onto her hands and knees. Pasahn kicked her backside to hurry her out of the circle.

"Are you all right?" I asked, when Jelsey sat heavily next to me.

"NESS!" Pasahn yelled.

"I'm fine. She's done that before." Jelsey rubbed her back and winced. "Pasahn hates Narine. She always makes practice harder on me."

Pasahn defeated Ness quickly. She rapidly dispatched the other girls in the class as well.

"You're the most hopeless group I've ever taught. We're going back to basics! Stand up and form a line! NOW!"

We could do nothing right, it seemed, especially me. We didn't run fast enough to the line, didn't hold the spears right, couldn't follow her most basic moves. I was glad when a whistle blew out and Jelsey explained we were rotating to another teacher.

"Where are you going?" Pasahn shrieked, when Jelsey and I headed over to the targets with the other girls of our class.

"I'm going to bow and arrow practice," I said nervously.

Her eyes bulged. "You're in my class all day long! Until you fight better than a seven year old child, you stay with me!"

My cheeks went hot when the little girls in her second group snickered at me. I was three years older than most of them, and I towered over their heads.

I learned the spear. Each class was about an hour long, and there were four of them. I spent every one with Pasahn. My legs buckled under me by the third hour, but she was relentless. I forced myself to stand and fight her again. By the fourth hour, my body trembled with weariness. Sheer rage at this awful woman kept me from falling again. The bruise I had given her swelled, an angry red color. When the whistle blew for the midday meal, Pasahn turned to me. Horrified, I wondered if she was going to make me stay through the meal as well.

"I'll see *you* tomorrow!" And she stomped away, throwing Jelsey's spear on the ground.

"Chaos-rot," I swore. Jelsey ran up to me.

"I had no idea she would do that. We've got to get you back to the camp, you look awful."

The anger kept me buoyant. "I'm not so bad."

"You're the color of dead fish. Lean on me, I'll help you back." Jelsey picked up her spear and then draped my left arm over her wide shoulders. We were the last off the plain. It was a slow journey back, even with Jelsey carrying a lot of my weight.

"I'll bring you lunch," she said, once we were outside the infirmary. "Just go on in and lay down."

"No!" I gripped her arm. "Listen!"

From inside the tent, the doctor's voice rang out.

"What in the world happened to your eye, Pasahn?"

"Nothing!" Pasahn's voice was as sharp to her as it was to the students. "Just put a cold compress on it and see if there's any ice in this infernal camp! Ouch! *That hurts!*"

"I'll get lunch with you," I gasped to Jelsey. We hurried away from the infirmary, clutching our sides. Once we reached the nearest cook-fire, I fell to the ground with Jelsey beside me. We laughed until we cried.

Chapter Thirteen

Becoming

I gave up Trae. During the time I had spent delirious in the infirmary, Trae and Jinda had claimed each other's hearts. And in the bewildering world of the Ilari, a world I wanted to explore and experience, Trae would be a hindrance I might find myself resenting. I loved her, but as Saasu said, my love should be a sister's love, and not a mother's.

The morning that the first snows fell, I left the sleeping tent that had been erected for me and met Saasu and Jinda in the temple of Ilari. I held Trae closely, my tears falling onto her light brown hair. Crusts of ice were forming along the edges of the pool. Jinda shuffled uncomfortably from one foot to another.

"You're still her sister, still her sister," she said. "You'll see her everyday."

Saasu touched my shoulder. "It doesn't mean you love her any less, Shannon. It means you are twelve years old, too young to raise your mother's infant, and old enough to recognize that."

"In the Valley, girls one year older than me are raising infants," I said. Jinda shook her head in disapproval.

"Is that fair? They're children raising children." Saasu moved her hand from my shoulder to Trae, who looked at her with big eyes. "There's time enough for motherhood when you're older. Right now you should be deciding what you want to do with your life, without an infant attached to the decision."

Decisions. I had more of those now than I had ever had in the Valley. A month ago I had chafed at every decision being made for me. Now I had more room to choose than ever before, and I found the freedom terrifying. To be a warrior or not. To be trained for scouting parties, hunting parties, or guarding parties. Jelsey wanted me to become a scout like her, but I didn't want to travel with Narine's group. I could even go to the settlement of Lorinn if I did not want to be with the Ilari, and there I could continue my schooling, or train as an artisan, or work in a shop or in the fields. Finally, I could choose to stay in the mothers' house and raise Trae. It was a tempting decision, until I realized that I would do it more to escape the rest of the choices.

I stepped closer to Jinda. Kissing Trae on her silky hair, I placed my youngest sister in Jinda's arms.

"Thank you," she whispered, her face lighting. "I want to see you every afternoon, understand? Trae should know her sister."

I nodded, feeling fresh hotness in my eyes. "I'll be there."

Saasu cleared her throat. "Shannon, when a baby is born or adopted into our clan, she is presented to Ilari by the Guide and foster mother and given her name. I'd like you to stay for the ceremony."

"You're not going to change her name, are you?" I asked, alarmed. "She's named for our mother."

"No, no, we're not changing her name!" Jinda exclaimed, anxious. "We're just giving her a full name. Trae, daughter of Trae ..." she paused. "What was your grandmother's name?"

I shook my head. "I don't know." I didn't even know what family in the Valley my mother had come from. Once a girl married, she had little contact with the family she had been born into. All that was left of my mother's existence was ten daughters who didn't know anything about her. And little Trae would not even know her mother's face.

"Then she'll be Trae, daughter of Trae and foster daughter of Jinda, woman warrior of the Ilari." Saasu lifted a case from beneath the bench. She snapped open silver latches and lifted the lid.

"But she's not a warrior," I said, straining to see into the case.

"We're warriors simply by refusing to be in the Valley and live by men's rules," Jinda said indignantly. Trae chortled in her arms. "The spear doesn't matter. Our presence is enough."

Saasu unwrapped a goblet. The cup and base were emerald green, and the stem was crystal. Two thin green strands coiled around the stem. *Ilari* had been written in silver on the cup.

Jinda and Saasu turned to face the statue. I stood to the side and watched.

Saasu spoke in a strong, clear voice, her words flowing over each other without a pause or break. It was nearly a song, the lyrics recited as smoothly as Beth could repeat the Codes.

"In the memory of the first fifteen," Saasu chanted, "to break the chains. In their honor, we dedicate a new warrior to the rebel clans of women."

Jinda's voice joined Saasu's.

"For Alda, Kalani, and Sude. For Liffa, Jannday, and Kyata. For Trelsa, Eline, and Sadira. For Rithe, Ilari, and Thrine. For Klia, Charney, and Anlon."

Saasu dipped the cup into the cold water of the pool. Once the cup was full, she lifted it to her lips and drank deeply. Then she handed the cup to Jinda, who also drank.

"We present Trae, daughter of Trae and foster-daughter of Jinda, woman warrior of the Ilari clan. In the names of the first fifteen," Saasu said.

"In the names of the first fifteen," Jinda echoed. Saasu held the cup so Jinda could dip her fingers into the remaining water. She dribbled the drops onto Trae's forehead. Trae squawked.

Saasu laughed. "Daughter of Ilari, we welcome you." She turned to me. "On the evening of a dedication, the baby is presented to the entire clan."

Shouting erupted outside. Saasu cut off her explanation, handed the cup to Jinda, and left to find the source of the noise.

I glanced at Trae. Her eyes focused on me and then slipped away.

Jinda deftly wrapped the cup with one hand and put it away. The three of us went outside. Light snow sprinkled to the ground and melted before it could collect. Saasu was nowhere in sight.

"I hope she's not cold," I said, fidgeting with the blankets wrapped around Trae.

There was more shouting.

"I wonder what's going on," I said.

"Saasu will take care of it," Jinda said. "I'll take Trae back to the Mothers' House now. And you, young woman, will be back this afternoon to see her."

I nodded and looked around the camp. There was no battle practice this morning. What was I supposed to do with myself, now that Trae wasn't mine to care for?

Jinda noticed my puzzled expression. "The children usually go to the north edge of camp when there's no practice. Why don't you go join them?"

Maybe Jelsey would be there. And the other girls my age had been friendly enough, all but Ness. Still, I stood frozen.

Jinda headed toward the Mothers' House, Trae peering over her shoulder. I hesitantly turned away.

"The north edge!" Jinda called, glancing over her shoulder. "They should all be there. Go on now. Go play!"

My muscles ached as I skirted through the tents. I had practiced on the field for a full week now, and every inch of me had some sort of ache, pain, or bruise. Pasahn was truly vicious. Though after that first day she allowed me to attend the other classes, she worked me hardest of all in the hour I was under her tutelage. Gray, the arms-woman who taught body combat, instructed me slowly and patiently. Archery was taught by Penlotte, swords by Tobi, and both tolerated my ineptitude with minimal shouting. When I finally hit the center of the target with an arrow, Penlotte voiced no praise but did nod her head in my direction. Jelsey cheered, "Finally!" and the girls burst into applause. It was embarrassing, but I was proud. It was Pasahn, only Pasahn, who could never be pleased with anything I, or anyone else, did.

The clamor grew louder as I headed for the north edge. I looked over to see Narine and Saasu, barely an arms-length from each other. Several women stood about them, two dressed in black, the rest in brown and white.

"... open your eyes!" Narine was saying. "How much longer are you willing to follow her? There are times I doubt her claims of being an Ilari blood descendant!"

Saasu slapped Narine. The crowd gasped. I remembered Jelsey's words and was appalled. No one could raise her hand to another Ilari! What was Saasu doing?

Narine rubbed her cheek and a smile crept across her lips. She opened her mouth to speak but Saasu interrupted.

"I apologize for striking you," she said icily. "But this cannot go on. I let you stay here after the Valley attack on the condition you keep your beliefs to yourself, and instead I find you here, like a viper, slithering from tent to tent for prey. I should expel you."

Narine scoffed. "No true Ilari will follow you any longer, Saasu! You are finished here! Everyone knows it." She addressed the other women standing by them. "I strive to end this war, nothing more. Take action! Don't follow Saasu like sheep to slaughter every spring. Let's end this war by any means possible!"

The two women in black moved to stand behind Narine. There were now five others in brown and white besides Saasu. Three of them laughed outright at Narine and stood behind Saasu; one looked curiously at Narine but then joined the three still laughing. The fifth remained where she was, looking at both Narine and Saasu, obviously considering.

"No more, Narine," Saasu said. "Go to your tent. Think seriously about your next move." Narine's eyes flicked to me as she walked away.

Why did Jelsey follow someone like her? I left the outermost circle of tents and heard girls' voices laughing and calling past a thin line of trees. I shivered in the cold, wondering if Ilaris had coats. My clothing shielded me somewhat from the winter air, but not enough. Snowflakes spun around me in the weak sunlight.

"Shannon!" Jelsey called. The black of her outfit was incongruous with the brown and white of everyone else.

"I hurt!" I complained when I reached her side. Many girls were in the clearing, most playing a catch game with a ball.

"You'll get used to it," Jelsey said.

Whether or not a girl planned to be a warrior, she was required to attend several years of battle practice. All girls and women in the camp had to be able to protect themselves. Most of the girls faced each day's practice with relish. The older women, those that battled each year, used the practice plain in the afternoon to perfect their skills.

"Shannon! Want to play?" one of the girls shouted. "Hold, everyone!"

I nodded and tugged at Jelsey's arm. "Show me how, I don't know this game."

All the girls stopped running to wipe sweaty hair out of their eyes and catch their breath. Mased, the one who had spoken, walked to us with a brown ball tucked under her arm.

"Come on, you can be on our team." She motioned to a group of ten girls. "We're playing Tackle. You try to get through the other team to the opposite end of the clearing. If you get past the first line of trees, you win a point for the team. We took off our animal teeth necklaces, and they left theirs on, that's how you know who's who."

I did not have an animal teeth necklace anyway. They were earned after a girl made her first kill hunting for food. The women in the main camp each wore one to signify their contribution of game. Narine's followers wore three for reasons I still did not know.

"Start!" Mased yelled. She lifted her arm to throw the ball to me. I readied for it. I was good at catching. Father had thrown things at me for years. But then as the girls on the other team charged for me, she laughed, put the ball under her arm, and raced across the clearing. One of the girls running for me realized her trick too late and collapsed on top of me. I fell to the ground. She jumped back up to her feet and ran off after the girl with the ball. I clambered up wheezing.

"That's why it's called Tackle," Jelsey hollered at me.

"Loose ball!" someone screamed. I looked up and saw the ball rolling away from a girl who had been brought to the ground by a pile of opponents. Jelsey was the first to get there. She scooped it up with one graceful swoop and sped across the clearing in my direction.

"Get her!" my team shouted together. I ran for Jelsey, but she darted away from me. As she neared the trees, one girl jumped on her. Four more piled down. One kicked her on purpose as they got up.

"Don't be a cow," Jelsey said to her.

"Shut up and play," Mased said.

We ran for hours. The snow stopped falling and the air warmed a bit. My knees were buckling with exhaustion when an older woman stepped into the clearing and beckoned us to follow her.

"I'm ravenous!" Jelsey said, limping up to me. She had received more than her fair share of tackles, and her black shirt was torn at the shoulder. Raking a hand through her curly hair, she ignored the nasty looks thrown in her direction from some walking out of the clearing. "Come on, let's go eat."

I floundered. "I'd rather not eat in Narine's camp."

Her face fell. "I didn't mean that. On our two rest days, everyone eats together in the main camp."

"Oh. I didn't know. Let's go then."

She brooded as we walked through the trees.

"I hope you're not mad," I said.

She shook her head. "No, not mad. I just wish people could understand why Narine believes what she does. Everyone should want what she wants! The end to the war, a chance to build a better society!"

"But what kind of society does she have in mind?"

Jelsey looked surprised. "I don't know. A better one. One

that doesn't have to go to war every year. One where girls wouldn't have to learn how to maim and kill other people."

"But you don't have to be a warrior if you don't want to. Girls aren't forced to fight like boys are."

"It's my duty to the Ilari clan." She led me around the edge of the camp to the east. The smell of food hung richly in the air. "I plan to serve in battle for ten years, then I want to go to Lorinn and find work. What I'd really like to do is join the mapping exploration group that Lorinn has. They set out every spring in a different direction."

"Why don't you join them now?"

"I told you," she said, "it is my duty to the Ilari to protect them as they have protected me. I'll serve until I've repaid my debt and then I'll go do something else."

"The Valley does the same thing," I said. Jelsey's eyes widened. "Men serve for twelve years and then come back to the Valley to work and start a family."

"I hardly think you can compare us with the Valley!" she snapped.

A line of women stretched in front of us. Ahead, I could see long tables laid end to end. Jelsey and I joined the line.

"But I forget you're a Valley woman," she continued berating me. "You're not a real Ilari, and that's probably the kind of ignorant remark I should expect you to make."

"Jelsey!" I exclaimed. "I didn't mean anything by it."

But she did not stop. "Narine's right. The only true Ilari is one born to an Ilari warrior, descended from the first fifteen. Not you Valley women runaways."

"What about the foundlings you take in from the Valley? They don't know any other life. Are they false Ilari as well?" I said, my voice dangerously close to breaking. My hands clenched into fists.

Jelsey blinked, flushing. "I ... I think ..."

"Why don't you go and ask Narine to answer? You let her think for you anyway!" I spat. "Why do you follow someone who's turning you into such a hateful monster?"

"We should have left you to die in the forest!" Jelsey roared. Abruptly, she turned on her heel and left.

The women around us were deadly quiet. I wanted to go after Jelsey, but a hand on my shoulder stopped me.

"Don't, Shannon," the doctor said, sympathy in her voice. "I know this is hard. But let her go."

My thoughts were gloomy that afternoon as I played with Trae in the Mothers' House. Jinda tended to the other little children. Every now and then, I felt her eyes rest on us, but she never came over. I would not have minded, but she obviously felt the need to show that Trae was still mine no less than before.

When the sun began to set, I gave Trae back to Jinda. Several girls came in with plates of food for dinner, and Jinda invited me to stay and eat with them and the other mothers and young children. The little girl Enon ate her food noisily and messily, ending up with more of it on her face than in her mouth. I stared again at her bright red hair. It seemed somehow rude to ask if she were a foundling; I knew I would always wonder.

Saasu came into the house when dinner was finished. "It's time for Trae's presentation to the Ilari."

Jinda and I wrapped Trae in several thick blankets and took her outside. I gasped. Everywhere I looked, Ilaris stood together. All of them smiled and yelled at the sight of Trae in Jinda's arms. Saasu raised a hand for silence.

"Clan of Ilari!" She waved everyone closer. "Are we all here?"

Heads turned. "Narine and her camp aren't," someone called.

I saw Saasu's lips tighten almost imperceptibly. "Fetch them, please."

We waited for what seemed to be a long time. Then the black-clad forms appeared, walking insolently to join the rest of the warriors.

"Good," Saasu said at the sight of them. "Clan of Ilari, we gather tonight for the presentation of a new warrior."

The crowd applauded. Jinda held Trae high so everyone could see her. I smiled up at Trae, glad for her welcome.

"I give to you Trae, daughter of Trae and foster-daughter of Jinda," Saasu announced when the crowd quieted. For a fleeting moment, I remembered my mother's wasted body at Trae's birthing. This new Trae would have a life worlds apart from our mother's. No man would control her destiny. Or mine. Joy rose in my heart. Trae and I may have been no more than pawns for Valley men, but the pawns had won the game.

The crowd went wild at Saasu's words. "We salute our new Ilari daughter. May she spend her life free!" The Ilaris lifted their hands to the sky and cheered.

"Trae, daughter of Trae and foster-daughter of Jinda, woman warrior of the Ilari clan!" Saasu said. "Blessed in the names of the first fifteen!"

Heads lowered. "Blessed in the names of the first fifteen!"

Jinda stiffened next to me. Behind all the bowed figures, Narine and her people stood with their arms crossed over their chests. I saw Jelsey. She smirked at me.

"Narine!" Saasu's voice burst out like a clap of thunder. "Bow your head!"

Narine looked at Saasu. "No."

Women gasped, and then hissed at her.

"I will bow to true Ilari only."

"Every woman in this camp is a true Ilari," Saasu said, her words clipped. "No matter where they come from, once they are here they are Ilari."

"No one born to a brainless cow of a Valley woman can have the strength of mind or body to honor Ilari's name." Narine said. "I do not welcome a foundling."

Horror made the warriors speechless.

"Then you can leave," Saasu said.

Narine spoke. "Don't welcome this Valley brat into our community. We don't need her blood. It's warriors like her that make us weak."

The mother of Enon pulled the little girl to her feet and strode off into the night.

"Narine, you're being ridiculous," said the doctor, who had come to stand behind me. "We are all the children of Valley women. Where did the first fifteen come from, after all?"

Narine passed over this. "How much longer will this war go on? We should want better lives for our daughters, not the same lives. Daughters of Ilari, we may not live with men, but still our lives are dictated by them!"

"This war will not be solved by stealing into a Valley market and killing little boys!" Saasu said.

And women, I thought.

Narine swept her arm out to include everyone. "You know I'm right. How was it wrong what we did in that market? How many of our lives were saved because of those I ended? With the help of all the clans, we can conquer the Valley. We can ..."

"You disgrace yourself," Saasu said. "You can leave and any who agree with you can go along."

The warriors in black raised their fists to the air. "True Ilari!" they shouted as one. "True Ilari!"

Those in brown and white laughed and jeered, copying them. "True Ilari! True Ilari!"

Narine faded into shadows. Jelsey, Ness, and the others vanished. Saasu took Trae from Jinda and thrust her again into the air.

Chapter Fourteen

Retreating into Stillness

"No! No!"

Footsteps pounded past my tent. I lifted the flap and saw women running in the direction of Narine's camp. Throwing my blankets off, I stumbled out into the cold morning and followed.

"They're gone, they've all gone without me!" Jelsey was choking through her sobs outside the dark tents, pushing away someone who had tried to comfort her. *"Why didn't they take me?"*

Trae. I ran back to the Mother's House to check on her, but she was safely asleep in her cradle

"I don't know what happened!" I heard Jelsey scream. *"I woke up and they were gone!"*

Jinda stood with me for a moment.

"Where do you think they will go?" I asked.

"I have no idea," Jinda said. "Perhaps to another clan, or off to start their own."

"Those filthy traitors!" Jelsey bellowed.

"Poor thing," Jinda said. "But she'll be better for it."

I agreed. "What made Narine like this?"

"What makes any of us what we are?" she said. "Don't worry. Jelsey will be taken care of. Go eat breakfast."

Weeks passed with no news of Narine. Ilari trackers determined their party had headed southeast, in the direction of the Sude clan. I heard the older women of the Ilari and Saasu had had an argument over whether or not to send a message to the clans about the rebels, but Saasu prevailed and no notice was sent. She seemed embarrassed about the whole situation, and soon no one mentioned it to her. The only reminder was Jelsey, who slunk around like a kicked dog.

Snow fell hard, covering the ground and piling up beside tents. The cold barely penetrated the thickness of my tent walls, and my animal skin blankets stopped that which did. I knew miles away my sisters were shaking with the cold. And with hunger. Many of the tents here held nothing but food stored for the winter, and the Ilari sent out hunting parties often. Some of the hunters were no more than seven or eight years old. When a young girl came back with her first kill, the camp cheered her at the dinner meal and Saasu placed an animal teeth necklace around the girl's neck. I was the only girl from age eight and older without a necklace. But since Jelsey wore three, perhaps we somewhat balanced each other.

Jelsey dressed in her black outfit for a week or so after Narine left. Then she strolled up to me one morning wearing brown trousers and a white shirt. I blinked in shock, but her expression warned me not to mention the change. She still kept her three necklaces, her one difference from everyone else. Her depression at being left behind lifted more quickly than I had expected it to, but reappeared at odd moments, almost as an afterthought. Without Narine around to distract her, Jelsey was great fun, and we became fast friends during the winter.

When the weather grew too inclement for practice, school studies began. I could read after a fashion, but as Pasahn said, my ciphering skills were abominable, *abominable*, ABOMINA-BLE. I could add and subtract small numbers with little difficulty, but when she curtly asked me about fractions and other sorts of trivia Old Mother Ica had never discussed, my resulting blank look earned me a seat with the younger children. Why did Pasahn have to teach school too? She was no kinder there than she was on the practice field.

Gray also taught in the classroom. Class-tent, everyone called it, laughing whenever I called it a room. Two of the larger tents had been converted into a study area for us, and we sat on rugs while the teacher stood in the center to instruct. After two hours of Pasahn's screeching, I was glad for Gray's quiet patience. She taught clan history and battle strategy. At the end of each week, no matter the weather, she took us to the practice plain and divided us into two groups. One from each group was put in charge, and the rest of us each represented a legion. The little Guides decided where we would be situated on the field, where and when we would attack, what weapons we would carry.

I loved the strategy games. It was miserably cold, but the Ilari had finally issued winter coats for each warrior. We could play for hours with minimal discomfort from the weather. At times, we became hot enough with our frantic activity to want to take the coats off, but Gray would not let us.

"Get used to discomfort. That's all there is in battle," she said. "Rodents in the food, bad weather, insects biting night and day, not a cot or blanket in sight."

We pulled at the necks of the coats to let cool air in, and I resolved to cut off my excess of heavy hair that night. There was a reason none of the Ilari had hair as long as mine. Pasahn snorted; she often came to watch the strategy games and provide us with her never-ending criticism. "Sweat, girls, sweat!"

"I think she hates us," I whispered to Jelsey, who was the little Guide that day for my team. Jelsey motioned to me frantically, and I looked up to see Pasahn looming over me.

"What did you say, warrior?" I gulped. *"Would I be doing this if I hated you? Would I be wasting my time in the freezing cold if I hated you?"*

"No, Pasahn," I mumbled.

Her eyes bulged. "I could be inside! I could have my feet up! I could be correcting your pathetic excuse of a ciphering slate!" My eyes slipped momentarily to Gray, who stood aside with an odd expression.

Pasahn finished her tirade and headed back for the main camp. Gray's face settled back to its usual calm look.

"I'm sorry," I said to Gray. "I didn't mean any disrespect."

"I know, Shannon. But you were wrong to say that; none of us hates you. It is just very hard to train you girls for war. Imagine how we feel when one of you dies on the battlefield?" She said no more and flapped her hand at us to resume the game. We faced the opposing team more seriously now, the fun gone away.

"Pasahn's still Chaos to deal with," one of the girls said at our next break.

Jelsey looked thoughtful. "I don't know. If I were an armswoman, I'd feel terrible knowing one of my students had died. I'd think maybe if I'd trained them harder, shown them one more sword move or leg twist, maybe they would still be alive. I think the guilt would eat me alive."

"One more game!" Gray called to us. We groaned and turned around. "Shannon, why don't you be the little Guide for this one? Do you mind, Jelsey?"

I was startled. Our team looked nothing more than relieved. Jelsey was not the best leader, and usually attacked the other team with one frontal assault and foolish weapon choices, like bows and arrows. Who could string a bow at close range? She just wasn't devious.

"Ten minutes to prepare!" Gray said. We separated into our two teams and went to opposite ends of the practice field. There were twelve girls to a team. Thinking quickly, I laid out my battle plan. I sent Jelsey into the forest, to skirt around the other team and stay hidden behind them until I whistled for her. We were forbidden from looking at the other team while they planned, so I did not worry about her being noticed. I sent two more girls, one east and the other west, to also wait at the other team's sides.

Nine of us left. We divided into three groups of three each, one with bows, another swords, and the last, spears. Two girls argued with my strategy, but as the little Guide, I had the last word.

"Ready!" Gray shouted. We broke our huddle and arranged ourselves on the field. The other team had all its members there in front of us. They spread out in a long line, probably planning to surround and box us in. I gripped the handle of the sword I held. It was wooden, with a blunt edge. The spears had rubbery ends instead of metal, and the arrows had the same rubbery points.

Gray shouted again. "Go!"

We yelled for attack. I whistled once and we charged forward ten paces. The other team advanced, the ends of their lines beginning to curve.

"Now!" I ordered. The three with bows let loose a small hail of arrows. The three with spears stabbed their weapons at the girls curving around us. Two struck their mark on the west side. Ten of the twelve other girls had swords, as had the two fallen ones, and the remaining two stood in the line's middle with spears thrusting forward.

"Archers, take out spears!" I called. They jumped back up and fired. The eight left with swords fumbled, their eastern end still curving and their west one fallen. One of their spears fell under a hail of arrows. The other threw her spear and nailed one of my archers in the chest. Grunting, the girl fell over.

I had eight on the field and they had nine. The three girls who had thrown their spears took out two wooden daggers each from their belts. The archers snatched arrows from their quivers and prepared to shoot again.

"Archers, attack west!" I shouted, just as the little Guide from the other team shouted, "Charge them!"

My two archers took out the last swords-woman on their western curve. The remaining forces ran for us. I nearly stepped back.

"Engage swords!" I advanced instead with my weapon drawn. Fear jumped in me, until I remembered the three girls I had sent into the forest. I whistled twice as loudly as I could. One of their swords-women whirled around to see if anyone was sneaking up from behind, but my archers pegged her with arrows before she could shout a warning. Jelsey, with a howl, jumped out from her hiding place and raised an arrow to her bow. The other two girls approached. The one from the west ran to join us, and the one from the east was swiftly cut down by the enemy.

Another of my archers fell. Jelsey quickly dispatched two swords-women, but then had the bow knocked from her hand with the swipe of another sword. She kicked the sword out of her opponent's hand and began fighting with her.

Swords clattered together. The little Guide of the other team pushed her way through the melee to get to me. I stood tall, trying to feign bravery. The shouts and screams melded together as she silently raised her sword.

Suddenly, her body stiffened and fell forward. An arrow bounced off her back. Jelsey's eyes met mine silently over the body.

"We won! We won!" a group of girls surrounded me, cheering. I counted, feeling inexplicable panic. Of the twelve I had started with, eight still stood. The enemy had been slaughtered.

"Hold!" Gray said. I looked down at the ground. Those that had been killed stood up and brushed themselves off. My stomach unclenched slightly.

Jelsey clapped my back. "Great game, Shannon! We only lost four, that's not bad at all."

Four seemed too many to me. I should have placed two at each of the sides and called them out sooner.

"Well, Shannon, you have the knack for strategy," Gray praised. "All right, girls, let's go back and eat."

My stomach felt hollow, but not with hunger. Jelsey chattered and argued beside me with the other girls about how I had placed them around the plain, but I barely heard her. Between two trees, I saw movement. It was Pasahn. She had been watching.

I shivered. When the girls went off to battle in a few years, it would not be a game any longer. Those that fell would stay fallen, not jump up and run to lunch minutes later. It would be real. Some of the girls I had played with would be dead. I looked into their laughing faces and tried to figure out which ones it would be.

Jelsey tugged at my hair. "What's wrong with you? You won, you won!"

I smiled. "I know. Nothing's wrong. I'm just hungry, that's all."

"I smell stew!" Jelsey sniffed hard. "Stew and bread."

A wave of nausea overcame me. "I'm going to go to my tent to lay down. I have a bit of a headache."

"All right." She walked off with the other girls. I ran all the way to my tent and collapsed inside. My eyes were hot, but no tears fell.

A rough voice intruded. "It's not a game, Shannon. You know that, don't you?" Pasahn spoke outside my tent.

"I know," I said.

"Then you'll be a better warrior than many of those fools."

I closed my eyes. Did I want to be a warrior? Watch friends be cut down? I did not notice Jelsey had entered the tent with a bowl for me until she snapped her fingers in front of my face.

"Gray's really impressed! She's telling everyone what a good Guide you were. Keep playing like that and you'll be the Charge of a regiment when you're old enough. Are you really all right? What's wrong?"

"What does the Charge do?" I asked.

"She leads her age group." Like Erlin, I thought vaguely, the second-command Ekklia had talked about. Tarien had led all the regiments, but Erlin and each leader of an age group had a voice in strategy. The clans were not as different from the Valley men as they liked to think.

"Jelsey, tell me about the warrior dedication ceremony," I said. She smiled.

"Do you mean it? You want to be a warrior?" she asked excitedly.

"I want to be a warrior and a Charge," I said.

"Then you'll have to fight me for it!" Her voice was competitive, but her eyes still friendly. "As well as Aryll and Mased!

There's only one Charge for an age group, and I'm going to be it."

Fight Jelsey? I smiled back at her.

"Then let's agree to a fair fight," I said, extending a hand to her.

She grasped it. "A fair fight, then. May the best warrior win."

We dug into the stew with our fingers. "Our first kill is going to be my braid, as soon as we're done eating."

Jelsey laughed. "Done." She sucked on a carrot. "With both of us in the regiment, we'll slaughter all the Valley for the pigs and cows they are." Not realizing what she had said, she laughed.

I watched her without responding, wondering how much she had really changed.

Chapter Fifteen

Hourglass Sand

Winter passed. The last of the snow melted to gray slush, and then vanished as the air slowly warmed. The forest was lush with spring when the Ilari warriors prepared to march away to battle. The night before they left, a dance was held in honor of the new warriors joining the ranks. The older women looked at the girls with worry, the younger ones were green with envy. To serve in battle was not a requirement among the Ilari, but even the most reluctant girl considered it her duty to fight for several years. The more enthusiastic planned to stay in the ranks as long as they could fight. Several of the women packing their clothes and weapons had hair white and thin with age.

The dance lasted far into the night. The women had brought out all sorts of drums from their tents. No two were alike; some were short and fat and had to be carried by more than one woman, others were skinny and made of a silvery metal. Sometimes, three or four drums had been banded together to make sets, and wide black straps hung from them to be placed over the musician's neck and shoulders. Many of the drums had striking sticks attached, but the rest were beaten by hand. One enormous drum had been suspended from a frame and would be struck by a large hammer stick.

Jelsey and I were shivering with excitement as the sun slipped down the western sky. We had been set to collecting rocks in the fringes of the forest with the other girls. Pasahn stood in the clearing shouting directions whenever we returned with handfuls of rocks for the large circle we were making.

"It's supposed to be a circle! *A circle!*" We heard her exclaim as we picked over the ground. "I want rocks! Not pebbles! ROCKS!"

"I wish she still went to battle and left us alone," Jelsey muttered. Mased and I laughed.

Pasahn fixed her eyes on me before returning to the girls at her feet scurrying to correct the bump in the rock circle they had made. I put mine down in a pile and went back for more.

"Hurry up, *hurry up*, HURRY UP!" came a furious shout behind me.

Once the circle was complete, Pasahn dragged us back to the camp, where venison was being cooked. Plates of bread and thick wedges of butter covered long tables, along with row after row of cider mugs. Jelsey and I chose plates and joined the line for meat.

"I can't wait until next year when I go to battle! If only I'd been born two months earlier, I'd be marching away now," Jelsey was saying, as I watched a group of new warriors fuss over their masks. "I've picked out the design I want for my mask. What kind do you want?"

"I don't know," I said. "Isn't it hard to fight when you're wearing a mask? Can you see properly?"

"Of course you can! Look how wide the eyes are. They're pretty light, too."

"They probably scare the men half to death," I said. "Look at that one with the black bear face!"

"They'll run screaming from mine," Jelsey bragged. "I'm not going to use an animal face like the rest of the girls. I'll have a skeleton face." She looked downcast. "Narine was going to help me make it."

"Anyone else would be happy to help," I floundered.

"You're probably right," she said. Her depression vanished. "Look, Saasu's calling them to Ilari's temple." We watched them go in.

"They have a private dedication before the dance," Jelsey

reminded me. I had not forgotten. We reached the front of the line and had steaming slices of meat piled onto our plates. The women gathered in the middle of the camp and sat on animal skins covering the ground. Jelsey and I joined Aryll and Mased, and we ate until we were bursting. I waved at Trae, dressed in tiny brown trousers and a white shirt, on Jinda's lap. Jinda picked up Trae's hand and waved it at me.

Saasu and the new warriors returned when dinner was nearly finished. They ate quickly, the girls excited and nervous. Then Pasahn shooed us to our tents to fetch our own gourd drums that we had made. Jelsey and I walked back together.

I wrestled my drum out from my tent and unwrapped it. Blue and white beads swayed back and forth on two long strings. On the other strings I had tied three white winterlark feathers. I admired my handiwork for a moment. Jelsey's could barely be seen under all her decorations.

"Aren't you finished with yours yet?" Jelsey asked tactlessly.

I glared at her. "There's a difference between quantity and quality, Jelsey."

Rage flashed in her eyes so quickly I barely recognized it. "Sharp tongue, haven't you? Come on, let's go."

"Chaos, Jelsey!" the doctor said when we walked by her to the clearing. "Is there actually a drum in there?"

"Yes!" Jelsey snapped. I stifled a laugh. The only part of the drum visible was a bit of the skin. The gourd had vanished under long strings of green beads twined into lumpy braids, each strand both beginning and ending with large tufts of red feathers. A lengthy golden fringe covered the outer portion of the drum skin, leaving only the middle discernible.

We entered the clearing. A fire burned in the middle of the circle, roaring high in the oncoming night. The new warriors stood motionless within the circle, their backs to the fire. Their masks hung still in their hands.

"Next year, next year," Jelsey chanted, hopping from one foot to the other. Her body quivered with excitement. I looked at the four girls standing around the fire in awe, and saw that their hands trembled ever so slightly.

"They don't look too excited," I said.

Jelsey waved her hand. "Oh, that's just first battle jitters. Everyone gets them at the thought of actually killing someone. The first kill is the worst, even if it is just a man. But then you get used to it."

"That's an awful thing to get used to, even if they are just men."

"I don't think so. I'll enjoy the dread on the faces of every man who meets his death on my sword," she said confidently. "They'll learn fear when I'm in the ranks next year!"

"I wish Trip were still warring!" I found myself saying. "He was the man I was supposed to marry, an awful brute of a man."

"They're all brutes," Jelsey said.

"But he wins the contest. I wonder what poor girl he ended up marrying in my place." I pitied her.

Jelsey and I joined the drummers in the circle. Warriors stood behind us, masks on their faces. Wolves and bears, wild boars and cats, even two or three snake masks loomed over us. A woman stepped between two drummers and stood at the edge of the circle. Her mask was a terrifying mix of the others, red-tinged serpent fangs below a long snout, beady holes for eyes and two pricked ears. The cheeks were studded with tiny, glittering black tiles.

"Begin!" the woman's voice called, unmistakably Saasu.

An old woman struck the drum hanging from the frame. A low boom shook birds from the trees. Pasahn nodded to those of us with handheld gourd drums, and we struck them in the pattern we had been taught, three strikes with the first beat loud, the second beat softer, and the third beat softer still. A pause, then we repeated the pattern.

The new warriors lifted their masks and held them high for us to see. A bear with lips curled in a snarl, a deer with bloody antlers, a screaming man's face, and the last, a choga flower outlined in black. The little girls gasped. Jelsey's eyes widened.

Saasu howled to the moon as the new warriors fastened their masks over their faces. I had not noticed the spears lying at their feet until they snatched them up and began to dance around the fire, holding the weapons over their heads.

The older women echoed Saasu's howl and struck their drums. At first the sound was discordant with ours, then the rhythm formed. During our three beats they struck only on the second, and then struck again in the pause. The women with the drum sets beat out an entirely different pattern, which quickened and then slackened, then quickened again.

Saasu's voice trilled. The older warriors threaded by the drummers and leapt into the circle to join the dance. Pasahn raised her hand and the gourd drums quieted. The other drums beat slowly and evenly with each other. With each beat the warriors took one step, creeping hunched over with their spears low. The pace became swifter, every other warrior in the circle whirling back to clash spears with the woman behind them before continuing on to stalk around the fire.

When Pasahn motioned to us, we began a new pattern. Five short strikes and a longer, louder one. The dance seemed to last for hours, until the warriors threw down their spears and faced the fire with their arms taut at their sides. They writhed like snakes. My hands stung from beating the drum, but I made myself go faster at Pasahn's scowl. Faster and faster, sweat streaming down my face and splashing onto the drum, until I gasped for air and looked up to the sky to see black birds wheeling above ...

The beat of the largest drum stopped us. Sound shook the air as Saasu and the warriors bayed like wolves to the moon. The cries lasted a long time, before fading into stillness. We were quiet leaving the clearing, too tired for words or goodbyes, and when I woke up the next morning, the warriors had left.

Those remaining, old women, new mothers, and children, began the move to the summer camp in the northern mountains. The Ilari statue was gingerly lifted and placed into a wagon. Four old women hitched up and rattled off to the settlement of

Lorinn, where the statue would be kept over the summer. It was too heavy to drag up the foothills and mountain passes. They would unload the statue, reload with food from the Lorinn settlers, and follow us to the summer camp. In exchange, the older warriors of the clans provided spotters. They rotated in one-month shifts, watching the surrounding areas so that should Valley men attack, Lorinn would be warned and ready.

We waited for the Sude clan, traveling from the southwest, to reach us. Each clan separated for the winter, and then came together with several others for the summer in remote areas. The Ilari and Sude clans would then join the Kyata clan in the east before traveling north. They had camped together for generations in the northern mountains. Jelsey told me the clans of Klia, Rithe, and Thrine traveled all the way to the Eastern Sea and lived on the beaches, while the Sadira, Jannday, and Kalani clans left the Beyond for the Sun Caves.

"I want to see those someday," Jelsey said. "Saasu actually went to them when she was a little girl; she told me everything she remembered."

I had no doubt I was about to learn everything Saasu remembered too. I grinned and thought of Ekklia, happily spilling every coveted fact she knew about the Autumn Night men.

"The Sun Caves are a huge webbing of tall white rock, with rivers running through some of the legs to a little pool in the center of the web. The ceiling of the caves is broken, so it's very light during the day and ... "

A shout rang through the camp. "Sude!"

The next hour I stood aside awkwardly, watching women embrace friends, small children chasing each other underfoot. The Sude were dressed in light gray shirts and darker gray trousers, all with shoulder-length hair drawn back in a green band. Every time Jelsey started to introduce me to one of them, she would spy another friend and hurtle away.

"I'm sorry, I don't remember you," one girl in gray said shyly. "Shara, is that what Jelsey called you?"

"Shannon. I just joined the Ilari clan, that's why you don't remember me," I explained, trying to make her comfortable.

"Just joined?"

"I'm from the Valley."

Her blue eyes widened with interest. "Like Priss, you mean."

Priss? "What? *Priss Dawidsdaughter?*"

The girl shrugged. "I don't know if that was her name. I think there was another Valley runaway in the Ilaris, years and years ago."

Priss, who had been carried off by a bear while picking choga flowers for Autumn Night. Priss had been an Ilari. I had to ask Jelsey. Just as I reached her side, fully intending to interrupt her conversation with several girls, Pasahn yelled.

"Let's go!" Jostled by women behind me, I forgot my questions and ran for the pack of supplies I would be carrying. Pasahn looked at me evilly. She pointed her finger.

"You, you, and you! Follow behind us and cover the footprints!"

I grumbled and hunted for a loose branch of pine needles. We left the camp and walked through the clearing, and then pushed into forest. At least a mile or so had passed before Pasahn let us drop the branches and join the rest of the women.

Two days passed as we traveled through nothing but forest. The trees above grew thicker until the sunlight was nearly nonexistent for hours at a time. Our party stopped to fill large buckets with berries and refill our canteens with water from the streams we crossed.

"I can't wait until we get to the mountains," Jelsey said. "There we can fish. Have you ever gone fishing?"

"Fishing is for boys in the Valley."

"Chaos to that! Come on, let's make you a fishing pole!" She searched for a long stick and told me to do the same. It had to be slender but thick, and bendy at the same time, and after we found one, she had me scrape the twigs and knobs from it with a knife. By evening, we reached the winter camp of the Kyata clan. Again, I stood by while the women milled about, laughing and greeting each other. The Kyata women wore blue, all sorts of shades put together. Put side by side, they looked like the sky in every season.

The next day, we left the forest. For a minute, I stood still, letting my eyes adjust to the bright sunlight. Hills rolled in front of us, climbing higher and higher until they turned to far-away mountains.

"Stop gawking! Let's go!" In Saasu's absence, Pasahn took control. The doctor mumbled something rude beside me. She saw that I had heard and forced a smile.

"I'll be at battle next year. Pasahn is by far the better deal."

"How can you go to war? Who will be the doctor?"

"The Kyata and Sude doctors are at the battle right now. We take turns, so that we get one out of every three years off. Next year, I'll work with the Kyata doctor at battle while the Sude doctor is here."

We traveled over the foothills. A wagon was being used for mothers with young children to ride in when they tired. Jinda sat with Trae in her arms. She was often passed around from woman to woman, to be petted and fussed over. Such a welcoming should have been every girl child's right, I thought fiercely. Our other sisters and I had never had that sort of attention showered on us. It made me jealous.

Once at the mountains, the spotters from both clans separated from us. Just an hour after they left, two wagons returned from Lorinn, packed with food. Pasahn directed us to a narrow break. We climbed for one exhausting day before the land leveled into the camp area. Mountains surrounded a clearing on every side, and by nightfall, some of the stars seemed to balance on the peaks.

Just like in the winter camp, arms practice swallowed our morning hours. However, the girls from each clan were instructed in one large group. Pasahn had far less time to terrorize the Ilari girls. She bore down on the Sude and Kyata girls just as much. We were all glad when the arms-women from the other clans taught spears.

The afternoons were ours. Jelsey showed me how to fish

in the lake beyond the camp. When I caught one and brought it back in triumph, I received my animal teeth necklace. Nothing about me, physically, marked me now as different from the rest of the warrior women.

From noon to night, the girls of Kyata, Sude, and Ilari, ran wild. We played games, dangled from trees, jumped off boulders into the lake. Sometimes we rode the horses and the other girls taught me how to ride, much to their amusement and several jolting tumbles on my part. Gray took us on frequent hikes in the neighboring mountains, pointing out all sorts of flowers and bushes that grew along our trail. A Kyata woman showed us the constellations at night. By the time we fell onto our sleep-rolls at night, there was not an ounce of energy left in our bodies.

One day, deep in the heat of summer, I remembered Priss Dawidsdaughter. Jelsey leaned back on a boulder next to me, lazily flicking her fishing pole in the water. She looked half-asleep in the humid air, which was like an unneeded coat.

"Jelsey."

A moment passed in silence. "What?" She yawned.

"Was there a girl in the Ilari clan once, a girl called Priss?"

Another yawn. She wiped damp curls from her forehead. "When I was younger. She was a Valley runaway like you. Did you know her?"

"Not really."

"She wasn't here very long. Her first battle was her last one."

I thought I felt a tug on my line. I stood up and pulled my pole back. The fish got away, if there had been one. I sat back down.

"Did she not fight well?"

Jelsey stretched. "I guess not. Valley girls usually aren't as good as warrior girls."

"What? I can nearly beat you any day."

"Nearly. You need to be trained to fight. The rest of us, it's in our blood."

I snorted. "Chaos-rot to that."

"I've got one!" She jumped up. The hook had punched straight through the fish's lip, and blood spilled out onto the water. Jelsey looked gleeful. The Valley girl in me just felt sick.

Chapter Sixteen

Lorinn

Summer heat boiled away to autumn briskness. The Ilari warriors would soon be traveling back to the winter camp, the men warriors back to the Valley. At times, I remembered Beth was only a few months away from marriage, and the twins were beginning their last term in school. But it seemed unreal, as if I knew the intimate history of someone I had never met. The women of the Ilari treated me as if I had always been with them, and the other clans followed suit.

We bid farewell to the Kyata and Sude clans and left the mountains. Mased, Aryll, Jelsey, and I made ourselves lookouts for our slow-moving party, and we practiced bird whistles and animal calls until Pasahn told us we were making her quite insane, and would we shut up before she strapped us to a horse's belly and had us taken back to the winter camp in that fashion.

"We were just practicing!" Aryll and Mased protested together. Pasahn's stare could have frozen water. They stammered, turned red, and finally apologized without Pasahn having to say another word.

We traveled through the foothills. The wagon carrying the mothers with babies and young children made tedious progress over the puckered earth, and often enough a wheel would stick in a rut and we would all have to wait until it was dug out again. No one minded the pace. The air was jovial, and quite often, the Ilari women would burst out in a warrior song. Some of them I knew the words to, others I was learning. A couple of the older women argued strategies they had used when they were in battle, and I followed closely behind them to listen. There were all sorts of names for strategies, the snap-string, the side crush, even one called the stomping foot.

"What's that?" I asked, laughing.

They laughed themselves. "I forget how ridiculous it sounds," a woman named Geda said. "We used that one night when the men tried to ambush us. We had fifteen warriors and they had twenty-five, so we climbed into the trees and waited until they were passing right below us. Our archers took out the first few, and then we jumped down right on top of them."

Another woman laughed and slapped her leg. "I was there that night. They didn't know where we were coming from and didn't stand a chance. I landed right on a man's head. He died without a sound."

"Oh, stop filling the girl's head with nonsense," Pasahn, astride a horse, snapped down at us. "Glorious battles and brave warriors. Tell her some of the strategies that didn't work. Tell her what it's like to watch a sister die." She kicked her horse and headed for the front of the caravan.

The other women did not get angry, like I had expected. Instead, they followed her retreating form with pitying eyes.

"But you weren't telling me battles were glorious," I said, needing to defend them in some way.

"She took her last year of battle hard," Geda said. "She lost several good friends."

"We've all lost friends," another said. And they nodded and began talking about defeats, doomed warriors, and death. About how a battle could change suddenly, rendering a well-planned strategy useless and its warriors stranded in enemy territory. How you could lose everyone who mattered to you in moments. What it felt like to watch a friend be cut down because you couldn't reach them in time.

"Some of the younger warriors are cut down right away. They charge into the battle ready to kill and never think for a minute that they might not win," Geda sighed. "The Guides for all the clans decided years ago to keep the first year warriors as the last line of battle. Mostly they work as cooks, medics, and scouts."

"They see horrible, horrible sights as medics," a woman named Iete added. "They aren't as foolhardy when they walk into their first battle."

"Well, most of them aren't," Geda said, shrugging. "The Valley woman we had a few years ago was struck down within minutes."

"Do you mean Priss?" I interrupted.

They nodded. "Priss was eager to kill the day she arrived. Insane with rage, really. She burned her dress and chopped off her braid, and she said it was a shame her husband wasn't still a warrior, so she could strike him down." Iete grimaced. "And then she fell without a blow to any man."

"Did she just run in when the battle began?"

"No." Geda tucked her whitening hair into a braid. "Pasahn and I ..." she stopped and looked at the other women.

"Please tell me what happened. Please." I stretched the truth a little. "I knew her when I lived in the Valley." Well, I knew *of* her through Ekklia.

"Priss was a good fighter," Iete said. "Quick of mind, quick of feet."

Geda looked ahead of us. "Pasahn taught her from morning until night. She wanted to go to war as soon as possible. Her mask chilled me. It was that of a long dead man, the face powdered white and rotting ..."

Iete cut her off. "An Ilari warrior picks a mask that will give her courage and strength. Some use a screaming face, because others' fear gives them power. Many use wild animals they respect for their cunning or force. A few use the choga flower, because they know the men have no cure for such poison, and the men's ignorance gives them the upper hand."

A woman who had been silent until now clasped her necklace. "I told her the men weren't worth this much hatred. They are worthy of our disdain, nothing more. She laughed in my face and told me I knew nothing of life with a Valley man. She had been married for several years, and said men were worth every bit of the hate she felt."

I heard Jelsey calling me, but pretended not to have heard her.

Geda shook her head. "She screamed and charged, swinging her sword wildly and hitting nothing. She was easy pickings for the men. Her sword never protected her the idiot way she thrashed it about."

"One struck her down and unmasked her. And then a man looked over and called her by name."

"Why did he unmask her?" I asked.

"The women wear masks to give them power. The men strip them to show they have no fear of women's power over them. After a man strikes a warrior woman, he pulls off her mask to watch her die."

"That's awful," I said in disgust.

"Finish and get it over with," said the woman still clutching her necklace.

"Priss stared at him as the blood bubbled out of her stomach. The man called her by name as he stood over her, and she called him Denny. She asked him to help her. He ... he knelt down then. And he slit her throat." Geda and Iete looked at each other before Geda continued. "Another warrior killed the man. Priss and he died next to each other."

"That was her brother," I said in shock. Denny had been one of the oldest boys in the school when I was very small. Something occurred to me. "Is that why Narine said Valley women have misplaced affection? Because of Priss?"

"Enough," said the one with the necklace in her hand. "That's enough for a child's ears."

Geda looked like she wanted to argue, but did not. At that moment, Jelsey shouted my name again.

"I think you're wanted elsewhere," Geda said quietly. "But know that Valley women do have a hard time on the battle field. You're going to kill people you know, even if they're just men. Think long and hard about whether you can do that, before you're standing on a battle field staring at a brother."

I did not have a brother. I nodded and walked down the hill toward Jelsey. How would I feel if I had to battle San Trelson, or Obal, as nasty as he was? Then I thought of Trip and the Crier. I could handle it.

Jelsey stumbled in her excitement when she saw me. "Shannon, great news!"

"What?" I thought of my father leaving Trae in the Beyond, and laughed with sheer malice. "Are we marching to battle this minute to spill blood?"

She laughed. "I wish! That, unfortunately, will have to wait."

"Then what?"

"Pasahn just told me that she's chosen you and me to join the party to Lorinn tomorrow! What do you think of that?"

I kept a straight face. "Well ... it's not as good as my idea, but I guess it will have to do."

We laughed together. Uneasiness at my remark surfaced time after time that day, but always, I shoved it back. Valley men beat their wives and daughters, ruled every decision that should rightfully be a woman's own. Why should I feel guilty about killing them? I would spare a woman's life with every man's I took away. And how could that be wrong?

The next morning, our party of six set out to Lorinn. Jelsey and I were the youngest, the rest were older women. Gray was one of them; to my delight, Pasahn was not. Though it was early, Jinda had dressed Trae and brought her out to wave at me.

"Wave farewell, Trae," Jinda said to her. "Farewell to your sister!" Trae gurgled and shoved her very chubby fist into her mouth instead.

I climbed onto my horse and rode to Jelsey's side. Two of the other women were driving wagons, and the other two slumped tiredly on the wagon planks. Gray snored, buried in a blanket she had bunched into a pillow.

"Let's go!" Jelsey shouted. "Come on, Shannon, I'll race you to that foothill over there!"

A hand clamped down on her leg. "You will not, Jelsey, or

neither of you will be going on this trip," Pasahn growled. I had not seen her approach. She glared at me until I looked away, and then she went over to the wagon and shook Gray awake.

We waited impatiently while they spoke. I stroked my horse's mane, pretending not to notice Pasahn's waving arms and wild gestures in Jelsey's and my direction. Gray nodded and nodded. Finally, Pasahn still raging, said, "All right, get going!"

The drivers clucked to the wagon horses. Jelsey and I nudged our horses to a very sedate trot, until Pasahn was too far in the distance to see us.

Jelsey looked over her shoulder. "Now let's race! Ready ..."

"Girls, please come over here," Gray called. Jelsey swore.

We rode over to the wagon. Gray thrust her feet up onto one of the food baskets and stretched. Empty bags and barrels were stacked at her side. They would be filled with food once we reached Lorinn.

Gray took her feet off the food basket. "Shannon, can you drive a wagon?"

"Yes, I think so." I had never done it, but I had watched my father long enough.

"Good. You and Jelsey will take turns driving the wagon we're picking up in Lorinn. You'll carry the Ilari statue back to the winter camp."

"When do we reach Lorinn?" I asked.

"How long will we be there?" Jelsey burst out. "Is there enough time for me to see the exploration team's maps?"

"We'll be there tomorrow, Shannon, early in the morning. We'll be there most of the day, so you can have an hour or so to look at the new maps, Jelsey, but not longer than that."

Jelsey looked pleased. "They went straight west this year. Imagine what they might have found!"

Gray smiled. "Probably what they found in every other direction. Mountains, plains, beaches, and rocks."

"Ness told me they found a settlement a few years ago, probably the descendants of one of the original ships that landed here." Jelsey's eyes were dreamy. "And they had no idea there were other people in this land! I'm going to ask about it when we get to Lorinn."

"You have an hour, remember that," Gray chided gently. "We have to be traveling by mid-afternoon, at the very latest."

"Enough time to hear a few stories, at least," she insisted. We traveled west over the foothills, the mountains at our right and vague shadows of forest at our left. The grass was thick and tall, occasionally trembling as a small animal ran through it. A cool wind flowed by every so often, and the sky was bright blue without clouds. I had never thought a place so lovely existed, and suddenly I wished my sisters could be with us, chasing each other over the hills, laughing and calling, their voices as clear as chimes. Nearly a year had passed since I had left the Valley. I felt I had traveled the world in those months, while they still walked only as far as the market. Their only future was Autumn Night, marriage, and children to feed. Compared to them, I had a wealth of choices.

"I miss home," I blurted to Jelsey, as we rode away from Gray.

Jelsey was appalled. "How can you miss the *Valley?* Being beaten and starved and ... "

"No," I interrupted. "I mean my sisters." It was the first time I had acknowledged them since I ran away. Jelsey listened while I described Beth, now old enough for marriage. Perhaps Lake and Damess had fostered her for Autumn Night. Beth, being Beth, would please them far more than I had. I talked about Roaninblue, not allowed the dignity of individual names. Dir, Synde, Balasar with her odd eyes, little Greda and Keluu.

And Ekklia, who probably had a child of her own. Her sweetness faded, her dreams of romance gone. What kind of person could she have been had she been lucky enough to be born an Ilari? Or Damess? My mother? Without choices, their lives had been wasted.

Jelsey disagreed. "They had choices. If Valley women banded together, they could break away from the men and live free."

"But when men direct your life from the day you're born, you have no idea you could choose to break free," I argued back. "You just follow the steps in front of you."

She snorted. "Then why are you here? Why aren't you following the steps?"

I had no answer for that question. I shrugged my shoulders and we continued riding in silence. I thought of that first day in the schoolroom, when Old Mother Ica ignored my presence even though I was marriage-bound and should have been at home.

That was how I had escaped, I realized when I woke up the next morning. It had been Old Mother Ica's quiet rebellion against the life laid out for women, letting me attend school when I was too old. It was my mother's refusal to teach her daughters the womanly arts. It was Gella's complaints at the festival, making me wonder if there was anything else. The acts of a few women striking back the only way they knew how, their passive streams of anger joining into a flood within me.

They weren't mindless pawns, bowing down to the way it was like so many of the other women. They weren't like Damess, who took her pleasure in smacking me around because she reveled in the small power the Valley world had allotted her. They were only unlucky. It was not lack of courage or weak wills that made many of those women what they were. It was fear and ignorance of anything different. Valley men, to Chaos with all of them!

By the time we reached Lorinn, I was in such a foul temper that I snapped at the first man I saw.

"Need any help?" a tall man asked at my side.

I snarled. "No. I'm perfectly capable of getting off a horse."

Jelsey's mouth dropped. The man looked surprised.

"Rot, Shannon, what's wrong with you?" she hissed when we swung to the ground.

I glared at the man's back. "I hate men! Why do they assume women can't do anything besides cook and clean? Of course I can get off a horse without his assistance."

Jelsey rolled her eyes. "This is Lorinn, not the Valley. He was going to help with the packs your horse is carrying, not you!"

"Oh." I blushed. "Well, I can manage my packs just fine as well."

She laughed. "It's a little bit different here."

"When you're finished, there's breakfast in the main hall," Gray called over to us, pointing at a log building. "And Jelsey, take your hour with the maps."

Jelsey whooped. "Want to come?"

"No, I'm going to go eat." We finished unloading the packs from the horses.

Gray called to one of the Ilari to take our horses to the stable. Jelsey sprinted down the street. I went to the main hall.

Lorinn was nothing more than one long street, with tiny buildings lining each side. The fields were green and gold in the early morning when we traveled past them, and the farms in the distance were red brick and white stone. The street had been empty when we rode in, the businesses dark. I could see a thread and scissors painted on one sign, indicating a tailor's. Next to it was a cloth store, with bolts of fabric lined up by the window. Across the street stood a bread-and-sweets store, jars of colorful candy just visible on the walls within. Next to it was the main hall, bigger than the others with a large golden bell hanging above it. As I watched, a girl appeared on the roof and rung it once. The sound echoed in the street.

I opened the door to the hall and went in. A few people were already in the large room, in a line at a counter or seated at round tables. They had eggs and pancakes on their plates. A boy tipped a brown jug at one table; thick syrup dripped down onto his food. My stomach rumbled.

I joined the line and took a plate and fork. It had been months since I had used a fork. I stared at it in wonder.

"Eggs?" a man behind the counter said, lifting a large spoonful. I saw the painting on the wall behind him of two wrinkled trees, stripped of leaves, and bent in a wind of white whirls. Their trunks settled in boggy earth, mottled browns and blacks disturbed only by patches of thin yellow grass. In the sky, a blue brilliant against the dull colors of the earth below, a white winterlark flew alone.

I had been there before. I had sat against those very trees, licking candy from my hands. How could a painting of the Mooring be here? Miles and miles away from an impossible world called the Valley? It could be no one else's work. A thin blue streak marked the initial I expected, but I had to be sure.

"Who ... who did that painting?"

The man looked surprised. "Why, he did." He pointed with his spoon behind me.

I turned around to see the person who had just walked through the door. I was staring at Jadan Trelson.

"Jadan." Something in my voice stopped the nearby conversations. Everyone looked from me to Jadan.

He had been laughing when he came in the building, propping the door open for a man with a cane.

"Shannon Wrightsdaughter?" And his voice was just as incredulous.

"What are *you* doing here?" I said accusingly.

The hall was so still I could hear the clink of a fork.

"I live here," Jadan answered, his voice just as accusing. He had grown taller since I had seen him last, his red hair darker. His nostrils flared.

I put my plate down on the counter and walked to him, not believing it was really Jadan. He looked like Trel. I had a sudden vision of the family portraits in Ekklia's hallway. Jadan had been no more than twelve or thirteen when he had done them, but his talent was undeniable. The day before Jadan went to war, his father had snapped his brushes and spilled the paint on the ground. San and Teff had told everyone the story in the schoolyard, laughing about Jadan's tears. Teff. Did he know Teff and Com were dead?

Gentle conversation began again in the room.

"Come on," he said abruptly. "Let's go outside."

The door swung shut behind us. Gray was still in the wagon. I felt safe with her there.

"I thought you deserted," I said, for lack of anything better.

Jadan's anger had gone. "Yes. Forgive me for shouting. This is such a surprise."

"How did you get here?"

He smiled. "It's good to see you, Shannon."

Obviously, he was not going to be hurried. A chilly wind swept down the street. I rubbed my hands along my arms.

"Is this your first time in Lorinn?" He began walking down the street. I hurried after him.

"Yes, it is."

"Then I'll show you around." We went past the tailor's.

"I liked your painting in the hall," I said when he was silent.

"Thank you. I've got paintings in a lot of the shops."

I had had enough. "How did you get here?" I repeated.

"I didn't want to fight the women," he said. I bristled.

"Why? Because you think they're weaker?"

"You've been with the Ilari for a while, haven't you? You look quite well."

I would not be deterred. "Women just can't do anything as well as men, is that it?"

"Did I say that?"

"You said you didn't want to fight women."

"I said, the women. I meant the clans. If they were full of men, I wouldn't have wanted to fight just the same."

"Why not? You're a Valley man."

"I'm no longer a Valley man. I don't want that way of life."

He was making it so hard to be angry. "Turn down a wife to serve at your beck and call? What kind of man are you?"

We had left the street minutes before. I had not noticed a thing. The road wound between fields of grapevines. Bunches of fruit hung heavy from the canes.

Jadan scrubbed his hands through his hair. "I don't know

what kind of man I am yet. I just know who I didn't want to be. And I know how you were treated in the Valley, and I'm sorry for it, but don't take it out on me."

I grunted. He started walking back to the buildings.

"No, wait, Jadan," I said.

"I mean, what do you think it's like to be a boy growing up in the Valley?"

I thought about my dead brother in Father's arms. "You had the world."

He shook his head. "I don't mean that. Did your father beat your mother?"

"Of course he did."

"My father beat my mother too. I tried to stop him once, when I was very small. And he told me it was his duty. One day, he said, it would be my duty to beat my own wife, to make sure she behaved herself."

Our voices were loud but not angry. A hollow formed in my stomach at Jadan's words.

"I hated my mother when she didn't behave because of what that meant he had to do to her. But that was the way it was done. And I hated going to war, but that was what I was supposed to do. It was my duty."

"But you deserted."

"I had to ... I just had to find something different."

"And have you?"

"It doesn't matter here if you're a man or a woman. Everybody in Lorinn does everything. I work in the mornings, but every afternoon I'm free to paint. Actually, I live with a painter. She gives me lessons."

We walked, not speaking, for a moment. "Teff and Com are dead," I said flatly, not knowing what else to say. "A group of Ilari went into the Valley and they were killed in the attack."

Jadan stopped walking, sucked in his breath and exhaled slowly.

"I'm sorry."

"I wish they'd had the chance to see this." He waved his

arm over the ripe fields. "I wish I could have given them this world."

"I'm sorry," I repeated, unsure of myself now. Jadan smiled sadly and patted my arm. I felt awkward. We spent most of our walk back to town in silence.

The sun set over the western foothills. The forest had darkened long before. We stopped to camp a mile from its edge.

"Don't like Lorinn too much," Jelsey warned. I had been speaking about it for the last hour.

"Why not? I think it's a wonderful place. Women and men all trying to get along peaceably," I said.

"Don't like it so much because it can't work. Sooner or later, the men will try to grab control. That's just how they are." Jelsey swiped her hair off her forehead tiredly.

"But Lorinn believes women and men are equal!" I protested. "Jadan told me boy or girl, each child is taught they can do whatever they want in the community. Men can be cooks or tend children, women can be hunters or historians. It's just like the old world Saasu told me about, where men and women considered each position equally important."

"If that kind of system worked, then the rebel ships wouldn't have left the old world to start with," Jelsey reasoned. "So women and men can't live together peaceably. Eventually, someone will try to control."

I tore bread from the loaf we shared. "I still like it," I said weakly.

"I like Lorinn, too. It's a great idea, peace between women and men, but it just won't work."

I threw a chunk of bread at her, suspecting she was right. She caught it neatly and threw it back. The Ilari statue cast dark shadows behind her.

I thought of Jadan's parting words that afternoon.

"Let the anger go, Shannon. It won't serve you." He tightened the knots holding the statue down. "No one is winning in the Valley, not the men or the women. Leave that world behind and make a new one for yourself."

"I can't let it go. And you're wrong, the men are winning." I clicked to the horse. "Farewell, Jadan. I hope to see you next year."

I had to strike back. For my mother, my sisters, and myself. Next spring, I would go to war for them. And when a man I knew cowered under my spear, I knew I would be able to strike the blow.

Chapter Seventeen

The Guide of the Ilari Clan

Saasu was dead.

The news stunned the winter camp, which had been preparing a feast and festivities for the warriors' return. The bright decorations should have, by all rights, drooped and wilted. But they sparkled brilliantly, ignorantly, in the sun, incongruous to the somber air.

"Saasu?" the old women kept asking. "She's dead?"

The ragged trail of returning warriors seemed to shrink in on themselves. If I had expected anything like the triumphant march of the Valley men back home, I would have been sorely disappointed. The Ilari warriors returned with weary faces, new wounds, and downcast eyes. They looked beaten.

I glared at the rich colors of the flowers in my arms. Jelsey, Aryll, Mased, and I had been put to flower gathering in the Beyond. The flowers we had already picked were leaning against the tents, opening their petals to the sunlight.

A younger girl had run out to find us in the Beyond, shouting of the warriors' return. We ran back, but I sensed the difference before we arrived. It was too quiet. The Ilari should have been singing and cheering, searching for friends and loved ones. But all was silent. We raced through the tents until we reached the eastern side.

Narine sat atop a tall bay horse. Jelsey froze at the sight

of her. The other warriors hung back behind Narine. Two were carrying Ness on a litter. Her eyes were closed.

The doctor and Pasahn pushed to the front.

"What are *you* doing on Saasu's horse?" Pasahn demanded.

A pause. "It went badly this year, very badly," she said finally. I noticed her clothes, though caked with mud, were tan and white beneath.

"But Saasu," the doctor said implacably.

"Saasu is dead." The breath went out of the camp.

"No, she can't be dead," I heard myself say. Someone cried behind me.

"How?" several pleaded. "Why didn't you send news?"

"It was less than two weeks ago," she said. "A man came to the women's camp and begged amnesty. He wanted to swish. But it was a trick. We took him in. And that night, he ... " She shook her head, unable to continue.

We moaned.

"What happened to the man that killed her?" Pasahn asked her in a terrible voice.

"I killed him myself." Narine slumped on the horse. "And Saasu was given a full ceremony in the warriors' camps, along with the Guide of the Janndays, who also died that night."

"You're back in Ilari colors," someone called.

"I would like to return to the clan, if you will have me. I realize Saasu and I saw things very, very differently, and I wasted a lot of time battling her, when we should have been working together. My past behavior ... troubles me."

She spied me, swung off Saasu's horse, and approached.

"Shannon Traesdaughter, I apologize for my inappropriateness at your arrival in the Ilari camp. I recognize you as Ilari."

Too flabbergasted to respond, I nodded my head before I realized what I was doing.

"I also apologize to your sister Trae." Narine found Jinda, who had Trae on her hip. She extended her hands questioningly, and Jinda put Trae in Narine's arms. Trae grabbed at one of

Narine's honey braids and tugged on it. Narine smoothed her cheek. I watched the nails on Trae's skin as if I expected them to turn into talons. It was not until Trae was safely back in Jinda's arms that I relaxed.

The doctor went to Ness and lifted her eyelids to inspect the motionless pupils. "We can discuss all this later. Put her in the infirmary," she ordered. "The rest of you who are wounded, come along. Jelsey, do you remember enough of your training to help me?"

Jelsey's mouth opened and closed without speaking. Tears ran down her face as she followed Narine's every movement. Her big hands wrung the material of her trousers.

The doctor's gesture to the women holding the litter broke through the shock rendering everyone immobile. The old women and older girls came forward to help the wounded to the infirmary. Voices warmed at the sight of the survivors.

Instead of festivities, the Ilari performed their own death ritual for Saasu that night. There was a dance in the clearing, and afterwards, everyone was given a thin candle to light and let burn until it put itself out. While the candles burned, the women ate cold meat and talked about Saasu, all they remembered of her life.

Narine had a wealth of stories about Saasu, told to alternately weeping and laughing crowds. Saasu had been a much older first cousin, and Narine had shadowed her adoringly for years. Narine had stood guard as a teenage Saasu and her friends raided the food tents. She had taken the blame when Saasu filled the tent of a disliked warrior with all the chickens in the animal hold. When Narine's mother had been killed in battle, Saasu had comforted her. Narine's eyes were somehow cold as they surveyed the reactions of the women at each story. No one noticed.

I should not have accepted Narine's apology. I had been so surprised that I had had no time to consider another reaction.

I found Jelsey standing near the edge of the clearing. Her eyes were on Narine.

"Are you all right?" I asked.

Her eyes were bright with tears, but they didn't fall. "Why do you think she didn't take me last winter?"

I remembered what Jinda had said. "Narine probably thought you were too young to make that sort of decision."

"Too *young?*" Jelsey's face crumpled. "I'm not a child!"

"No, but you're not an adult either."

She looked at me balefully. "She hasn't even spoken to me. I'll show her."

"Show her what?"

"I'll show her that she should have trusted me, no matter my age. I'll be the best warrior she has on the field."

"That sounds good," I said, not sure where she was going.

Her candle burned out. "I'll kill every man who sets foot on the field. And when I'm old enough, I'll lead the expeditions to the Valley and slaughter every man or boy in sight."

She turned and melted into the darkness.

Ness died the next morning, despite the doctor's desperate ministrations. The camp was subdued that day and the festivities a few days later were forced.

As Saasu's closest blood relative, by tradition the role of Guide fell to Narine. During the muted celebrations, she refused to take it, saying acceptance back was all she sought. For now the clan would be run by a council, until the shock had worn off, and contenders could be put forth and voted for.

Afterwards, we tried to settle back to routine. Narine eased back into our lives unobtrusively, her former fire quenched, perhaps for good. The suggestions she made were small, hesitantly put forth for the council's approval. Her steps around the camp were timid. When she proposed that there be no more scouting parties at the Valley's edge, her reasons were that no woman should put herself at risk in the terrible winter weather we were having. We needed as many able bodies as we had. To lose one to sickness or a wild animal would be wasteful.

But with no scouting parties, an exposed Valley girl had no chance of survival. She was gently overruled, and she took it well. But the scouts and hunters were then limited to those old women who had stopped warring and childbearing. Nobody who warred or would one day war would be put in any danger. With this change, an eerie energy moved through the tents.

The Ilari camp filled with whispers.

Jelsey joined me as I walked back to my tent from a quiet meal. Her face was ebullient.

"Narine was afraid Saasu wouldn't allow me to leave with them. She didn't want to start another battle, so she left me behind and planned to come back for me when I was old enough. Narine didn't want to leave me. It was Saasu who would have had the problem with it."

"Did Narine tell you that?" I did not like that explanation, even though it had a ring of truth.

"Of course she did."

"Why didn't she tell you she was leaving at the time? Why simply abandon you?"

Jelsey, taken aback, fought for an answer. "They wanted to leave early that morning, and not attract any more attention."

"What an excuse," I said. Jelsey turned red.

"Who are you to judge? I knew Narine was trustworthy, everyone knows that now. All except you, with your nasty, suspicious mind."

I had a dim memory of Beth saying something similar. Beth, just married. Had I stayed in the Valley, I would be marking my first anniversary of married life.

"I don't see why everyone trusts her all of a sudden, especially you!" I said. "Don't you remember what she did in the marketplace? To women?"

"I don't think her decision was that bad. What's a Valley woman?"

I slapped her. She blinked in shock and threw herself at me, punching and kicking. We fell into the snow, my loose hair in her fist, her shirt tearing under my fingers.

"I'm a Valley woman! You're the descendant of Valley women!" I screamed in her face. Why could she not understand? Her hand smashed into my nose. We rolled over and I pinned her. "They're just like you, those women are *just like you*, and only fortune had you born here and not the Valley. Had you been born of a Valley man, you'd be one of them!"

"Never!" she bellowed, breaking my hold on her. She threw me over and scrambled up, her chest heaving.

"Don't think what happened to those women couldn't have happened to you, Jelsey. It's not their fault they're down in the Valley. They don't deserve the abuse they get, or the blame you give them for taking it."

"The women let themselves be abused." Blood trailed from her lip. "I think they must want it."

"Want to be beaten?" I thought of Damess showing me how to cover up the marks of my husband's beatings. "You're just as ignorant as the men."

"Don't compare me to a *man*," she hissed. "Animals."

"It wasn't men that came to the marketplace, killing those boys and girls."

"Who cares about the boys, anyway?"

"What if Jadan had been down there? He wasn't really one of them, but would Narine have given him a chance?"

"Why should we take the chance that one boy out of dozens may have a change of heart? Who cares? That's how Saasu got herself killed. Let's just get rid of them all and get on with our lives."

"'And build a better society?'" I quoted Narine.

She missed my sarcasm. "Exactly!"

Blood poured from my nose and into my mouth. "Go away, Jelsey," I said. "Killing boys and women before they have the chance to learn any different is insane."

"Are you saying you won't go to war?"

"I'll go to war. Those men have made their decision, and I hate them for it. I'll fight by your side."

"Is everything all right?" a woman asked.

"We're fine," I answered, and my rage melted. She went away.

"I shouldn't have hit you," Jelsey said, after a long moment.

"Me neither." But neither did we apologize for what we had said. "Come on, let me get a rag for your nose." We patched each other up in the infirmary and made our peace.

The winter snows were deeper this year, and stayed through the chilly spring. The council held the vote and Narine was voted Guide by a very small margin. To placate nearly half the clan, it would be under strict supervision by the council until she had proved her worth, and there was no stricter supervision than Pasahn.

Jelsey, Aryll, Mased, and I made our battle masks. Aryll and Mased had snake masks, and Jelsey did a skeletal face, powdered white until it gleamed. After careful consideration, I created a mask of a girl's face. It was a girl of Autumn Night age, with delicate skin and blonde curls that fell onto the forehead. I touched the dimples with deep red, and gave the nose a sweet, upturned twist. The lips quirked with a demure and deferential smile, the expression of a girl hoping the man approaching her fancied a dance or a place at her table. But below the plump curve of the upper lip, in place of the front teeth, I put in two sharp fangs. The tips were tinged blood red, real blood I had squeezed from my pricked finger. Innocence and death together, I thought when I finished, pleased with my creation. Perhaps I would make some man wonder about his Autumn Night woman, that maybe the mouth she was not allowed to speak with at the table was hiding something.

Narine led the four of us to the Ilari temple the night of the warriors' dance. We lined up at her bidding and looked to the statue, each of us carrying a spear in our hands. Narine reached for the silver and green goblet and filled it with water from the pool.

The ceremony was short. Narine stood by Aryll but addressed all of us.

"When Ilari made her first spear, she vowed to the other escaped girls that it would have no mercy, spare no man the pain of death. The clans forget this when they take in swishes, and it cost Saasu her life. Remember that it can be hard to kill. War is an unforgiving work. But we have to do it."

Narine tipped the point of Aryll's spear toward Ilari.

"Aryll, woman warrior of the Ilari clan, will you be merciless in battle?"

"Yes," Aryll whispered. Narine poured a little of the water over the spear.

"Then let this spear know blood and rejoice. Know with every man's life you take, you have won freedom from tyranny."

She stepped in front of Mased and repeated her words. I was next.

"Shannon, as a Valley woman, you need to be sure of your answer. Can you strike the fatal blow to a man you've known all your life?"

"Yes," I said firmly. She repeated then the words she'd spoken to the others.

After Jelsey had her spear drenched with the remainder of the water in the cup, Narine put it away and appeared to ponder her next words.

"There may come a time, warriors, where you may kill other than on the battlefield. You know I led an expedition to the marketplace in the northern Valley." I looked at her warily. "We killed many of the little boys we saw there. It seems cruel, I know, but I want you to understand why I did it. The three-year-old boy looks innocent, yes, but already he is poisoned with the hatred Valley men have for women. What difference does it truly make whether we kill him today or in fifteen years? Think of the lives I've spared by eliminating that child. He will never kill one of us in battle. He will never father sons to fight our daughters. It's hard to think of him as the enemy when he's only a three-year-old child. But he is."

I wanted to protest. Narine looked at me.

"I am not asking you to agree with me. I just ask that you consider it. If we were to have expeditions into the Valley, the men wouldn't have as many warriors to replace their ranks."

Her eyes burned with a strange, yet familiar fire.

"Daughters of Ilari, I welcome you to the ranks of women warriors in battle. Now come, let's have dinner and go to the dance!"

We filed out of the temple. Aryll and Mased spoke to Jelsey. I walked apart from them, confused about what to think. Had Narine changed at all? Why did her words make so much sense to me now when they never had before? I thought of the things she had not said. Killing Com Trelson had not only kept him from the battlefield, it had kept him from marrying had he survived his warring years. Some unborn girl had been spared his husbandly attentions. Several future daughters would never experience his scorn. His sons would never make other women miserable.

But Com could have been like his brother Jadan. He could have gone to the battlefield and found himself unable to kill another human being. He might have been a swish, running to Lorinn for another kind of life. But what were the chances? There were never more than a few swishes a year. Was the chance he was different worth the risk of sparing him?

The four of us stepped into the circle for the dance. I knew the steps so readily that they needed no conscious thought, unlike that long ago practice for Autumn Night. Pasahn watched Narine with an unreadable expression for the last time, for at war she would be the doctor's problem. Little girls pointed at my mask of the girl with bloody fangs. The mask I had struck away from Narine was back on her face, the visage no longer scaring me. Drums pounded until their rhythms echoed in my bones.

The next morning, the warriors woke early. Narine rode Saasu's horse. I looked back once at the winter camp. It could be the last time I saw it. Just because new warriors had duties like drummers and medics did not mean they were safe from danger. Not all the girls to leave last year had returned.

We traveled quietly, every warrior lost in thought. Aryll, Mased, and Jelsey voiced the only words for days.

"I'm going to send them screaming back to their mothers," Mased bragged.

"They'll think twice about leaving the Valley next year!" Aryll added.

Jelsey ran her finger over the point of her spear. "Let it know blood and I will rejoice."

The other warriors ignored them. I said nothing.

Chapter Eighteen

War

There were no heroics or glory. Only blood, and death screams, and warriors on both sides trying to stay alive one minute longer. Aryll and Mased cried beside me. Jelsey was pale. I could only watch, unable to turn away from the carnage that was war.

A surprise rain had dampened the earth, giving the warriors difficult footing to fight upon. The heels of their boots sank into the wet dirt, gouging out holes for others to trip over. The grass was slick. No one waited for an unbalanced opponent to right himself or herself before striking. The first kill had been a man slicing through a woman who had stumbled. Her blood had sprayed. Her dying body had been trampled on. And her screams had lasted a very long time.

Few deaths were clean, I learned. Another woman was struck down. As she fell, pressing her hands to her spurting stomach, the man unmasked her. A warrior of the Kyata clan turned and saw him. She loosed an arrow from her bow and hit him in the back. He ran ten paces before falling, frantically trying to reach the arrow in his back to pull it out. He died slowly, screaming as high-pitched as an infant.

Blood. It soaked the ground just as the rain had, filling the deep footprints, staining then drowning the grass. Warriors fell with a splash. Many of the women fighting were so covered with blood that I could no longer make out their clan colors.

The men were just as drenched. Had it not been for the women's masks, men and women would have been nearly indistinguishable.

A spear punched through a man's eye. I vomited. Hands moved on my back, on my arms, leading me away. I heaved through my mouth and nose, feeling like I was losing every meal I had ever eaten in my life. I choked and Jelsey pounded on my back. The screaming faded away as I let the hands guide me to the camp.

A bit of cloth was pressed into my hand. I wiped my mouth and tried to straighten. Aryll was still as stone. Mased, crying, ran into the tent we shared.

Jelsey tried to smile. "We'd better get back to the infirmary."

I shook my head. There was no way I could sit and roll bandages, after seeing that. "Let's go back in the tent, just for a little while."

Aryll followed us, her steps wooden. Mased had her face pressed into a pillow. Her body shook.

"We should have stayed in the camp like we were told," I said to no one in particular.

"It's better we saw that." Jelsey disagreed. I took a sip of water, hoping my stomach would hold it.

We had reached the forests of the southern Beyond a week before, the last of the clans to arrive. The women of nine clans came together to form an army with hundreds upon hundreds of warriors. The camp was overrun with a rainbow of clan colors. I saw the Kyata blues, Sude gray, Ilari tan and white now least of all, for these three clans were smallest. It seemed every other woman was either wearing the mahogany of Thrine or else the Kalani greens. The Sadira clan was almost their size, full of loud, laughing women who walked around the camp with confidence radiating from every step. They wore bright yellow shirts with sun necklaces and multi-colored trousers that looked more patches than anything else. The Janndays stuck together, in gloomy colors, and I never saw one alone. The Rithe and Klia clans were closely allied, even camping together in the winter. Their clothes were very similar, purple shirts and pleated white trousers for Rithe and lavender shirts with plain white trousers for Klia.

The Ilari clan camped next to Thrine, the clan they had broken off from generations ago. It was like living next to an army of benevolent mothers, pleased to see the successes of Ilari, their daughter clan. The girls my age were friendly but overbearing, checking constantly on our health and happiness. When Jelsey revealed my origins as Valley-born, they stamped their feet and whistled.

"Have you started raiding the Valley for your warriors, Ilari?" a tall Thrine girl asked. "Good for you! Take their breeders right from under their noses!"

"No, she's a runaway," Jelsey explained. "Does your clan raid?"

"No, not yet. But we have been known to steal away a girl who ventures too close to the forest." The Thrine girl looked mischievously at another. "And last year our scouting party heard a man beating his wife in one of the more remote farms near the Beyond. We went right in and beat him instead! By the time he came to, we'd stolen away his wife and three young daughters. What a lark it was!"

The other girl laughed. "And you, Ilari? Perhaps you could swell your ranks by raiding, for you're yet a small clan."

"We collect the exposed girls when we're at our winter camp," Jelsey said tersely. "But the northern Valley isn't nearly as large as the southern." And besides, I thought, certain Ilari would rather kill Valley women.

"We meant no offense," said the first girl, catching Jelsey's tone. "Say, is that your Guide waving to you? Best be off."

Indeed, Narine was beckoning to us as she strode through the Thrine tents. In her hand was a small blue package, carefully wrapped.

"Come with me, girls," she said. Jelsey shouted to Mased and Aryll. We followed her to a quieter place in the women's camp. She unwrapped the cloth package to reveal four teeth like the ones on our necklaces. Not exactly alike, I realized, looking more closely. They were bigger than the ones we wore, and did not shine the same way.

"Take off your necklaces." Narine held up one of the teeth gingerly. A tiny hole had been drilled through it. "I want you to replace one of the teeth you have with the one I'm about to give you."

"Why?" Mased asked, untying her necklace.

"Sometimes, women are captured during battle. If you are, this will be your last chance. Look at it carefully."

"It looks like the special paper we used to make the masks," Jelsey said.

"This is simply a mold of a tooth. Within it is a tiny fang that has been steeped in choga poison for several days."

We gasped. I noticed the larger, duller tooth on one of Narine's three necklaces.

"You do not want to be their prisoner. I do not have to tell you why. So I'm giving you an escape. Every woman warrior carries one of these somewhere on her body."

She gave a tooth to each of us. I shivered, almost expecting the black poison to start creeping up my fingers.

"The mold is heavy. Don't worry that you'll unintentionally poison yourself." Narine folded the empty cloth. "But if you're captured, break that mold and pull out the fang. The fastest death is to scratch your face or neck. If you can't do that, then as a last resort, just swallow the tooth. Your death will be longer and more painful, but just as certain."

I plucked out one of the teeth in my necklace and threaded its deadly replacement onto the string.

"No warrior has been taken alive for many years now. We know death is preferable to a life enslaved." She watched us tie our necklaces back on. "The first battle will be tomorrow. You four will be on medic duty. Go see the doctor now and she'll tell you what you'll need to do."

I looked at the warriors' jewelry with new eyes as we headed for the infirmary. The Sadira clan's sun necklaces. The deep purple bracelets on the wrists of the Klia and Rithe clans.

The teardrop earring each Thrine warrior wore. Each woman walked with death.

The doctor cursed over an entanglement of bandages, soiled with dirt. She told us to carry them to the river east from the camp and wash them. They would dry overnight and we would roll them the next morning.

"All this way to wash bandages," Jelsey grumbled on the way to the river, while we were washing and all the way back. "I want to fight! Chaos-rot!" She had been made Charge of the four of us. With Narine as Guide, I had not expected the role to fall to me, no matter how skilled I was at strategy. Or perhaps it was just that Jelsey fought better than I did. While I could hold my own with a bow and spear, the art of the sword was not a natural skill.

When we returned with the clean bandages, the doctor set us to hanging them on a line stretched between tents. Once we were done, she sent us to gather firewood and when we finished with that, she set us to scrubbing pots. The rest of the day passed quickly in the various, and apparently unending, tasks the doctor gave us.

We were awoken in the morning by the sound of trumpeting horns. Jelsey was out of bed with a whoop and ran out of the tent while still jerking on her clothes. I pushed the blankets off me and went after her. The smell of sausage filled the air. The clans of Thrine and Sude were on cook duty.

I saw the doctors and their apprentices huddling over their meals, speaking in low voices to one another. The new warriors of the Kyata and Rithe girls would be going to the battlefield today, I heard someone say, to work as medic assistants. The Ilari girls were to stay at camp and prepare for the wounded, lay out cots, have bandages clean and rolled, sun-warmed blankets ready for those cold with shock, water boiling over a fire for sterilization of the doctors' instruments.

The warriors lingered over their food. Jelsey watched them enviously as they polished their weapons, formed rank lines, and started south for the battlefield.

Mased, Aryll, and I pulled down the bandages we had left

out to dry. Jelsey would not help until the last warrior had vanished into the trees. We poured water into the large pots and stacked wood for the fires.

"Let's go watch," Jelsey said suddenly.

Horns blew from far away. Jelsey looked like she had a fierce itch under her skin. Aryll and Mased set down the cots they had been carrying. I arranged them into a line.

I shook my head. "We need to prepare the camp. I'll need help carrying out those tables."

"It can wait a few minutes. Come on, don't be such geese! Let's go and watch." Jelsey turned on her heel.

Mased and I looked at each other. Aryll shrugged and we caught up with Jelsey.

The voices of the warriors led us right to them. We hid behind the last row of trees, crouching down to peer between bushes at the huge field in front of us. Men lined one end of the field, women the other. A horn blew three times.

The war began. Jelsey's excited whispers died. I had aged years by the time the spear pierced through the man's eye. Spilling blood, dismembered body parts, reedy cries. The girls who had disobeyed and left the camp a short while before were not the same ones who returned. The doctor of the Thrine appeared, two medics behind her with a litter.

"Why aren't you ready?" she screamed at us. "They're coming now!"

I stared at the woman on the litter. The doctor had the medics put her on an operating table.

"You!" the doctor said to me. "Help me! Danae, Vell, get back to the field!" The two medics ran, the litter dragging behind them.

"Hold her down." I slowly approached the table. Was it really a woman there? Blood and mud covered her face, caked her hair, frothed from her nose.

The doctor shook me. "Snap out of it! Hold her down!"

Blood spurted from the woman's neck. I finally saw the shaft of an arrow protruding from her skin, the arrow embedded somewhere inside.

"Chaos!" the doctor swore. I reached over and clutched the woman's hands, frantically trying to remove the arrow with blackened fingers.

"Shh. It's going to be all right," I said, pinning the woman's hands down to her side. In the muck on her chest, I saw the outline of a sun necklace.

The doctor pulled out an odd pair of scissors. Thin forceps, I remembered dully from my lessons in the camp.

The woman was trying to talk. I shook my head. The doctor reached down and pushed the forceps into the woman's wound. Blood sprayed my face. I sputtered.

"Don't let her go!" the doctor warned. An eerie keening sound came from the woman and filled the air.

The doctor pulled the arrowhead from her neck and threw it to the ground. She snatched a needle and thread that had been stuck in the collar of her shirt and put her fingers back into the woman's neck. Had I had anything in my stomach, I would have lost it.

Minutes passed. The keening sound stopped. The doctor stepped back.

"Is she all right?" I asked hesitantly.

The doctor stared at the Sadira. "She's dead. Dress her for burial."

I looked in horror at the woman. Her eyes were fixed and still.

More medics arrived with litters. Jelsey and I wrapped the woman clumsily in two large sheets, tying off the ends. We laid her gently down away from the cots and tables. Later, she would be identified.

My hands, face, and clothes were stained with the woman's blood. I had no time to wipe it off.

"Every hand, every hand!" The calls rang in the air. Every unharmed woman was carrying the injured, arranging them on cots, yanking blankets and sleep-rolls from tents when the wounded outnumbered the cots. Those walking wounded were sent to another part of the camp. The doctors had no time for them, so several other women tended to their cuts or breaks.

"You!" a doctor pointed to Jelsey and me. "Start dressing the dead and clear these tables!"

We grabbed sheets. I tilted the dead woman while Jelsey twisted the first sheet around her body, then Jelsey lifted her while I wrapped around the second sheet. Body after body we carried to a growing pile. Two Sadiras, one Sude, three Kalanis. An Ilari.

Jelsey's face was grim, what little I could see of it. We slipped in the blood on the ground as we carried the dead Ilari to the pile.

"She was a great warrior," Jelsey said when we put her down.

"What a waste," I said furiously as we went back to collect another.

The sun was sinking, I realized with a start. Where had the day gone? Women returned to the battlefield to retrieve those that had died there. I watched them carry bodies over their shoulders as I held down the leg of a flailing warrior.

"No, don't! No, don't!" she screamed.

"Be thankful it's only a finger!" a doctor screamed back at her. A loud crunch filled my ears. I let go of the leg and heaved dryly on the bloody ground.

A hand touched my shoulder. I looked up and saw the Ilari doctor.

"We don't need you here anymore," she said.

"No, I'm fine," I said. "I can still help."

She wiped a line of blood from her face, streaking it. "No, child. There's no one else to help with."

I looked around. All the bodies being carried out of the forest were still.

"Go get dinner, and then you'll be collecting wood," the doctor said. "You too, Jelsey."

Jelsey's curls were matted to her forehead with sweat and blood. "Is it always like this?"

The doctor pulled a filthy rag from her belt and tried to clean off her hands. "Sometimes it's a lot worse. Be thankful this part was all you saw."

Jelsey locked eyes with me about the secret we shared. Even after this day, she wanted to war. I wanted to run away and never look back.

That night, after the dead had been identified, we burned them. There was not the energy for any other sort of ritual or ceremony. The women simply stood around the flaming pyre and watched the bodies of friends and family turn to bone and ash.

"Next year," Jelsey said in frustration. "They'll pay."

"Sometimes I think you really want to die," I said.

She snorted. "I won't die. The men will die."

Perhaps three days passed. One of the worst wounded, a Jannday who still lived with an arrowhead lodged in her brain, was quietly given an overdose of sleeping medicine by her clan. All the Janndays stood around her bed as she died, singing to her.

Another battle challenge was issued by the men, trumpet bursts through the Beyond like thrusts from a spear.

"They turned it down again," said a wounded Thrine from her cot, after a staccato of trumpets and drums.

"Turned what down?" I asked.

"The peace treaty. The men always turn the treaty down."

I was scandalized. "We send out a *peace treaty?*"

"Every time. We'll live in the Beyond, they'll stay in the Valley, and we'll leave well enough alone."

"Why would they take it? They're animals," Jelsey said. "They live to war."

"Maybe accepting a truce means defeat to them," I guessed. "Being a man means warring."

"Well, you'd know," Jelsey said. I glared at her.

The Thrine considered Jelsey. "A lot of the women are beginning to think that being a woman means warring as well."

Jelsey rolled her eyes.

Then the wounded poured from the trees.

Time was marked in screams and clashes. In what could have been the fifth or seventh or twentieth battle, I bandaged and held, wrapped and sterilized. I washed cold faces of blood and filth for identification, led the living past the dead and waited for that gasp of recognition. Some could not be recognized. I grew to hate the sound of trumpets.

On the morning of another battle, two medics came from the trees screaming.

"The line's broken! The line's broken!" They wheeled away.

"Yes!" Jelsey shoved her fist into the air. "Shannon, all of you! *Get weapons!*"

I snatched a bow and quiver from the medical tent. They were red with someone's blood. Mased and Aryll found swords. Jelsey found another bow just as men burst into the camp.

Two young Thrine warriors ran behind them, firing arrows. I lifted my bow to my shoulder.

Five men, at least. Then four. I fired but missed. Mased screamed somewhere near me. Then three.

I fired. Two. Then a Thrine fell as one of the two turned back and swung his sword.

The last warrior ran to me. Jelsey shouted my name. For one frozen moment, his eyes met mine.

It's not someone you know, I thought sternly, pulling back an arrow.

"Don't shoot, don't shoot!" the warrior, *the boy*, screamed at us. He stopped running and threw his sword to the ground, his belt dagger after it. "Please!"

"It's a trick!" Jelsey ran for us, but she was so far away.

The boy sank to his knees, staring at me as if I were the only person in the world.

"Please, please, please ..." he begged. An arrow whispered just over his head. Cursing, Jelsey snatched another arrow from her quiver and stumbled.

He lowered his head then, and waited. Streaks of blood glistened in his brown hair. I lowered my bow.

"Kill him!" Jelsey screamed at me. She lurched to her feet and drew back her arrow.

"*NO!*" I stepped between her and the boy, pointing my bow at her.

"What are you doing?" she screamed back.

"Get up! Get up!" I grasped the boy's forearm and yanked him to his feet.

"*Traitor!*"

"Run!" He and I veered away from Aryll and Mased, who stared at us in utter shock.

What to do, where to go? We ran through the tents and into the forest. West. The Valley was west of us. We had to go north. I was still holding his arm. I let go and made a quarter turn to the right.

The boy tried to gain enough breath to speak.

"Shut up," I panted, before he could. "I need to think."

Saasu died for a swish, I thought.

Someone was following. We ran.

Chapter Nineteen

The Boy

The boy fell behind me. Cursing, I hauled him back to his feet. Any moment, I expected Jelsey and the others to erupt from the trees and kill us.

"Move, *move*, MOVE!" I ordered. He gasped for air, bending in half with his arms clasping his chest.

"I ... I don't think ... I can run another step."

Neither did I, but fear filled me with energy. I pulled on his collar.

"Leave me alone, woman!"

I kicked out his knee. "Don't speak to me like that, *man*."

He fell. I resisted the urge to kick him a second time.

"Now get up or I'll pull you up by your ear."

He got up. I listened to the forest around us.

"I don't hear anything," he said.

"Me either. Let's keep on going though."

We walked. I wiped the sweat from my face.

"Where are we going?" he asked.

I did not answer.

"I asked you a question!"

"I don't know. Just away!"

He was quiet. We came to a small clearing and I looked up to check the sun's position.

"North," I muttered.

"What's north?"

"Lorinn," I said, surprising myself. "It's north of the Beyond." We would be safe in Lorinn.

"What's Lorinn?"

Tired of his questions, I spoke shortly. "It's a settlement."

The boy looked priggish. "Do you mean the heathen towns? The ones ruled by women who keep men slaves?"

I stared at him. "What are you talking about? There's no such place as that."

"I heard the older men talk about them. We can't raid those towns because you women protect them. It's a disgrace how those unfortunate men live, as women's pawns."

"What about the Valley? The women there are nothing but men's pawns, aren't they? And Lorinn's not like that."

"Women aren't men's pawns! They have good lives, and we care for them. Besides, we have to. They're weaker by nature."

I tripped him. He fell flat on his face in the dirt.

"Do I look like I need to be protected? Do the women you fight look weak to you?" I shouted, not caring if every single warrior in the Beyond heard me.

He sputtered, spitting dirt out of his mouth. "You women aren't natural! If you'd only come to the Valley and see how our women live, you'd understand how much happier you'd be!"

"I am from the Valley, fool! I ran away because of how badly I was treated there!"

"You weren't treated badly. You ran off in a child's tantrum. See? Women are weaker, especially in mind. They can't see when something is being done for their own good."

I fumed. He stood up and grinned at me smugly. I advanced on him, until we were nose to nose.

"I should have let Jelsey kill you. I should have done it myself. You're nothing but Valley trash, fit for slaughter. You've not once in your life tried to imagine what it's like to be a woman, have you?"

"Why, of course not!" Uncomfortable with my proximity, he stepped back.

"What do you think your life would be like?"

"I'd worry about my hair and having pretty clothes!" he said nastily. "I'd scream at spiders! I'd wonder what kind of husband would pick me at Autumn Night and what color dress my father would choose for me."

"That's what I expected," I sneered. "Maybe you shouldn't come to Lorinn. The men there would despise you for that answer as much as the women would!"

I turned and walked away from him, not caring if he followed.

A minute later, I heard his voice behind me. "How would a Lorinn man have answered your question?"

I did not look at him. "The Lorinn man I know would have said he hated the imagining of a Valley woman's life."

The boy fumbled for words. "It's not like a Valley man's life is all fun and games. We have to war."

I snorted. "Why don't you just accept the peace treaty? The war would be over with then."

The boy began to speak but then stopped. He shook his head.

A stick snapped. I looked around in dread. The forest was still.

"I'm Gace Shellsson," the boy said.

"Shannon Traesdaughter."

"Trae's a woman's name! Your father is named *Trae*?"

"Trae was my mother's name. It was my mother who bore me and raised me, why should I not carry her name?"

"Your father earned the money that fed you. You're supposed to have your father's name!"

"Chaos to that! Men are supposed to war. Women are supposed to marry and have babies. But here we are. I'm unmarried and you've defected."

"I'm a swish now," he said, his eyes widening.

"Then go back," I said. "You seem perfect for that way of life."

"I don't want to kill."

"Then do something else."

"I can't. Men are supposed to ... " Gace trailed off.

I grinned in spite of myself. The sun burned down as we passed out of the trees into a thin field.

And then the warriors were upon us.

Not Jelsey, the Ilari, or any woman warrior for that matter. My first wave of panic convinced me it was hordes of men warriors, shouting and swinging swords. Gace yelled in surprise beside me and fumbled for his belt dagger, forgetting he had dropped it. I snatched my bow and an arrow and pointed it at the man closest to me.

"Get away!" I shouted, searching for the others. But there were only two of them, men nearing the end of their warring years. They had harsh faces, one whose nose had been broken many times, the other with a scarred face. Both had malicious smiles.

"Looks like the swish has found a wife!" said the one inching around Gace.

"Bounty hunters," Gace whispered with despair.

The man's scars creased as he smiled.

"Come on, there doesn't have to be a fight!" he simpered in a singsong voice. "Put the bow down, that's a good girl."

Out of the corner of my eye, I saw the second man come closer to Gace. Gace dodged behind me.

"Little coward!"

"Why try to talk me out of a fight? Are you afraid I'll win?" I said, bluffing for all I was worth.

He jumped towards me. I loosed the arrow and reached for another. The other man lunged. No time, no time ... a sharp whistling ...

A spray of blood splashed down on us. My arrow had lodged in his chest, but a second had gone through his neck. He clutched his throat with desperate fingers. Then he hit the ground heavily.

The second man backed away. I looked behind me. Jelsey lowered her bow.

"Well, well, well," Narine said beside her, arms folded over her chest. "Misplaced affection, indeed."

Jelsey's lower lip trembled. The man curled on his side. His nails scrabbled weakly in the grass.

Suddenly, the man with the scarred face had my hair in his fist, the side of his sword tightly pressed to my neck. I flailed and dropped the bow. His sword cut into my skin, and a line of hot blood spilled down to my shirt.

"Back off!" he shouted to Narine and Jelsey. "Or I'll kill her."

Narine began to laugh, a hard sound. She put her hand on Jelsey's bow, keeping it down. "Do it. This one's no loss."

"Narine, no!" I begged absurdly.

Her eyes were coldly pleased. "Kill her!"

The metal pressed into my throat even harder. I gagged and thrashed in his arms, trying to get away.

Gace, who just stood watching, touched the man's arm with his hand. "Let her go. I'll go back with you."

The man sneered. "Men show no mercy, *boy*."

"How amusing," Narine said, leaving the trees to walk into the clearing. "Neither do I."

Jelsey shook herself. "Narine, don't! He'll kill her!"

One step. Another step. Narine advanced until she and the man were only paces away. Spots danced in front of my eyes from the pressure on my throat.

Thunk. I crumpled to the ground, pressure gone.

"What? Jelsey, no!" Narine was shouting.

The man clutched the torn material of his shirt. An arrow had sliced his left shoulder.

"Come on, quick!" Gace put out his hand to me. The man swung his sword, nearly striking Narine.

Narine's sword collided with the man's. They circled each other above us. I took Gace's hand and we threw ourselves past the dead man. Jelsey watched us, her face expressionless.

The man lashed forward. Narine met his blow and forced him back. They circled again. She jabbed, baiting him. He backed another step.

"Is this how you fight, little man?" she asked.

He leaped for her, sword flying, driving her all the way back to the trees.

"Let's go!" Gace whispered.

I looked back to Jelsey. The man raised his sword too high, giving Narine the chance she had been waiting for. She slashed across his belly. He choked and bent over double, dropping his sword. Narine looked at him dispassionately and brought her sword down.

Gace and I darted across the clearing, but we weren't fast enough. Narine cut us off ten paces from the trees.

"Your turn!" she said. Blood pattered down her hands from her sword. She spoke over her shoulder. "Do you understand, Jelsey? Valley women are born different from us. The first chance she had, she ran back to the men's side."

"That's not true!" I shouted. "Jelsey, don't listen to her! You saw the boy throw down his weapons!"

Narine smirked, coming closer. "Only to beg sympathy, so he could kill us in the night."

"No, Narine. He's leaving the army. He can go to Lorinn!" I had no weapon but a small belt dagger. The bow was lost in the grass. I needed a sword.

Gace stood up and tried to place himself between us. "I'm not an infiltrator."

She ignored him. A sword, a sword ... the man Jelsey and I had killed had a sword. I twisted around and ran back for him with Narine on my heels. I dove over his body, grabbed the hilt of his sword, and rolled to a standing position just as Narine's sword whistled out to strike me. I faced her, sword ready.

"Jelsey, help me!" But Jelsey watched like a confused child.

"She won't help you," Narine said. "She knows you're just a Valley woman, nothing more than a pretty pawn to be passed around between men. You can't rise above what you are."

"Let us live, Narine. I want to go to Lorinn, I won't trouble you anymore."

"Lorinn!" she spat. "We can't live together in peace. You

can't reason with animals. One day Lorinn will be what the Valley is."

I had only one thing left to bargain with. "Let me go, please. I've kept your secret. You owe me for that. I don't want to fight you."

Her sword smashed into mine, tearing it from my grasp. I ran to retrieve it.

"Jelsey!" I screamed. "Please, I can't fight her alone!"

Jelsey jumped at my voice. She stared at Narine with a strange light in her eyes.

"Jelsey!" I grabbed my sword and whirled back to Narine.

Narine was inches behind me. The sword sliced across my cheek. I howled and staggered.

Jelsey shook her head. She climbed to her feet.

I coughed up blood onto the grass. I had thought she was a friend. "Please, please."

Eyes wild, Jelsey turned and ran into the forest away from us.

Narine was upon me. I clumsily blocked a heavy stroke to my side and lost my balance. On my back, I stared at the bright sun in a moment of total silence. Then the darkness of Narine's form stood over me.

I turned my head away. A bloody sword lifted from the grass by the second dead man.

"Stop!" said a thin voice.

"Wait your turn, boy!" Narine said. A cold point of metal touched my chin. Slowly, I tightened my fingers on the hilt of my sword. One swing, enough to get her away ...

She blocked my feeble attempt to wound her. But she did not move fast enough to block Gace's.

Blood pattered down like rain. She stared in disbelief at the deep cut on her arm. Back on my feet in an instant, Gace and I stood next to each other with our swords raised.

Narine lunged at us. Two to one, but she had battled for years and years. We struck at her, but she viciously drove back each blow. My shoulder soon ached from trying to maintain my hold. Gace took each blow with a grunt, jumping when she slashed for his legs. But then she kicked out her foot, tripping him. He landed on his knees. She brought down the full weight of the hilt onto his head. Without a sound, he crumpled.

She bore down, a bear on a rabbit. My sword was out of my hand before I realized she had struck me. I blinked my eyes and found myself crawling as she followed me with sure steps. For a second, I saw my sisters with their heads bent counting to thirty as I escaped Father's wagon.

The air snapped.

"NARINE!"

The warrior Ilari took up her spear.

No, not the warrior Ilari, but her warriors rained down into the clearing. Narine was gone. The doctor's voice was around me, all around, in the air and the grass, and I closed my eyes.

"Drop your sword!"

I opened my eyes. Narine stood five paces from my feet, her face sulky. Tan and white surrounded us, arrows poised in taut bows.

"Shannon!" Jelsey burst into the circle and collapsed beside me.

Taking the rag she offered, I tried to staunch the flow of blood from my neck and my face.

"*Why,* Narine?" the doctor demanded.

Narine glared back. "It's a man and a Valley woman. What's the difference?"

"Shannon is an Ilari and the boy is a swish! And even if Shannon were a Valley woman, there is a rule among the clans not to raise their hands to them! You seem to have forgotten that! Women will not win their independence by slaughtering each other."

"Our women won't win at all," Narine said, her lip curling in distaste, "Because of your sympathies for the Valley woman's plight! We should kill them!"

"You already have," I said hoarsely. "You didn't spare the

women and girls any more than you did the young boys in the market."

A warrior gasped. The doctor looked at me.

"Is that true?" she asked.

I thought of the screams and the fire, the dead girl whose blood had pooled at my feet. "It's true. When I first arrived at the camp, she threatened to kill Trae if I told."

The doctor's eyes were terrible when she looked at Narine.

"Did you kill women during that Valley raid?"

"Yes. But ..."

"There is no *but!* Warriors, take her back to camp and call the Guides together!"

"No!" Narine shouted as two women grasped her shoulders. More came to assist; she began fighting. "It was justified, you fools!"

"And trying to murder Shannon, an Ilari warrior, was justified? Or the swish?"

Gace. Jelsey was at his side, his wrist in her hand as she took his pulse. His body was still.

"We need to take him back," she said to the doctor, who left Narine to crouch at Jelsey's side. The doctor beckoned a warrior, who lifted the boy into her arms and followed the pack around Narine into the forest.

"Do you think you can stand?" the doctor asked me.

I nodded. "I can."

With Jelsey on one side and the doctor on the other, we went back through the forest to the women's camp.

Epilogue

There never would be a formal punishment for Narine. That night, while she waited judgment from the other Guides, she broke open the mold of the phony tooth on her necklace. She removed the tiny fang inside and traced the heavy scar on her face. By the time someone found her, it was too late.

The next day, the Ilari held the funeral pyre separate from the rest of the clans. We burned the small candles and talked about Narine's life. There was little, unlike Saasu, which was amusing or noble.

The next morning, I spoke to the Guides as a Valley woman. They asked what I had seen at the market and I told them of the children slain, both girls and boys. The women and old men. It was almost funny to me that in the Valley, it was only the death of the men and boys that were registered on the marble block. In the women's camp, it was only the death of the women and girls that mattered in their court. The rest of Narine's followers would have to be judged for their part in the attack. I did not want to stay for it.

When the mid-day meal had ended, I went to the infirmary. Gace had not regained consciousness, and the doctors were not hopeful. When I walked into the tent, Jelsey looked up at me from the boy's bedside.

"He's worse," she said. "I'm sorry, Shannon." I looked at the still form, head shaved and criss-crossed in black stitches. A slight grayness flushed the pink of his face.

I touched his hand. His skin was cooling. Then I left the tent with Jelsey behind me.

"Are you going?" she asked. I nodded and spoke impulsively.

"Come with me. It may not be too late to join the mapping expedition."

She started to shake her head, then hesitated. "They've already left. But ... maybe next year?"

I smiled. "Thank you for bringing the Ilari. Even if it was just for a Valley woman."

She smiled, knowing I was teasing. "They were already following. I just made them hurry. And I had to bring them *because* you were a Valley woman. You need to be taught how to fight better."

"Farewell, Jelsey. Please ... check on Trae every now and then, will you?"

"Of course."

The doctor told me to visit the Ilari summer and winter camp whenever I wanted, so that I could watch Trae grow. I hoped one day she would join me in Lorinn, but it was her decision to make when she got older.

"Shannon!" Jelsey shouted, as I walked away through the camp. I turned.

"Why are you taking your mask and weapons?" she called.

I felt the mask dangling down my back, the weight of the spear and the bow and arrow. "Unfinished business at home, Jelsey."

"Well, be careful then." She went back into the tent where Gace lay.

Lorinn was my final destination. I lifted the pack in the tent I shared with Jelsey, Aryll, and Mased. It was heavy with rations and a sleep-roll. More rations than necessary for one person to get to Lorinn, but I had reasons for that.

I waved more farewells and headed into the forest. I walked north until night fell, then camped and ate sparingly. The next three mornings I went north again, until the forests of the Beyond curved west. But instead of leaving the forest and following the foothills to Lorinn, I curved with the Beyond and went west.

I traveled just above the northern Valley, barely hidden in

the trees. I peeked out occasionally to see the small world of my childhood. The town, the fields, the schoolhouse. At the sight of the schoolhouse I picked up my pace. My timing had to be perfect.

Once my father's cabin was a distant spot below me, I dropped my pack and climbed down the slope into the Valley. It was not as steep as I remembered. I pulled the mask over my face and hurried to the road where my sisters would walk in a few short minutes. I huddled in the wildness of my father's land, waiting, waiting.

Beth had been married, so she would not be among them. Grief rose in my throat, but there was nothing I could do for her. And the twins, Roaninblue, would be home with Father or fostered elsewhere. I checked around me carefully. Father was nowhere in sight.

Their voices rang through the air. Keluu and Greda giggling, Dir scolding Balasar for skipping the first day of school. I peered between the branches of a bush and looked at them. They were taller, with thin legs and white faces. I paused. One of the twins was among them, her hair braided. I stepped onto the road, spear lifted in my hand.

My sisters froze. I could imagine how I looked to them, tall and frightening. Just as Synde opened her mouth to scream, I yanked the mask away from my face.

"Shannon!"

I stood over them. "Come with me. I want to show you something." My voice broke. I turned and walked away. Please follow, I begged them silently.

I left the road and turned north through Father's land, never looking back. The silence tortured me. I kept my back straight and my steps sure, my weapon still drawn as I stared into the darkness of the Beyond. I would not look back, not look back ...

"Shannon?" said a tentative voice. I closed my eyes briefly to stop the tears. Then I looked down at Keluu.

"Where are we going?" she asked.

I stroked her hair. "To a safe place."

She thought about this. We left Father's land and walked

through the fields to the Beyond. I half-expected to hear a scream for Father, but all was quiet.

Once we were at the bottom of the slope, I turned. Dir and Synde held Greda's and Keluu's hands tightly. Balasar stood apart, her odd eyes fixed on me. Only Roaninblue remained at the end of Father's fields, watching us. Her heavy brown hair had been pulled into a clumsy braid that coiled around her head. She looked at us, then back at the Valley.

I helped the girls up the slope silently. It had to be her decision.

"Come on, Roaninblue!" Keluu called excitedly.

I called to her, warrior to Valley woman. *"Your life is your own."*

She stood motionless. I helped my youngest sisters up the slope.

"Isn't she coming?" Dir asked. I shook my head, put my spear away, and hefted my pack onto my shoulders.

"She decided to stay. Come, girls, let's go." I showed them a tiny passage through the thick line of trees. "Don't worry, you're safe with me."

They pushed into the forest. I looked at Roaninblue one more time, and then followed them.

"Wait! Wait!" I turned. Roaninblue was running, the wind pulling loose her awkward braid until her hair tumbled free down her shoulders and back. She forced her way up the slope on her own. The others cheered when she stood up in the Beyond.

"I'm glad, Roanin ..." I stopped. "Roan."

A slow smile crept onto her face at the name, the one name.

"That goes for all of you," I said sternly. "Your life is your own, understand?"

They didn't, not yet, but it didn't matter. I took Roan's hand and led my sisters away. The trees closed behind us, hiding the Valley from view.

About the Author
Kerrigan Valentine was born in 1976 in Wisconsin and grew up in California where she lives today with her partner of nine years. She has a bachelor's degree in Classical Studies. After graduating in 1999, she worked for several years in education with mildly to severely disabled children, and now divides her time between writing, occasional teaching and seasonal viticulture positions, and learning how to cook with limited success. *Legacy* began as a short story when she was fourteen years old for a tenth grade creative writing class. Although she earned a good grade for it, the short story never felt complete and she expanded it into a book just after college. Currently she is at work on a science fiction book for adults.

Contact the Author
Contact Kerrigan through the publisher, information below. Kerrigan is available for booksignings and discussions. *Creatrix Books LLC* will forward all correspondence directly to Kerrigan.

About *Creatrix Vision Spun Fiction*
Legacy is another invaluable addition to the *Creatrix Vision Spun Fiction LLC* imprint. *Creatrix Vision Spun Fiction* specializes in woman empowering mythic fiction. For further information about any of these books, please contact us through *Creatrix Books LLC*, information below. *Creatrix Vision Spun Fiction LLC* is a Wisconsin Limited Liability company and a *Creatrix Books LLC* company.

About *Creatrix Books LLC*
Creatrix Books LLC is woman owned and operated and was founded to give a voice to Goddess and Her children via the written word.

Creatrix

Creatrix Books LLC
PO Box 366
Cottage Grove, WI 53527
www.creatrixbooks.com